Fisher Amelie

http://www.fisheramelie.com/

First Edition: October 2016

Printed in the United States of America

THE TRUE STORY OF

Atticus and Hazel

For baby Gabriel, I think about you all the time. I love you.

CHAPTER ONE

"Hazel, don't look."

Immediately, I whipped my head around. "What?"

"I said don't look. Gaw, you never follow directions!" my best friend gritted. Her hands shot out to situate me. "Let's try this again. *Don't look* but there is a boy sitting in the back of the room who is burning a hole into the back of your head. I'm shocked you can't feel him."

"Etta, tonight is the airing of the grievances. We are not here for the boys."

"Well, well, well, Hazel," she continued, ignoring me, "I think this one might be striking up the nerve to come over." She looked at me. "You look like an idiot." Her eyes dragged to my favorite baby-doll dress. "I see you found that paper bag again, and I thought I'd hid it better this time."

My eyes blew wide. "I knew it! I knew you'd hidden it again. I asked and asked and you swore up and down you didn't know what I was talking about and—"

"Hazel, hush!" she whisper-yelled. Her body stiffened and I followed suit, unable to help myself. "Oh my word, he's coming over here. Here," she said, fluffing up my hair then squeezing my cheeks.

"Ow! Stop, Etta."

"Shh!"

"You're treading a fine line."

"Shh!" She pushed a pink fingernail into my thigh. "Cross your legs."

"Etta!"

"Shh! Quiet, he's coming."

She made a move to fluff my hair again and I shooed her away, which only prompted her to fluff more wildly. We ended up in a battle of slapping hands as we heard someone clear their throat to my left.

Etta pushed my hands at my side and straightened, turning toward our interloper. "Hi," she greeted sweetly, like she wasn't made of salt and vinegar.

"Hello," a deep voice crooned.

I turned toward the bar and refused to look at him just to spite Etta.

"How are you ladies doing tonight?" he asked.

Original. I snorted. Etta elbowed me.

"We're well," Etta laid on thickly. "How are you, baby?"

"I, uh," the poor sap struggled. He cleared his throat again and I rolled my eyes. "I'm well, thank you."

"What happened? Losing your nerve?" I asked the bar top.

Etta's head whipped my direction and she shot daggers. "This is my rude, stupid friend. Don't mind her. She's kind of whiny today because her boss harasses her at work. She's not usually this way, though." A boldfaced lie. "She likes to act all tough and moody like this sometimes because she's scared of almost everything, yet she refuses to acknowledge this fact."

"Etta!" I protested, finally turning her direction.

When I did, I caught a glimpse of the guy and nearly fell from my chair. My eyes climbed his body up to his face. The corner of his mouth lifted in a bashful grin, his head bent, and his hand went to the back of his neck. There were tattoos as far as the eye could see. I mean, the guy was covered in them, from the tops of his hands all the way up his throat as well as, I could only assume, everything in between. He had a ring in his bottom lip just off center to the left, and his chin-length hair sat tucked behind his ears. He was built but not overly so. His clothes were worn and layered. When his hand dropped, the leather of his jacket moaned in complaint.

"Hi," he quieted.

I swallowed. "Hi."

"What's your name?" he asked me.

"Hazel," I answered.

"Nice to meet you," he told me, holding out his hand. I slid my fingers into his warm palm, which caused satisfying tingles to dance over my skin. "I'm Atticus."

"Nice to meet you as well."

He let my hand go. "Are, uh, are you from around here?" he asked me, looking unsure of himself.

He was standing awkwardly in front of us, and I was starting to feel a little sorry for him, which I never did, because I thought men in general kind of sucked and I liked to watch them squirm on occasion, but he felt different for some reason, and it made me sad to see him uncomfortable.

"Do you want to sit down?" I asked, shoving Etta off

her stool.

"Hey!" she yelled.

Atticus's eyes popped wide. "No, no, that's okay," he said, beginning to back away.

Shit, I've scared him off.

Etta glanced at me and rolled her eyes. "She doesn't mean anything by that. She's just *socially inept* is all." She pointedly stared at me then turned back to Atticus. "Come," she invited him, "sit on my stool. I'm heading out anyway. My auntie will be waiting up and every minute I'm past eleven p.m. she thinks I'm 'caught underneath a boy and up to no good.'"

Etta leaned over and kissed my cheek but not without a parting jab. "Scare him off and I'll kill you."

"Look who's talking, Dexter," I whispered.

She faked like she was going to hit me and I flinched.

"Made you blink, white girl." I popped her on the butt and she squealed. "You're a brat," she complained.

"I know."

"Love you," Etta threw over her shoulder.

"Love ya. See you *mañana*."

"Tomorrow!" she yelled, heading for the door, not bothering to turn around.

I turned toward Atticus.

"So you and Etta," he stated, "you're good friends?"

I almost laughed at his facial expression. "Etta and I shared a playpen. We're more than good friends; we're practically sisters."

"Thus the nonexistence of normal social boundaries?"

"Thus."

"Cool," he said, bobbing his head. He sat in Etta's abandoned stool and balanced a heavy boot on a bottom rung.

His hands went to the bit of stool between his legs and I found myself mesmerized by them. I loved men's hands. I don't know why. I loved the callused skin there, how sensitive they were, the way the muscles bunched and contracted, the shapes of their fingers.

He mistook my staring at his fingers for my staring at his tattoos and brought them up for me to see.

"Do you like tattoos?"

"I don't care either way, to be honest."

He gave me a cheeky grin, and I felt my stomach flip on itself. *What is this?*

"Most people love them."

"Yeah, well, I'm not most people."

He laughed. It was a deep, throaty laugh. I watched the line of his throat, the skin there, the lean line of his neck, his defined Adam's apple. He was pretty spectacular.

Have you ever met someone with whom you felt an instant chemistry? That was this stranger for me. It was instantaneous, intoxicating, and overwhelming. It was the most smack-you-in-the-face, deep attraction I'd ever felt. His teeth were beautiful, his skin a perfect peach color, save for the attractive bits of red that would paint his cheeks when he talked. He kept taking his fingers and tucking his hair behind his ears.

His fingers drummed with incredible skill at the lid of his stool.

"Oh no," I said, my stomach sinking. "You're a musician."

He looked taken aback. "How did you know?" I gestured at his drumming fingers and they stilled. "Oh." His hands went to the tops of his thighs and he leaned forward. "What did you mean by 'oh no'?"

"I don't think this is going to work out," I said, standing up.

Atticus looked shocked and stood quickly. "Wait, what are you talking about? We were just chatting here."

I smiled at him. "Yeah, have a nice life, drummer boy."

"Wait," he said, stopping me by lightly touching my forearm, "don't jet off just yet. Take a seat, have a drink with me? Just stay for a minute. Hell, tell me what it is about musicians you don't trust."

"Besides every stereotype ever imaginable? Beside those?"

He laughed. "Yes, please?"

I shook my head. "Probably going to regret this, but okay, one drink."

He helped me to my stool, which earned him one Hazel point, and signaled for the bartender. "What'll you have?" he asked me.

"Guinness," I told him. He nodded and turned toward the bartender. "Hey, Sam, can I get two bottles of Guinness, please?"

"Sure, man," the bartender answered and dug into his ice pit for two dark bottles, propping them up on the bar top, and popping the tops of each before handing them over to us.

The bartender walked off, which surprised me.

"You drink for free here?" I asked.

He smiled that knowing grin. "Something like that."

"That's cool."

"Sure," he said, lifting the bottle and taking a small swig. I did the same then set the bottle on the bar top. "Etta was saying something about your boss harassing you?"

I sighed, exasperated. "Yeah, the bastard is just yucky."

Atticus laughed. "Well, like how?"

"He makes excuses that he needs to *fix* things underneath my desk, which makes no sense because there's nothing under my desk but my legs and a small outlet for my drawing table. I guess he doesn't think things through all that well. Anyway, the first time he did it, I didn't think much about it, but the second and third time? I was like 'what's up, man' and he just shook off my questions. He works in the desk in front of mine and the other day he placed a mirror on the top edge, settling it so he could get the perfect angle to watch me. I guess he doesn't think I can see him in the mirror, but I can."

"What the hell? That's pervy as shit."

"Right?"

"Why don't you turn him in? Or leave?"

"Aye, there's the rub. I need this job. Like, really need it."

"What do you do?" Atticus asked.

"I hand paint animation cels for sale. I'm only one of three people in the company who has the position. I do it to pay my bills so I have the freedom to finish school as well as freelance, which is my real passion."

"Wow, that's cool. Would I have seen your work?"

"You know that big brick building on Elm with the painting on its side?"

"Holy shit," he said, studying me a little closer, "the one that looks like the bricks have fallen away, revealing strange people living inside compartments?"

"Yeah, that one."

"You did that?" he asked, leaning closer.

"That's me." His eyes cut down to my hands. I held them flat on the bar top. "Yeah, can't ever get the paint all the way off."

"I can't believe you painted that."

"Why?"

"When I have writer's block I'll sit on the bench across the street from it and stare at that painting, imagining the people you drew were alive, and letting their world take over."

I swallowed. "You do?"

He looked at me, really looked at me. "I do."

"What do you write?" I asked.

"Music, Hazel."

"That's right," I realized out loud, as if a bucket of cold water had been dumped over my head. "I almost forgot. You're a musician."

He watched me closely and the intrusion wasn't unwelcome. "Who was it?"

"Who was who?"

"Who was the musician who tainted musicians for you?"

I laughed. "He was older."

"Of course." He smiled.

"I was seventeen and naive, hopeful, and trusting."

"Naturally."

"I fell hard, fast, and without any guard up. I wasn't careful. He chewed me up and spit me out before moving on to the next girl. It was pretty humiliating because I was left reeling and didn't know what was up."

"That can happen," he added, "but you have to admit that was only one guy."

"Right, that's what I thought too, then I met Simon. He

was so charming, so believable, so convincing."

"Oh no." He laughed.

"Then he dropped me like a bad habit when the next pretty bauble walked by."

Atticus laughed, really laughed. "Like children, musicians."

"Exactly!" I told him, smiling. "Needless to say, I've had my fill."

"Were both of them singers?"

"What difference does it make?" I asked.

"It makes a huge difference."

"Then yes," I confirmed.

"Well, there you go. You're dating the wrong band members," he told me.

I shook my head. "Uh, no, it's a musician's personality. It's inherited by all of you. Even good ol' Beethoven was afflicted. You're *all* charming," I said, gesturing down his body, making him laugh, "sweet, funny, hot as hell. I can admit this to you because nothing will come of us so I have carte blanche to say whatever I feel like without fear of sounding like a dweeb."

He grinned at me. "You think I'm hot?"

"Like the surface of the sun, Atticus."

"Huh," he replied, then bit his bottom lip to keep from smiling and studied the bar top.

"Anyway, you're all scoundrels."

Atticus shook his head back and forth, the smile he'd been fighting finally making an appearance. "We're not all that way, Hazel. I promise."

Not caring how he might interpret it, my hand reached up to tuck a stray lock of hair that had fallen out from behind his ear. "But don't you see, Atticus? That's what they all say."

"Then I'll let time do my talking for me."

He spun me in my stool so we faced one another, our knees interwoven. His incredible hand found mine; his long fingers curled around mine and brought it in front of his face. "This is one awe-inspiring hand," he told me, echoing my own sentiments about his. His eyes met mine. "Have you painted anything else in the city?"

"Lots," I whispered, unable to find my voice.

"Sam," Atticus threw out at the bartender, keeping his hand on me, his eyes focused on mine. "Hand me a pen, will ya?"

"Sure," Sam the bartender complied, tossing a pen and a pad of paper near Atticus's elbow.

"Here," he said, letting go of my hand and gathering up the pen and paper. "Write them all down for me."

"All of them?"

"Don't leave a single one out, Hazel."

I picked up the pen and set its tip on the paper. "Okay," I said, lining each address up one after the other.

There were fifteen pieces I'd done across the city. I started with the one nearest to the bar we sat in and worked myself around.

"There," I said, sliding the paper over to him.

Atticus took it and ran his thumb over the indentations of the pen markings then tucked the list into the pocket of his jacket.

"Fuel for the muse," he said with a smile.

"Those thieving birds," I mock complained, not expecting him to get its reference, despite his being a musician, but secure in it still making sense.

"Hang strung from an empty nest," he responded,

shocking me.

"Stop," I ordered him.

"Stop what?"

"Charming me."

"You go first," Atticus insisted.

I smiled at him. "You see this? This is how it starts, Atticus." My smile fell. "You'll put me under your spell, and I'm susceptible to spells. They do things to me and I struggle to get out from underneath them."

He shook his head at me. "I promise not to put you under a spell, Hazel."

I leaned back, away from his intoxicating smell, his inviting smile. "I don't know you, though. I don't know your promises."

"We'll start small, then. I promise not to touch you again tonight, even if I'm dying to, *unless* you ask me."

"Not even a brush of your elbow?"

"Not even a whisper against your cheek, Hazel."

"Fine, we'll see how that goes."

"Good," he told me.

I sat back and crossed my arms to study him. "Tell me something about yourself, Atticus, something unappealing, something to break this tension bubbling up between us."

"Okay, let's see, " he played along. "I'm allergic to peanuts. Does that shatter the illusion?"

I looked at him again. "No, unfortunately it doesn't. You're still as hot as ever. Damn."

He laughed at me. "Okay, try this on, I have crippling stage fright."

I took him in yet again. "No, it's not working; you're still too much to take."

He swallowed audibly and studied me for a moment.

"So you feel it too?"

"Without a doubt," I answered.

"It's crazy, right?"

"I've been attracted to boys before but this," I said, pointing between the two of us, "is on some nuclear level."

"It's definitely teetering on explosive," he admitted. "It's not helping that we're acknowledging it. I thought it would, but it's not."

"For me, it's your hands, your teeth, your throat."

"For me," he admitted, "it's your hands as well, but also your eyes, your face, your hair."

"Should we just walk away?" I asked.

"I don't think I could," he said, his body stiff beside mine. "I don't want to. Do you?"

"No," I told him.

He stared at me for a moment. "I have an idea."

"What?"

"Take me to your painting. Show me all the little things my eyes are probably missing."

"I don't know," I said. "I want to trust you, but I don't know you."

"Here," he said, taking out his wallet and pulling out his ID. He set it on top of the bar. "Take a picture of it and send it to Etta. Tell her we're going on a walk to your Elm painting and you want someone to know who I am and what we're doing."

"I don't know." I hesitated.

"Send it to her. I'll take care of you."

I slid his driver's license closer and considered his face. "Oh my God, you even look hot in this picture." Atticus blushed red, which made me want to roll my eyes or possibly my lips over his skin. The lips one. I'd take the lips option. I huffed. "Fine."

I unlocked my phone and took a picture of his license, sending it to Etta.

I'm taking Atticus to see my painting off Elm, I texted her.

You hussy, she replied.

shut it, Etta

Why send me his license?

bc I want you to have proof of who he is if I'm found murdered in a ditch

you're ridic

it was his idea!

that doesn't make me feel better

not the murder part, dumb ass, the picture part. He did it to make me feel better

Good idea. Fine. I have your evidence. Have fun. Love you, booger butt

Love you, my chocolate covered cherry

I locked my phone. "You've been entered into our database. Proceed."

Atticus stood. "Here's where I would normally offer my hand to help you off your stool—"

I jumped off. "Duly noted." One more Hazel point.

"Sam, I'm out," he called out to the bartender.

"Later, dude."

"Shall we?" he asked, holding out a hand toward the exit.

I started walking toward the door, but he edged around me to open it for me. "Thank you," I told him.

"My pleasure."

The warm night air rushed around us, disturbing leaves

that lay on the street, swirling them around and around with a pretty crackle as they slid in unison across the cobblestones they lived upon. Stars shone bright and sweet in the sky, peppered between tall buildings built at a time when it meant something to build and the moon hung soft and magical, throwing her light on us in beautiful greeting, telling us she was vigilant, she was there for us.

We walked in silence, neither of us feeling uncomfortable, it seemed. Atticus smiled at me and stuck his hands into the pockets of his jacket. I thought he did this to give himself something to do. He seemed to possess a pulsing energy that needed to be addressed constantly. Two blocks away from my painting, he finally spoke.

"How long did it take you to finish it?" he asked.

"Took me about two weeks total, five hours a day. Sometimes I'd work late into the night and would set up these large, crazy lights. The neighbors weren't happy when I did that."

He smiled at me once more. "A small price to pay. I'm sure they regret making any kind of fuss now."

"I don't know, Atticus, not everyone appreciates art."

"People who don't appreciate art aren't living a full life. Art, whether it's music, paint, words, whatever the medium, busts veins of color that usually lay dormant beneath our skin. It gives life love. It opens the mind for greater pursuits. I wonder how many mathematical theorems were bolstered or how many scientific breakthroughs were motivated while listening to Radiohead or looking at a Ron Mueck."

"It's beyond measurement," I agreed, growing more and more attracted to him by the second.

No, Hazel. Go ahead and stop this right now.

My painting was on the side of a three-story brick building. It sat on a corner facing a park newly built by the city. It was prime real estate that caught the attention of several people, thus paintings two through fifteen.

Atticus led me to the bench across the street facing the painting and we sat down.

"What was the hardest part?" he asked me.

"That bit there," I said, pointing to the top right corner of the painting.

"What made it difficult?"

"The subject matter."

Atticus looked at the girl then back at me. "Ahh," he realized, "you're that girl."

She was by herself, a 3D effect gave you the impression she was reaching out of the painting, but you didn't know what she was reaching for unless you looked closer.

"To see what she sees, you just have to look at the reflection in her eyes," I told him.

He leaned closer. "It's too dark." He turned to me and smiled. "What's in there?"

"You'll have to see in the light of day. I don't know if you could handle it here in the dark," I teased, only half kidding.

He laughed. "You're an intriguing girl, Hazel."

"So they say," I hedged.

"Okay, are there any other hidden gems in this masterpiece?"

"Masterpiece, shmasterpiece."

"It's an incredible painting, Hazel. You do know that, right?"

I cleared my throat, uncomfortable with the praise, and ignored his question. "There are twenty-two hidden pieces in there. I painted them for me. Not even Etta knows them."

"Is the reflection in the girl's eyes one of them?"

I swallowed and nodded, afraid to speak.

"I'm honored you told me one then."

He sat back and studied every inch of the painting. I didn't bother looking, I knew the thing by heart, by tears, by sweat. I would be able to recall it even on my deathbed. Instead, I watched him.

"What's your favorite part?" I asked.

He smiled at me, but it felt shy. "I'm afraid to tell you."

I laughed. "Why?"

"Because the part I love the most, that I've always loved the most, it's so obviously you now that I look at her."

I knew exactly what part he was referring to and looked directly at the girl hanging in the center of the painting.

"So you know what part I'm talking about," he stated.

"What do you like about it?" I asked him.

"The way she precariously hangs from the floor above her but doesn't seem to care at all she might fall. I love the way she looks over her shoulder directly at you, the way her eyes haunt you, the shape of her body." I swallowed. "She looks exposed, laid bare, like she's begging for you to catch her but she refuses to ask." Atticus turned to me. "Are you falling, Hazel?"

"Maybe, I don't know."

"Would you like to be caught up?"

I stared at him. "I'm not sure."

He nodded. "How old are you?"

"Twenty-one. How old are you?" I asked.

"Twenty-six. Did you grow up here?"

"No, I moved here for college with Etta and we never

left. Her aunt followed us up three years ago. She's the only family of hers nearby."

"Are you finished with school?" he asked.

"No, but this is my last semester."

"And your family?" he asked.

"I've only my grandma, and she's back home in Austin."

"What's her name?" he asked.

"Hazel."

"Makes sense," he said with a smile.

"Are you from here?" I asked him.

"Yes, born and raised. I've done a fair bit of traveling, though, so I don't feel stuck or anything. I like it here."

"What about your family?"

"I've got five siblings."

"Six kids then! Wow, that's cool. Christmases must be fun there."

"They're awesome. Lots of fighting, lots of food, lots of laughs, lots of lots."

The thought made me grin. "How many brothers and how many sisters?"

"All brothers."

"Oh my God, your poor mother."

This made him laugh, really laugh. "Please, she can throw down with the best of us."

"What does she think of your tattoos?"

"She calls them my 'devil marks.'"

I couldn't help the laugh that came bursting out of me. "That's frank."

He smiled. "To say the least."

"Are you the only one with them?"

"No, all of us boys are covered in them, much to her

dismay."

"That is hilarious. So what are their ages?"

He looked up into the sky as if the numbers were written there. "Let's see, the oldest is thirty-one and it trickles down every year to me."

"You're the youngest then."

"They never let me forget it," he stated, but there was nothing playful in the admission. It felt bitter.

I decided I wouldn't ask.

"Your dad's a pretty fertile guy," I teased.

He laughed. "We all are, apparently." He stretched out his lean, muscled legs and bounced the heel of one boot off the sidewalk. "This city is crawling with Kellys."

"Atticus Kelly," I repeated.

"That's me," he teased with a smile.

"So, Atticus Kelly, do you have any of these supposed little Kellys running around?"

He snorted. "You know the benefit of having five older idiot brothers all tied down to early families because they couldn't keep their shit in their pants?"

"What?" I asked.

"You have the advantage of learning from their mistakes."

I sighed in relief. "Ah, that's good."

"Very good."

Atticus plucked the sheet of paper with the list of my paintings on it and read the next address on Commerce out loud. "Should we?"

"I don't know," I told him.

"Text Etta."

I slid my phone from my bag and unlocked it. My thumb hesitated over Etta's and my last text conversation.

Atticus gently removed my phone from my hand and wrote something to her, hitting send before I could approve. He handed it back to me.

Etta, this is Atticus. Is it okay if I take Hazel to her painting off Commerce?

Have fun, was all she replied.

"Etta thinks it's okay."

I rolled my eyes at him. "Fine, let's go."

We both stood and began walking the two blocks to my next painting.

"You live close?" he asked.

"Yeah, I've got a little studio about seven blocks that way," I said, pointing down Malcolm X. "You?"

"I share an apartment with my brother Aidan uptown."

"Fancy, dude."

He laughed. "Not really. It's his apartment. I just rent. I also help him out from time to time when he has his daughter."

"That's cool."

"My parents live in OC, though."

"Also cool."

"Not really." He laughed. "It's not in one of the new hipster neighborhoods or anything. It's in one of the patchy, watch-your-back, everybody's-packing-a-piece neighborhoods.

"Is it the house you grew up in?"

"Yeah, it was a little rough sometimes. I learned how to fight pretty early on."

"Have you been in a lot of fights?"

He cleared his throat. "A few, yeah."

"Atticus Kelly, are you a little bit dangerous?" I teased.

He smiled and it reached his eyes. "I don't think so. I

will admit that trouble likes to find me a little bit, though. Does that count?"

"Oh, it counts."

"What's your last name?" he asked.

"Stone."

"Hazel Stone." He studied me. "It fits you."

I felt my cheeks heat up. "Thank you."

"Am I changing your mind at all about musicians?" he asked.

I almost choked on the laugh that bubbled from my throat. "Uh, no, Atticus, you're only confirming everything I already thought."

"Just need more time then," he promised.

"More time my ass."

He smiled wide at me then bit at his bottom lip to control its eagerness, I thought. I became fascinated with the ring near his teeth. "When did you get that?" I asked him, pointing at his incredible mouth.

His fingers went to the piercing before falling back down. "I forget it's even there. I think it was about three years ago."

"I like it," I told him.

"Do you?" he asked, coming to a stop. I stopped as well and he leaned in close.

The proximity made my stomach flip over and over. "It's sexy, Atticus, as you are well aware."

The crinkle of his smile met his eyes. "I didn't think so at the time, though, Hazel. I only thought it was cool."

I nodded. "It is, Atticus." The wind picked up around us and blew his scent my way. I took a deep breath and closed my eyes. It was something natural, something woody and aquatic, a hint of patchouli and warm fruits.

"Oh my God," I whispered, my eyes popping open. "If I could, I would lick your skin. What is that?" I asked him.

"Some cologne I smelled at a store once and bought on a whim."

Not bothering with how embarrassed I might find it later, I leaned forward and took a deeper breath.

He bent his neck back but kept his soulful eyes on me. "Go on then," he taunted. I looked at him and he straightened his head. "Chicken?"

I gulped. *That's exactly what I am. A big fat, yellow chicken with a side of fraidy cat.* "No," I bit back, lying through my teeth. "No touching, remember?"

"Ah, yes," he breathed, "*that's why.*" My heart hammered in my chest. "Hazel?"

"Yes?" I whispered.

"We're here."

I turned toward my second painting, surprised we'd already arrived. We stood side by side; the adrenaline from the rush he'd given me still pumped through my veins.

"Um," my voice broke. I cleared my throat. "This is *Evensong.*"

We stared at it under the low glow of the streetlamp. I looked on him then at the painting, trying to experience what he was seeing for the first time. It was an androgynous child, allowing them to be whomever you wanted them to be, a metallic crown set on their head, their face an explosive set of colors dripping down their gorgeous face, down their chin, their throat, down their shoulders, over their clothing and pooling onto the concrete parking lot below. I kept the child's eyes closed. It was a metaphor for life, really. All of us, well, most of us, are living with our eyes closed, sightless to the ironically blinding bright colors of the world around us. Our noses to the grindstone, to our feet, to our hands, to our tasks.

"So busy building a life, we forget to live one," Atticus spoke.

"What?" I asked him, my chest panting from the statement.

"She's blind, isn't she?" he asked.

She. To him the child was a she. "Yes.

"She doesn't live the colors you've painted on her. She merely wears them."

All the breath rushed from my lungs. "Yes, Atticus."

"What's her name?" he asked me.

I looked at him. "Her name's whatever you want it to be."

"What would you name her if you wanted to name her?" he asked me.

"It doesn't matter. That's the point of any painting, though. It belongs to the admirer and only the admirer in the moment they're absorbing it."

He nodded. "Her name is Juniper. I'll call her Juniper then."

"Juniper is a beautiful name for her, Atticus."

He smiled at me. "She's a beautiful child. She deserves a beautiful name."

Atticus looked across the street at a popular pizza place in Deep Ellum. It was packed. It was always packed, though.

"Want to grab a slice?" He glanced at his phone. "It's only midnight."

I didn't know how to answer. I wanted to grab a simple slice of pizza with him more than I had ever wanted to do anything in my entire life but I also knew if I did that, I'd fall fully under his spell. I was already beginning to fall, plummet, more like.

"I don't know, Atticus."

"It's just a slice, Hazel," he said, raising a shoulder.

My heart beat in my throat. "Just a slice, just a look, just a smell, just a mouth, just a throat, just a pair of incredible hands."

Atticus's teasing face dropped. "Just hair begging to be touched, just a pair of haunting eyes, just provocative lips, just a beautiful face, just two talented hands."

"Just." I swallowed.

"Just," he repeated.

"Just a slice," I whispered.

"Just."

We walked quietly, afraid to kick up the explosive chemistry that lay at our feet, bubbling up, ready to boil over. When we reached the door, he opened it for me and we walked beneath the shop's revealing lights. Those fluorescents confessed something terrible to me about him. It betrayed every doubt I'd saved up from the moment I'd met Atticus until then. He was, unfortunately, beyond anything I could imagine. His skin more tempting, his mouth, his throat, his *hands* looked made for me. They weren't a figment of my imagination. He was real.

We stood behind a line ten people deep. The noise was deafening, a cacophony of shouts, laughs, and yells.

"What'll you have?" he asked, gesturing to the old-school sign that hung above the service counter.

"A slice," I answered, afraid to speak, afraid to look at him.

He laughed. "Yeah, a slice, but what kind?"

I took a deep breath to clear my head. "Pepperoni, duh.

What other kind is there?"

He nodded. "It was a stupid question, excuse me." He smiled down at me as I looked up at him.

"Oh no," I quieted.

"Oh no, what?" he volleyed back.

"It's happening," I told him.

"What is?"

"I've forgotten why I don't date musicians."

His smile fell away. "Good."

I shook my head slowly back and forth, mesmerized by him. "No, not good at all."

He didn't reply as we were next in line and they called us forward.

"What'll you have?" pizza guy Dave asked.

Atticus signaled for two slices of pepperoni. "Feel like sharing a Coke?"

Oh my God. "Sure." I was barely able to speak.

"A Coke, please, Dave."

"What kind?" he asked.

Atticus looked at me. I cleared my throat. "Just regular, Dave."

"No problem," he said, sliding two giant pieces of pizza onto paper plates and filling a cup.

Atticus slipped cash over the counter and Dave made like he'd make change. "No," Atticus said, "keep it."

Dave nodded at us both and we each grabbed a plate. As I said, the place was packed but regulars knew in the back corner of the restaurant was a steep staircase leading to an upper floor that looked down on the first. It was quieter up there, darker, more intimate. Atticus went straight for the stairs.

Once we'd climbed them to the top, we picked a table

near the railing and in the corner. We slid into our seats and laid our plates in front of us. I wasted no time folding my pizza in half and taking a bite. Atticus smiled at me then did the same.

Without a word, he reached over and yanked two paper towels off a holder at the far end of the table. He handed me one and I took it from him. He wiped his mouth then brought the Coke to his mouth, his lips around the straw, his eyes on mine, and took a sip. When he was done, he offered the cup to me. My hands clenched the edges of the table as I leaned forward, wrapped my lips around the same straw he'd just drunk from and took a sip. After I swallowed, I sat back, my hands still at the table's edge, and stared at him.

"Thank you for the pizza," I breathed.

He smiled at me and took another bite, wiping his mouth yet again. I followed suit then wiped my own. Slowly, I reached for the cup and brought the straw to my lips before taking a sip. His tongue licked at his bottom lip as I extended my arm and tipped the cup at him. He bent toward the straw and wrapped that incredible mouth over it once more, drinking deep, then sitting back.

"You trying to kill me?" he finally spoke.

"Are you?" I asked him.

He didn't answer. Instead, he said, "More to drink?"

"No, thank you, I'm fine."

"That's too bad."

After a few seconds' pause, we picked up our slices again and took another bite. We stared down at the people below us. A few of them I recognized. I stared at a face I knew.

"Who is that?" Atticus asked me.

I looked at him. "Just someone I used to know," I vaguely explained.

He shook his head and smiled. "How did you know them?"

I sighed. "They're jackasses. My freshman year, that one," I said, pointing at a jock-looking idiot with a popped collar, named Brett, "paid me to *tutor* him," I explained with finger quotes. "Let's just say it was a subject matter I hadn't agreed to."

"French?" he teased.

I fought a smile. "Something like that."

"Did your grandmother raise you?" he casually asked me.

This was a forbidden topic. I knew this. Etta knew this. Grandma knew this. But Atticus Kelly didn't know this.

"Uh, yes, she raised me."

"That's cool," he said.

I nodded, not wanting to talk about it anymore.

"So nothing personal then," he stated with a small smile.

I tried to smile back. "My mom is an addict who had me at sixteen and is God knows where, and I don't even know who my father is. My grandma is my only parent."

"And you love her," he said.

"More than anyone in this entire world."

He nodded. "My mom and dad had my oldest brother pretty young as well. Right out of high school, actually."

"It's cool they stayed together."

Atticus snorted. "I guess."

"What?"

"Nothing."

We finished our pizza and tossed the plates in recycling

then stood next to our table, staring at one another. Atticus made a move for our shared cup and brought it to his lips one last time before doing the same for me. As I drank, he leaned over me, his mouth near my ear. "I should get a refill," he joshed. I pulled away and swallowed.

"Should we?" he asked, throwing a head toward the door. I nodded my answer.

We descended the stairs and made our way toward the exit when Brett recognized me and called out my name. I stopped in my tracks, my shoulders involuntarily hunching up in disgust of the guy.

"Hazel!" Brett shouted. His buddies started laughing at how uncomfortable he made me. "Come on, Hazel, turn around! You remember me, right?"

I cringed. Quietly, Atticus faced me, studied me. Our eyes met and I visibly relaxed.

"Touch me, Atticus," I begged.

A look of relief flashed across his face. His long fingers wrapped around the small of my back and he culled me into his tall, muscled body, the metal on his jacket rattling in singing chimes. As he led me toward the door, his arm around my body, his scent against my nose, he turned toward Brett and gave him a look to kill. All the bravado left Brett and his idiot friends. Brett sat in his chair, turning toward his food, not another word spoken.

"Thank you," I told him.

"I can't accept it, Hazel. If you only knew the thoughts running through my head right now."

I smiled at him. "Would it help if I told you they probably matched my own?"

He looked down at me. "Maybe just a little."

He brought his arm out from around me and I wanted to beg him to put it back.

"Should we walk to your next painting?" he asked me.

"It's cool with me," I told him before looking on him. "Do you want to? If you're tired we can call it a night or whatever."

Atticus stopped, his boots scraped against the bits of gravel on the walk it was so abrupt. "I would stay up for days with you, Hazel. Weeks. Months, if I could. I'd walk the entire city five times over with you if you were willing."

"Why?" I asked, curious.

"I think you're the most interesting person I have ever met, Hazel, that's why."

"But you don't know me."

"I know enough to recognize I want to know more."

We continued walking.

"Do you want to text Etta?" he asked.

I bit my bottom lip in thought before I answered. "No," I whispered.

A look flashed over Atticus's face, something similar to satisfaction, but I didn't really know for sure. I studied his body. He looked nervous—kept tucking his hair behind his ears, his shoulders lifted rapidly over and over in quick breaths. We kept glancing at one another.

Atticus swallowed audibly. "Where is this new painting?"

"It's a little ways. A few blocks to Pearl near the cathedral."

We walked until we came upon the empty parking lot facing the side of a parking garage. The painting was my largest to date at the time and had taken me a total of seven weeks. It was a jumbled mass of words using typography. I studied hundreds of different fonts to find the perfect ones to fit within one another like a giant puzzle. I drew it at least a thousand times on paper before I got it exactly as I wanted. It was beyond tedious.

"What do all these words mean?" Atticus asked.

"There's a pattern to them. Once you figure it out, it reads like a letter."

"Teach me."

I looked at him. "I can't, Atticus."

He nodded. "I can respect that. One day, um, do you think one day you would show me?"

"You think we'll have more than this day, Atticus?"

He got really quiet then sat on the concrete below, extending his legs away from him, and leaning back on the palms of his hands. He tossed his head to the side, signaling he'd like me to join him, so I did.

"Do you want more than these few hours with me?" he asked.

"What do you want me to tell you?"

"I want you to tell me the truth."

"I have two answers for you then."

"What are they?"

"My loud, thumping heart wants to say yes," I admitted. "My rational, cynical mind says no."

He nodded and stared up at my painting. "Your heart is the only honest part of you then."

I bit back a laugh. "How do you know?"

"Because her answer is the only answer you need, Hazel."

"How about we play it by ear?"

Atticus laid flat against the concrete and stared up into

the night sky, so I did the same.

"Fine with me," he answered. "Hey, Hazel?"

I turned my head to look at him, our cheeks pressed against the warm lot.

"Hmm?"

"I have to admit something to you."

"Go on," I urged.

"I want to kiss you. So bad," he divulged. He stared at my lips and swallowed before looking into my eyes once more.

"Atticus," I whispered.

"Yes?" he asked quietly.

"I want you to kiss me too."

He smiled. It grew and fell then grew then fell, like he was fighting words. "I won't do it, though."

This surprised me. "You won't?"

He shook his head from side to side. "No."

"So what should we do instead?" I asked. "Stay here? Lay on this parking lot?"

"Yes," he said, staring back up into the sky.

We sat quietly, the sounds of a sleeping city all around us save for the occasional siren or car passing by. After five minutes' time, he looked at me once more and slowly raised his hand, turning his palm toward me. "Take it, Hazel."

Hesitantly, I fit my palm inside his and he threaded his fingers with mine. The heat from our skin—the electricity from our attraction—made the simple act an incredible experience. I had never in my life reacted to someone like I did with Atticus. It was like a bass drum thumped through my chest, making my skin vibrate, my fingers and toes tingle.

"Wow," I spoke aloud.

He nodded slowly in agreement. "This," he barely got out, "is insanity." He peered at me harder. "Is this real life, Hazel?"

"I don't think so, Atticus."

"Good." He looked at me. "Do you feel this?" he asked, squeezing my hand a little.

"Yes, I feel it."

"What is that?" he asked me.

"It's attraction, Atticus."

"No," he argued, "this isn't attraction, Hazel. This is gravitation."

I squeezed his hand a little in return just to feel the intensity rise.

"Are drums the only instrument you play?" I asked him, suddenly obsessed with the idea that I wanted to know everything about him.

He shook his head. "I play all percussion, piano, guitar, bass guitar, banjo," he said, trailing off.

"Oh, is that all?" I teased.

He smiled at me. "Yeah, just those."

"What do you do for cash?" I asked him.

"I produce albums at The Sink."

This surprised me. "That's kind of cool."

"It's a cool gig, yeah."

"Are you any good?" I asked him.

He squeezed my hand again and my belly floated across the world then back to me. "I'm okay," he said, though I felt he was probably being modest.

"Could I hear some of your stuff?" I asked him.

He licked his bottom lip, and I followed the movement with eager scrutiny. "Of course, Hazel."

He let go of my hand then stood up and crouched over my body, offering it one more time to help me stand. He didn't let go, though, once I was up.

"Let's go back to the bar. If you're cool with it, I can drive us over to The Sink."

I felt a bit shocked because it was then I instantly discovered he could have had said anything at all and I would have agreed to it as long as he still held my hand. "Okay," I agreed.

The walk to the bar was much shorter than I wanted it to be. The butterflies it gave me increased with every step. He led me to the parking lot behind the bar and pointed at an old black '64 Impala. It was in rough shape but it was beautiful.

"Damn, Atticus, this is sweet," I told him.

He smiled at me. "I've had her for years. Can't seem to get rid of her. Every time she breaks down I promise myself she's going to the junk heap, but I always end up finding a way to fix her anyway."

He followed me over to the passenger side of his car and opened its door for me. "Thank you," I told him.

He closed the door behind me and scaled the front of the car, his keys hanging from one of the belt loops of his pants bounced with every step he made, and I followed them as they swung back and forth. *Oh my God*, I thought.

He opened his own door and slid in next to me. When he did this, his cologne wafted over to my side of the car and I had to stop myself from leaning into him. He turned his key in the ignition and the engine rumbled to life. He went to put the car in gear just as another car peeled into the parking lot at an incredible speed.

Atticus's hand shot out and landed across the top of my

chest.

"Fuck, it's my brothers." He turned toward me. "I'm sorry."

"For what?"

"You'll know why in a minute." The car swung itself in front of Atticus's Impala and four huge guys, who looked a lot like him, piled out. They were all beautiful, if I was being honest. It was really no wonder they each had little kids running around. "At least Aidan isn't here," Atticus admitted.

He opened his door and stood but left one booted foot resting inside.

"Well, well, well, look at what we have here. Hello, Atticus," the driver said, and the other boys laughed.

"Get the fuck out of my way, Cillian."

"Make me," the boy he called Cillian responded.

Another boy bent down and eyed me through the windshield. "Oh shit! Atticus has himself a girl in there."

"Shut the fuck up!" another boy shouted.

They all started to box in around us, so I opened my door and stood next to the car.

"Holy fucking shit. She is hot, Atticus!" one boy yelled.

"Seriously?" Atticus said, his hand going to his face. "You are embarrassing as fuck, Malachi."

All his brothers laughed. "What's your name?" Malachi asked me.

"Hazel," I told them, trying to smile, but it didn't translate. I was too intimidated, to be honest.

"What kind of name is Hazel?" Cillian teased.

"I don't know," I shot back. "What kind of name is Cillian?"

A chorus of *oh* sang out around me. Atticus laughed

loudly and shook his head. "You're in for it now," he told me.

I eyed Cillian up and down. "I think I'll be all right," I answered, which sent them all reeling.

"You got a problem, little girl?" Cillian asked.

"You're the only one who seems to have a problem, dude."

Cillian paused for a moment and looked me over. "I like her," he finally said, and I rolled my eyes.

"What are you guys even doing here?" Atticus asked them.

"We're looking for you," one of the boys, not Cillian or Malachi, answered. "Mom told us to come get you."

They were all quiet as they stared me over. Atticus snapped his fingers to get their attention. "Feel like telling me what she wants, Liam?"

"Yeah, she's pissed as shit at you."

Atticus sighed, exasperated. "What now?"

"She's mad you didn't show up to dinner tonight."

Atticus looked over at me, stared at me. "I had something come up," he explained.

"I can see that." Liam laughed. "But you better get your ass home and at least apologize to her."

"I can't," Atticus said.

Malachi and Liam got visibly upset. "You can't do Mom like that, asshole," Malachi threw out.

Mama's boys, apparently.

"I'm sorry, Hazel, it looks like I'll have to show you the studio some other time."

"That's fine," I lied.

"Unless you want to come over," Cillian offered.

"Cillian," Atticus scolded, "she doesn't want to meet

Mom and Dad right now, dude."

"Hold up, fool, why don't you ask her?"

Atticus turned to me. "Uh, I'm sorry. He's an asshole."

I laughed. "It's okay."

"You should just come over," Malachi urged.

"Yeah, Mom won't care," Liam offered.

"I mean, you could come over, if you want. I mean, if you're cool with that or whatever," Atticus said.

The idea of meeting his mom and dad at one in the morning felt odd, but I didn't want to stop hanging out with Atticus. All five boys stared at me with pleading eyes. It would have been hilarious if they hadn't all looked so dangerous.

"Okay, I guess that would be cool," I told them all.

All Atticus's brothers piled back into their car. Their tires squealed as they pulled out of the lot like their car was on fire. Atticus and I got inside his already running car.

He looked at me. "Again, I'm sorry."

I laughed. "What the hell was that?"

Atticus's head fell onto the back of his seat. "That was four out of the six Kelly boys."

"That was insane."

"I know." Atticus put the car in gear. "Listen, you don't have to come. I mean, they're crazy, so I understand if you want me to just drop you off."

I looked on Atticus's face illuminated by the dull lights of the car. "If it's okay, I'd like to hang out with you a little more, get to know you better."

I followed the line of his throat as his Adam's apple bobbed up and down once. "Of course it's okay with me. I-I want to know your skin again, Hazel. You're addicting."

He glanced at me and held his hand out for me, so I took it. When we arrived at a stoplight, he peered down at our hands and memorized the tops of my fingers with his thumb. "You're so soft, Hazel."

"It's the cleanser I use to take the paint off. It exfoliates really well. Because of that I have to use really good moisturizer. It makes for soft hands."

He brought that hand to his mouth and kissed underneath the bend of my knuckles, which sent shivers throughout my entire body. He let go of my hand and unfolded my fingers before placing them at the side of his neck. My thumb found his Adam's apple as he swallowed. Atticus closed his eyes when I did this, which made me want to do it over and over again. He took my hand again and kissed the pad of my thumb, making my stomach plummet to my feet.

The light changed, but he kept my hand in his between our seats. "Will your parents care that I'm coming over so late?" I asked him.

"Did you see my brothers, Hazel?"

"Yeah?"

"Do you think this is the first time we've ever brought someone over this late?"

"I don't know," I told him.

"It's not, Hazel. Though," he cleared his throat, "this is the first time I've ever brought someone over."

All my breath left my lungs in a rush at the thought. "I see."

"My whole family lives at night. Most of my brothers are bartenders at the bar we met at. My brother Aidan owns it."

"Ah, it all makes sense now."

We drove through a part of the city I hadn't ever really seen before. He wasn't kidding when he said it was a little run down. We pulled up to a rough-looking house, although it was the best looking on the block, not that it was saying much. The paint was chipping off to the point you couldn't even tell what the original color was. There were kids' toys settled all throughout the unkempt lawn. All the lights were on, though, and there were loud voices spilling out from inside. I could hear them all the way in the car.

Atticus shut the engine off. "If this is too much for you, just tell me. I know what it looks like because I lived in it. If you want to turn back, Hazel, I can. I'll take you home right now."

I looked away from the house into Atticus's face. "This is so crazy."

He laughed. "I know."

"I'm not going to lie, I'm nervous as shit."

He laughed again. "As you should be. Tell me, Hazel, do you want to go home?"

I took a deep breath. "What the hell, let's just go inside. If I want to go, we can always leave."

"Of course," he said.

He stared at me for a few seconds before exiting the car. I made a move to open my door but he pointed at me through the windshield to keep me where I was.

"Let me open your door for you, Hazel," he said, swinging it open.

My hand found his as he helped me out. He closed it behind me and we traversed the overgrown walkway to scary-looking porch steps. Those loud voices got louder and louder as we ascended the stairs and reached the front door. Atticus swung open the creaky screen door and led me inside.

The noise was almost deafening. Boys were shouting and laughing, a television was blaring somewhere. He led me down a short entryway and around a wall to an open living room connected to a worn kitchen. All the furniture looked old but was covered in plastic. The whole place appeared surprisingly clean. In fact, it smelled like lemon Pine-Sol and a baking cake. It seemed as if Atticus's mom did the absolutely best she could with what she had, and she did a damn good job. The inside, although not new, appeared sweet and homey. It didn't look anything like the outside. I breathed a little bit easier before I realized the whole house had gone deathly quiet and everyone was staring at us.

Without realizing it, I leaned closer into Atticus.

He cleared his throat. "Everyone, this is Hazel Stone. Hazel, you've met Cillian, Liam, and Malachi." I waved at them and they waved back, making me blush. "That's Brendan. He was in the car, but I don't think he spoke."

"Hi," I said.

"Hey, what's up?" Brendan greeted.

"And this is my oldest brother, Aidan," he said, pointing to an older guy, but Atticus's spitting image.

Aidan nodded his head at me.

Atticus walked toward two older people, both blond, both handsome, both with happy expressions, and brought me with him. "Mom and Dad, this is Hazel. Hazel, this is my mom, Sarah, and my dad, Casey."

"Nice to meet you," I said.

Sarah and Casey looked shell shocked I was there, and I

started to get a little uncomfortable.

"I'm sorry, I realize it's late, but the boys said it would be okay to come over." I started to back away, looking to flee. Atticus stopped me by swinging me closer to him.

"Give them a minute," he whispered in my ear.

After another thirty seconds, they looked at one another then at Atticus. "Atticus, you're bringing girls home now?" his dad asked him.

Sarah shook her head as if to clear it. "I'm sorry, baby, where are my manners?" She stood and offered her hand out to me and I took it. "Very nice to meet you. Hazel, is it?"

"Yes, ma'am," I answered.

Casey stood next to her. "You look like a nice girl, Hazel."

"Thank you?"

"Casey, oh my God." Sarah laughed. "I'm sorry, dear, but we don't get many nice girls come through here."

"Hey!" Aidan said.

"Except for your Ellie," Sarah amended, rolling her eyes playfully.

"What are you doing with this bum?" Casey teased Atticus with a wink.

"Jesus, Dad."

"Oh, I'm just teasing, son."

"She *is* too hot for you, Atticus," Cillian chimed in.

"Cillian!" Sarah chided then looked at me. "I did try to instill some manners into these knuckleheads," she explained, "but they didn't stick. Excuse him." I smiled at her. "Here, here, sit," she said, dusting imaginary dirt off the plastic couch surface. Atticus and I sat next to each other on the sofa. I was grateful the television was on.

Otherwise it would have been dead silent in that room. It seemed they were all waiting for me to speak.

"You have a nice home," I told Sarah.

Sarah chuckled. "Oh, darlin', you don't have to worry yourself with that. I know what it is."

"Oh, come now, Sarah," Casey said. "You've made it a real home, babe."

Sarah blushed a little, which I thought was sweet, and smiled. "Thank you, sweetheart."

"Mom," Atticus said, "I'm sorry I missed dinner."

"You should be. It was a good one," she said, shaking her head.

"I'm sorry. I'll be here for next week's. I promise."

"You say that every time, Atticus."

"I came last week, Mom."

"I know, but you're not consistent enough. I raised you better than that."

"I know and I'm sorry."

She leaned forward in her chair and kissed his forehead. "Fine, baby, just be here next week?"

"A promise is a promise."

She nodded once. "You can bring Hazel if you want!"

"Oh, uh, I don't know if Hazel is going to want to do that. She might not want to come," Atticus sputtered out.

"What's the matter?" Aidan asked. "Embarrassed of us?"

"Yeah," Liam ribbed with a blazing smile, "we promise to be on our best behavior, Atticus."

"And a promise is a promise," Malachi teased.

"This was a mistake," Atticus whispered under his breath, making me want to laugh.

"What do you do, Hazel?" Casey asked, ignoring his

sons.

"I paint," I told them.

"Lord alive, another artist," Sarah teased. She winked at Atticus. "I can see why you two would like one another," she added.

Atticus abruptly stood. "Well, this has been sufficiently embarrassing," he said, grabbing my hand and pulling me up beside him, "but we have to go."

"But you just got here!" Casey said, looking confused.

"Yeah, sorry about that. I just came to apologize to Mom. I've got to get Hazel home."

Atticus rushed me through the living room as they all stared after us. "Nice to meet you!" I shouted as we bolted through the door and down the steps.

"She is definitely too hot for Atticus," one of the boys said.

Atticus opened my door for me and I sat. Within seconds, he was in the driver's seat and had started the car.

"That was fun," I told him, and genuinely meant it.

He laughed. "Sure it was."

"No, really, I thought your parents were wonderful."

As we sped down Atticus's parents' dark street, he smiled at me. "Thank you. I also like how you left my brothers out of your compliment completely."

It was my turn to laugh. "Your brothers are, uh, interesting."

"Interesting," he parroted. "Yeah," he said sarcastically.

"Where are you going?" I asked him.

"Anywhere but here," he said, taking a turn down a busy connecting street. He looked at me. "There's a two a.m. showing at the Anjelika, would you be down?"

"Yeah," I answered without hesitation. He smiled at

me. "This is the strangest night of my life," I told him.

"It's a good strange, though?" he asked.

"A great strange, Atticus."

The Anjelika was just down the road from him, and we bought tickets to a film neither of us really cared to see. The lobby was surprisingly full for two in the morning.

Atticus gestured to the concessions. "You want anything?"

"No, thank you," I told him.

"Are you sure?" he asked again. "We could share another Coke," he teased, making my blood race.

"No," I told him, "we won't need it."

He audibly gulped, which made my cheeks warm. He grabbed my hand as we approached the ticket guy. The guy tore our tickets in half.

"Last theater on your left," he droned out.

The theater was pretty packed already, full of noisy and buzzed patrons. I spotted two secluded seats in the top right section of the theater. We raced up the stairs and sat down before realizing the reason they were empty was because two fence bars obstructed the view.

"I don't care," he said.

"I definitely don't care," I agreed.

He rubbed the palms of his hands down his jeans and let out a shaky breath as the lights came down and the first preview began to air. He stared at me and lifted the armrest between us. I lifted and bent my left leg on the seat and turned more fully toward him, my right knee resting against his. He turned as well.

"Can I touch you?" he asked.

"Yes," I whispered.

His incredible hands found my hips and ever so slowly,

he slid me closer to him. He memorized my face before he brought his hands up and threaded them through the top of my hair. My head fell back a little, exposing my throat. He moved his hands down the sides of my neck and placed his lips just above the skin below my ear.

"Can I kiss you here?" he whispered.

I made the slightest nod before I felt them on my skin. My hands found the shirt underneath his jacket at his rib cage and gripped the fabric there. He moved his lips down an inch.

"Can I kiss you here?" he asked again.

"Yes," I whispered.

His lips found my skin once again and my hands tightened even more. He moved his lips another inch.

"Here?"

"Yes."

He kissed me yet again and I began to pull at his shirt, making him laugh into my neck. He moved his mouth to the base of my throat, right at the top edge of my collarbone.

"And here?"

"Please," I begged.

His kissed the dip there, his tongue darting out for just a moment. "Atticus," I breathed.

He placed his lips at my ear. "I have never in my life tasted anything as incredible as your skin, Hazel."

I turned my head so my own mouth found his ear as well, but I had no secrets to tell. Not yet, anyway. Instead, I drew his earlobe into my mouth, running my tongue around the edge. I felt him shudder against my body and smiled at how satisfying it felt to have that kind of power over him.

Atticus's right hand found the hem of my shirt, his bare fingers located the skin at the small of my back, and a small gasp escaped my lips. His hands scorched me there, branded forever. I committed the feeling to memory, wishing I could relive the experience over and over without cease.

"Haze," Atticus spoke against the skin of my throat. "I don't want to be here anymore."

"Atticus," I answered, "neither do I."

He shot up a like a rocket and dragged me back down the stairs with him. We practically ran through the lobby. Atticus threw open the outside doors and we sprinted to his car. He swung me toward him, tightly against his chest; his hands found my jaw and his mouth found my lips. Atticus kissed me like he was dying, and I found myself wanting to go with him, willing to follow him into a dark abyss if that was where I could find him just so I could know his mouth, to know his hands, to know his skin.

He pulled open the door to his back seat and swung his body inside smoothly, bringing me with him. Shrugging off his jacket, he tossed it in the front of the car. I stopped for a moment and studied the exposed skin there at his arms.

"Oh my God," I told him. "These are beautiful."

He swallowed, his chest panting. "Thank you."

The night was dark, the light was minimal. My hands went to the skin of one bicep and pulled it closer, shoving up the sleeve. "Oh my God, Atticus, this is Bosch."

"Yes," he told me quietly, letting me run my fingers up and down the painting he'd had drawn there. "He is one of my favorite painters."

He dragged a thumb across my forehead, shifting a lock

of hair that had fallen there. "Nobody knows Bosch's work." He looked on me and smiled. "I guess a fellow painter would know his stuff, though."

I looked at the floor of his car. It was littered with paperbacks. I picked up book after book after book after book. "You've read *The Screwtape Letters*? And *Utopia*? And *1984*? And *The Count of Monte Cristo*?"

"Yes, Hazel," he answered, kissing my cheek.

Hit with the unmistakable feeling I found someone I was destined to find, I also found myself overwhelmed. My hands went to his face. "Are you real, Atticus Kelly?"

"Are you?" he asked, smashing his mouth against mine.

We tumbled backward against the cushion of his back seat.

And that's the story of the night I, Hazel Stone, lost my virginity.

CHAPTER TWO

The light crested through the window and I was shocked awake, not used to morning sun since my studio apartment had blackout curtains. I was lying against someone's chest. *Atticus's chest.* And half dressed.

Carefully, I pulled myself up, scaled the front seat, bent back over to retrieve my bra and my bag, stuck my bra inside, and crawled through the open window of his driver's side door. I stood in the empty parking lot of the Anjelika, the gray morning surrounding me like a humid blanket. I took a deep breath and reached into my bag for my phone. It was dead. I peeked back inside the Impala and caught a glimpse of Atticus, shirtless, his arm thrown over his face.

"Oh my God," I whispered, my stomach filling with incredible butterflies again.

I looked down at myself, at the blood that had run down my leg and dried there, at my bare feet on cool asphalt, at my blurry, disheveled reflection in the side of his car. *This wasn't how this was supposed to go. I wasn't supposed to lose it to a practical stranger in an old car in a parking lot.* Tears began to fall down my face. *Oh my God, oh my God,* I kept repeating.

Without thinking, I ran as fast as I could, not bothering to pull my boots out of Atticus's car. I had to go, had to run, had to leave. I couldn't stay there anymore. I couldn't face him, couldn't talk to him. *What if he's not who I thought he was?* I asked myself. *I don't even know him. What the hell was I thinking?*

I ran until my breaths burned cold in my chest, my limbs tingled, my bare feet ached. I ran toward the direction of my studio apartment and didn't stop until I reached my front door. Once inside, I tossed my bag on the floor before remembering Etta was probably worried sick. I stuck my phone in its charger, peeled my clothes off, and practically fell into the shower, sitting in the tub and letting the warm water cascade over my tired, sore body. The blood on my legs ran off in rusted rivulets down the drain. I felt sick to my stomach.

"Hazel Stone!" I heard from my living room, making me jump.

"Etta, I'm in here!" I yelled back from my bathroom.

Etta stormed through, tossing back the door and standing in all her heated glory, hands on her hips, her braids dangling at her shoulders.

"What in the actual fuck, Hazel!"

"I know. I'm sorry. My phone died."

"Are you just getting home?" she asked.

I swallowed, fighting the tears. "Yes."

Etta started to look genuinely concerned. "Are you okay?"

"Yes," I assured her.

"Why are you sitting like that?"

"I'm a little sore," I admitted.

Etta fell on top of the closed toilet. "Oh shit, Hazel. You gave your virginity to that boy."

I nodded my head up and down.

"Why?"

"I don't know how it happened, Etta. He was so incredible. Do you know he likes Bosch? Had him painted all over his body. And he reads, Etta. He reads and he is so beautiful and his skin drives me crazy and I have never been more attracted to anyone in my life. And he smells like someone I could eat with a spoon. And his hands move like no one else's. And the things he says and the words he promises and his mouth on my skin and his fingers in my hair," I trailed off.

Etta looked at me carefully. "He sounds perfect for you, Hazel."

I sniffed back my tears. "He is or *was*."

"*Was?* He didn't force himself on you, did he?" She started to stand and adopt her mama bear stance.

It was comical and I laughed a little. "No, no," I insisted, and she sat back down. "No, he was really kind and gentle with me. He was so sweet, and he took really good care of me, but we shouldn't have done it. We should have stopped."

Etta sighed. "Okay, well, maybe you should have, but what's done is done. *What are you going to do now, though?*" she asked.

"What do you mean what am I going to do now? I'm not going to do a damn thing, Etta. I'm going to pretend this never happened, forget all about him, work on my studies, and focus on my art."

Etta rolled her eyes at me. "You are a mess, white girl.

Come on, get up, wash yourself, then crawl into bed. You have to work at ten today and you need to get as much sleep as possible."

I sighed, ready to cry. I felt overwhelmed. "Okay."

Etta bent over and kissed the top of my head. "Try to calm down a little, maybe think about calling him, maybe think about taking things a little slower?"

"No. No way. I couldn't anyway. I don't have his number. Besides, I couldn't ever face him again." I looked at Etta. "I think I got blood in his car."

"Well, that's what happens, dumb ass. How can you be the smartest yet most unschooled child I have ever met in my whole damn life?" She stood and ranted all the way to the front door, closing it behind her. I heard her turn the locks with her own key and made a move to stand myself. I washed my body, cleaned and conditioned my hair, got dressed, and climbed into bed. I set my alarm for nine a.m.

I fell asleep quickly and woke just as quickly, it seemed, with the incessant beeping of my phone alarm. I wanted to kick my own ass. I did my hair, brushed my teeth, and got dressed, grabbing a muffin from a glass container on my kitchen island next to my keys. I hauled to work after walking the few blocks to Normandy's, Atticus's brother Aidan's bar, where my car was.

I walked in five minutes late and my boss, Tim, caught me. *Oh shit*, I thought. My workmate, Madison, looked at me with pity. *Sorry*, she mouthed, knowing what was coming.

"You're late," Tim shot out.

"I know. I'm sorry. I forgot I left my car at the bar last night and had to go pick it up."

His jaw gritted. "*Did you go home with someone?*" he asked me.

I was appalled. "Excuse me?" I asked him.

He stood, panting, his nostrils flared. "Nothing. Never mind. This is your third offense, though. You'll have to be written up."

Tired and sore and sad, I yelled, "What the hell are you talking about, Tim? This would only be the second time I've ever been late in a year."

"Third."

"There was the time my car broke down and when?" I asked, incensed.

"Two months ago, when you brought the donuts in."

Madison looked at Tim like he'd grown two heads.

"You *asked* me to get those, Tim! I wouldn't have been late if you hadn't asked me to get them!"

"Not my problem. You should have left your house earlier."

I huffed a little in disbelief. "Fine, whatever, write me up."

He made a big show out of going to his overgrown desk and pulling out a sheet of paper. His pen bit down as he wrote; I could hear how hard he was pressing on his table. I fell into my own chair and tossed all my stuff at my feet, breaking out all my paints and my latest cel. When Tim was done, he stood up and walked with purpose toward me, slamming down the paper in front of me.

"I need you to sign this," he said.

I made a move to pick up the paper but his stupid hand stayed on top in a show of authority. It was disgusting. I stared at his hand until he removed it and glanced at what he wrote, at each offense.

"I'll only sign this if you let me add that I was late the second time because you asked me to pick up donuts before work."

"No," he said.

Fed up, I stood. "Tim, if you don't let me add that to this sheet of paper, I will walk out that gosh-damn door and never come back."

He stood fully from his crouched position. "Is that a threat, little girl?"

Madison stood as well but stayed at her desk. "Wait, wait, you guys," she said, trying to defuse the situation.

"It's not a threat. It's a fact." I studied him. I decided to call his bluff. "I don't think you want me to quit, Tim. I think you'd be upset if I did. We both know you need a talented painter, and Madison and I are the best in the city. You'll let me add this one thing or I walk."

Tim's shoulders deflated and his face softened. He looked at me as if he wanted to eat me for breakfast, which disgusted me, but I kept my composure. He crumpled the paper in his hands and returned to his desk without another word. Madison sat as well but glanced at me, her hand over her heart, looking visibly shaken.

Sorry, I mouthed at her.

She waved me away with a hand and started back on her work.

I threw my apron on and sat down but as I began to work, I became distracted by thoughts of Atticus, of things he'd said, his skin, his mouth, and my hands began to shake. I stood up and grabbed some water from the water cooler to calm down. When my hands steadied, I returned to work. Tim refused to look at me, which was just dandy with me. I trudged through the first couple hours and when lunch came, I gathered all my stuff and followed Madison out the door.

"You only have twenty-five minutes now," Tim threw out.

Madison looked at me and I shook my head. "Fine, Tim."

As we walked out, she turned to me. "That guy is an idiot, Hazel."

I sighed. "I know, babe. Let's not think about it anymore. Let's get away from this place. What do you want?" I asked her.

"I don't care. We can hit up the food trucks if you want."

"Okay, cool."

We walked down to the food trucks near Klyde Warren Park, got a couple of sandwiches, and sat in the park as we ate. Five bucket drummers hit out a lunchtime concert that made my stomach plummet when I'd begun to imagine Atticus as one of the drummers.

"I've never seen you stand up to Tim like that," Madison commented.

"Dude, I am so sick of his crap. He's constantly threatening to fire us but he never does. It's a power tactic, and I'm done with it."

She nodded as she chewed then swallowed. She looked at me. "You look tired today, babe, what's going on?"

"Madison, uh, I did something kind of stupid last night."

"I kind of figured since you had to go pick your car up this morning."

I set my sandwich down on the wax paper on my lap and let out a slow breath. "I slept with someone."

Madison almost choked. "You didn't."

I nodded, the tears surfacing. "I did."

She set down her food as well and grabbed my hand. "Oh, okay, okay, don't cry. I can't take it when you cry. You look like a Precious Moments doll, and that breaks my heart." I smiled at her stupid reference and wiped the tears away. "Are you okay?"

"Yes, I'll be fine. I just need to get through this day," I said. Little children running through one of the fountain features giggled loudly behind us and we turned to watch them. "I need to get home. Eventually call my grandma."

"What is she gonna say?"

"That I'm a freaking idiot? I don't know, actually."

"Who was the guy? How did you meet?"

"We met at the bar."

Madison's eyes bugged. "What!"

"It sounds bad. It sounds really bad, but he was too much. He was everything I didn't know I wanted and it got to me, through me, and I forgot everything my grandma taught me."

When we were done eating, Madison held my hand and we watched the children running through the water together before heading back to work, back to Tim and his annoying self.

It was late in the year and the sun was starting to set earlier, which meant when I left work, it was dark and that depressed the crap out of me. Etta was at my house when I got home, and we decided to walk the short distance from my studio to Deep Ellum since it was Friday and all the locals came out to play.

As we passed by a telephone pole, Etta snatched a piece of paper off it.

"What is this nonsense?" she asked, shoving the paper in my face.

Hazel, what happened?
Call me, please.
214.555.7986

"Hazel, what happened? Call me, please. 214.555.7986. Oh my God."

Etta snorted. "What did you do to this poor boy?"

We kept walking and there were more. Hundreds of pieces of notebook paper tacked to every surface possible all over Deep Ellum, it seemed. "Etta," I whispered, taking them down as we came upon them. I had a stack at least fifteen thick.

"Call him, Hazel."

I brought my phone up to my face. My thumb hesitated over the unlock button. "I can't."

She shook her head at me. "You are a fool, babe. What would the harm in it be?"

I closed my eyes and tried to steady my beating heart. I dropped all his posters except for the first one and stared at it before folding it up and putting it in my bag along with my phone.

"You're going to call him eventually. You might as well just get it over with. Put the poor fool out of his misery," she said, walking ahead and yanking down new poster after new poster after new poster.

"I can't, Etta."

She rolled her eyes as we headed for the Curtain Club.

One week after Atticus

"Hey, Dave, can I get a slice, please?"

"Sure, babe. How are you?"

"Good. You?"

"Great. Have you called Atticus yet?"

"Not you too, Dave," I whined.

"I can't help it. He's moping around here, making me leave these damn posters all over. Just call the boy."

He handed me my pizza and I gave him cash. "Bye, Dave," I said, heading out the door.

"Call him!" he sang out after me, making my heart race.

Atticus, I thought over and over and over.

***

Two weeks after Atticus

"Hey," Madison greeted. "Have you seen these flyers all over town?" she asked, laying one of Atticus's posters on my desk.

"Yes," I answered simply, grateful Tim wasn't in the office yet.

"Is this your boy?" she asked.

"Maybe."

"*The* boy?"

"Maybe."

"What's his name?" she asked.

"Atticus."

"Call Atticus, Hazel."

Atticus, I thought over and over and over.

Three weeks after Atticus

"Etta, shut up about it already," I demanded, making her laugh.

"I'm just saying we should go to Normandy's tonight. See if he's there."

"No. My word, Etta."

"I'll even let you wear the baby doll again."

I considered the offer. "No," I finally decided.

"You are a fool, babe. Poor, Atticus."

Atticus, I thought over and over and over.

Four weeks after Atticus

"Hey, Etta. Hey, Hazel," someone called out to us on the street as we made our way to the Gypsy Tea Room.

He crossed the street and met up with us.

"Hey, Brandon," I greeted. "What's up?"

"Nothing, gonna hit up the Velvet Hookah. You guys wanna join?" he asked.

"Nah, we're gonna go see The Future Cast at Gypsy."

"Damn, I forgot they opened for Air Review. You know what, do you guys care if I tag along?"

"No," Etta said, "come on, though, or we'll be late."

"Yes, my queen," he teased, making Etta laugh.

"Oh shit," Brandon said, grabbing my arm. "I just realized something."

"What?" I asked.

"You're Hazel. *The* Hazel."

Etta laughed loudly, and I elbowed her in the gut, making her grunt.

"Do you know Atticus Kelly?" Etta asked him.

Brandon nodded his head up and down. "Yes, dude, I know Atticus well."

Damn, I thought.

"I can't believe you're *the* Hazel. The whole damn town has been looking for you. The freaking *Observer* did a piece on you two."

My hand went to my face and pulled. "I know."

Brandon cleared his throat. "You should call Atticus, Hazel."

Atticus, I thought over and over and over.

Five weeks after Atticus

Etta entered my apartment using her key just as I doubled over my bathroom trash can.

"Damn," Etta said, running over to my side. "You okay,

Hazel?"

"Ugh, I don't know. I've got a bad flu."

Etta stood up. "I love you lots, babe. I'd take a bullet for you, but I can't get sick."

"Some friend you are," I teased, wiping my mouth and standing to empty the trash can.

When I had dumped and rinsed the contents into the toilet, I sat at the edge of the tub. Etta walked in and leaned against the doorjamb.

"Did you hear the Toadies were playing the fifteenth?" she asked.

I took a deep breath, trying to control my nausea.

"No, that's cool."

"We should go on Friday if you're feeling better."

"Wait? What?"

"We should go Friday if you're feeling better," she spoke slowly.

"No, no. This Friday is the fifteenth?"

"Yeah."

I stood up in a rush, my head spinning. "Oh shit, Etta."

"What? You're scaring me, Hazel."

"Oh shit, Etta."

"What!"

"I'm late."

"For?"

"My *period*."

"No, no. That can't be right," Etta assuaged.

"No, Etta," I said. "I'm late. I'm never late. Today I am ten days late."

She walked backward until her backside met my bed. "Oh my God, it's Atticus's," she said.

Atticus, I thought over and over and over.

"What are we going to do?" she asked, lifting me just a little bit when she said the word "we."

"I don't know, Etta," I said, sitting back down on the edge of the tub.

"Let's go get a test," she said. "No, stay there," she rationalized. "I'll go get the test. Stay there," she said, standing up and running for the door.

Fifteen minutes later, I could hear Etta swing open my door and slam it closed. "I have it!" she shouted. "I have it."

"I peed in an old Solo cup already. Do you think that's okay?"

"Yeah, I guess." She turned the box around and read the instructions. "It says it needs to be a clean cup."

"I don't care anymore, Etta, break it open."

With shaking hands she tore open the package and handed over a test.

"Okay," she said, "it says you have to hold it in your urine stream or in collected urine for five seconds. Blah, blah, blah, okay, then replace the cap, set it flat, and wait three minutes."

I swallowed and soaked the test strip portion in my pee for five seconds, replaced the cap and laid it flat. Etta and I leaned over the little plastic test and watched as the strip under the window portion turned wet. Eventually two solid pink lines appeared.

"What does that mean?" I asked.

Etta turned the instructions over and pointed at the results portion. "It," she gulped, "it means you're pregnant, Hazel."

My world turned upside down. I fell back a little, unable to stand. Etta grabbed my arm and led me to the bed. We both sat, her arm around my shoulder, neither of us able to say anything for a solid five minutes.

I fell back onto the bed and she followed. I felt numb. "Etta, what the hell just happened?"

"We discovered you do not have the flu, Hazel."

"I can't be pregnant, Etta."

"Hazel."

"I can't, Etta. I can't be pregnant."

Etta sighed. "We need to call Atticus."

I shot upright. "Oh my God, no, Etta!"

Etta sat up as well. "What are you talking about? You have to tell him."

"I most certainly do not have to tell him."

"Hazel!" Etta yelled, standing up and beginning to pace. "You have to tell that boy. He has a right to know. We'll gauge what we do based on what he says. Let's be honest, he'll probably run," she reasoned, "but that's just a bridge we'll have to cross when we come to it."

"Right," I agreed. "He'll probably run. I mean, boys don't want babies." I paused for a moment. "Oh my God, what if he runs?"

"Hazel," she said, grabbing my hands, "no matter what happens, you'll be okay, you know that, right?"

"How can you stand there and say that to me, Etta? I have three months left in the semester too. Oh my God, how am I going to go to class with this freaking nausea! Oh my God, Tim is going to fire me. I'm going to get fired."

"Hazel!" Etta yelled, grabbing my chin. "You're going to finish the semester out before Christmas. You're not going to tell Tim anything until we have to, and you will not get fired. We're going to do this."

I started breathing normally again and felt a little bit better and in control until the nausea hit again. "Out of my way!" I ordered, practically crawling to the toilet and heaving everything in my stomach.

"First things first, you have to find Atticus Kelly," I heard over my shoulder.

CHAPTER THREE

Etta threaded her arm through mine as we approached Normandy's.

"I can't do this," I told her.

She tightened her grip. "Just do it, Hazel. I'll be right out here," she told me, pointing at a patio table.

"You're not coming with me?"

"Girl, are you crazy? I can't go in there while you tell him this difficult-ass personal thing. Man up!"

"Fine, sit out here."

"I love you," she said.

"I love you too, but I don't like you all that well right now."

"That's fine. Now go."

I opened the big, creaky door to Normandy's and stepped inside. It was busy, as always, so I meandered through the crowd and approached the bar. The music pulsed above. My heart raced when I saw Atticus's brother Cillian. I knew the exact moment he saw me.

"You!" he yelled, pointing at me. He leapt over the bar with a look that told me he was going to catch me if I dared attempt to run, and from that look I was thinking about it. "Liam! Brendan! Malachi!" he yelled over his shoulder. "It's Hazel!" I watched as the other three followed their brother's movement and each caught me in their line of sight.

It scared the shit out of me, to be honest. I started to back up a little, ready to bolt, but Cillian caught me by the elbow and smiled at me. "I don't think so, Hazel. Do you mind coming with me?"

"I do, actually," I explained. "I'm looking for Atticus."

"That's splendid then," he said, "because I'll be calling him up here in just a moment."

"Did he say *Hazel*?" one dancer asked another, catching the attention of a few others.

My eyes darted all around me. People had stopped dancing and started whispering.

"It's Hazel," I heard over and over.

"*The* Hazel?"

"*Hazel* Hazel?" one girl asked her friend.

Liam, Malachi, and Brendan joined their brother's side and all four towered over me. "Take her to the office," Cillian told Malachi. "I've got to get back to the bar." Malachi guided me toward the back. "And don't let her leave until Atticus gets here!" he threw out.

Malachi led me down a dark hall; the bass of the music shook the walls around us. "Here you go," Malachi yelled. He opened the door and let me inside. "I'm sure it won't be long. Atticus is just down the road," he promised, making the butterflies in my stomach race at an unbelievable speed. He winked at me and shut the door.

I sat on the edge of my chair, my knee bouncing up and down. I placed my bag on the chair next to me, thought twice, placed it on the ground next to my feet, then stood, unable to sit still. I paced back and forth in what I assumed was Aidan's office when the door opened abruptly and Cillian came sauntering in.

"Hello, Hazel," he greeted cheerfully, a wide smile on his face.

He plopped down in the chair and propped his feet on the desk.

"Hello, Cillian."

"Fancy seeing you here tonight," he stated.

"Listen, I'm looking for Atticus—" I began.

"How ironic. In case you didn't know, Atticus has been looking for you, or have you not seen the thousands of posters he's posted around the city?"

I gulped. "I saw them."

"Is it true you only met him that night?"

"Yes," I answered, settling in my chair again, satisfied the conversation would keep me distracted.

"Do you know that Atticus doesn't date, Hazel?"

My breaths started to speed up. "I didn't know that."

"He can attract them. He just can't ever keep them. He's too cerebral for most and they end up getting bored, they can't keep up. You see, Atticus is the family Good Will Hunting, so fucking smart he got a full scholarship to MIT but gave it up because he wanted to pursue music. The whole family was beyond pissed he did it but, hey, it was what he wanted."

"That's incredible," I admitted.

"So you can imagine our surprise when he brought you over."

I swallowed again. "I see that now."

"The next day he couldn't shut up about you,

wondering what happened to you, if you were okay. He actually called hospitals just to make sure you weren't hurt."

My blood started to race. "Oh my God, I hadn't even considered that," I told him.

"Yeah, maybe you should have, though. Left a little note after you stomped all over his gosh-damn heart?"

I felt my face flush. "That wasn't my intention. I swear."

Cillian studied me for a moment. "Maybe. You know what I really want to know?"

"What?"

"Why now? Why this night? After weeks of posters and his dogged search for you?"

"I need to talk to him."

"You're a hard girl to track down, you know that?" He ignored me. "You're not listed anywhere, not online. It's like you're a ghost, Hazel."

I nodded. "I have to stay hidden or my mom tries to find me and hit me up for cash," I told him truthfully.

He opened his mouth to say something else when the office door blew open, bringing in music and noise from the bar and making me jump.

"Hazel," Atticus promised with a low voice. His eyes swung to his brother and he nodded. Cillian stood and left, closing the door behind him.

Atticus moved beside the door, his back leaning against the wall. He was a mere five feet away from me and I realized time hadn't done anything to diminish the attraction I felt for him. He wore black tattered jeans, a white T-shirt, and a pair of black chucks. His hair was a mess on top of his head, parted on the side. His left hand rested on the handle of the door, and my eyes went to his fingers.

He moved to the desk and sat in the chair there; his forearms rested on its surface.

"Hi, Atticus," I greeted, but he didn't anything.

He didn't answer me. He could only stare, his mouth parted slightly.

"Atticus, I—" I began, but he held up his hand to stay me where I was.

His eyes perused me up and down, and the look sent violent shivers throughout my skin.

He breathed in deep through his nose and leaned back in the chair, throwing out his long legs much like he'd done the night we sat on the bench.

"I've been looking for you," he told me.

"I know," I admitted.

He raised a sardonic brow.

"Atticus," I said, scooting forward in my chair. "I have something I need to tell you."

He licked his bottom lip and stared at me, looking bored, and he waited.

"Um, that night," I said, my throat growing dry.

"That night?"

"I, uh, well, that was, um, my first time ever."

"I'd discovered this," he said. "The blood was a little confusing," he explained, mortifying me.

"I'm sorry. I should have told you."

"Yes," he agreed, his face passive, "you should have."

"I don't date musicians," I told him.

"Yes, you've told me this already."

"I woke up that morning and I felt a little overwhelmed. I'd just lost my, well, you know, and I hadn't expected that to happen."

"I wish you would have told me," he said, a little bit of honesty coming out in his voice.

"I-I wish I had too." I looked down at my folded hands on my lap. "I *really* wish I had said something. Anyway, I'm getting off topic. I have to tell you something."

"What do you need, Hazel?" he asked, making me feel small. He sighed like he was bored, and something switched inside me.

Oh my God, I have to get out of here.

I stood up, sure I'd made a huge mistake in coming that night. He watched as I moved slowly toward the door. He sat up in his chair and leaned forward. "Don't leave, Hazel," he warned.

"I, um, I'll try and—" I stuttered when my back reached the door and my hand found the knob.

Atticus stood in a rush, his face passive, but stalked toward me with purpose, boxing me in. "Say it, Hazel."

"I can't."

"Why?

"I'm a little afraid to."

"You don't have to fear me. I'd never hurt you."

"I know this."

"Then what are you afraid of?" he asked me.

The smell of his skin made me feel dizzy. "I found out something today, and it affects the both of us."

"Oh yeah? And what did—?" he started to say before stopping stone still.

His eyes frantically searched my face, and the tears I'd been trying to hold back came streaming down my face. I sucked in a breath. "I'm so sorry," I told him.

"Wait a minute," he said, staggering back a few steps. His hand went to his mouth and drew down. He folded his arms and sat at the edge of the desk. "Are you telling me you're pregnant, Hazel?"

I nodded, unable to speak.

He let out a breath and stood, both hands went to the top of his head, and he paced back and forth.

"I'm so sorry. I feel like I've ruined your life," I sobbed.

Atticus stopped. His hands fell at his sides and he turned toward me, looking confused before wrapping me up in his arms.

"You haven't ruined my life, Hazel. This is something we did *together.* This is the consequence of what *we* did. Now we just have to sit down and figure out what to do."

He held me in his arms for a long time while I got myself together then sat back, putting his hands on the sides of my neck. "How are you feeling?" he asked.

I laughed a little. "Like shit," I told him truthfully.

"I'm sorry for that."

"It's okay."

"Have you been to a doctor yet?"

"Not yet. I just found out today. Took a test."

He nodded, looking a little shell shocked. "Well, we can guess how far along you are then."

"Yes," I told him. "Atticus?"

"Yeah?"

"I'm scared shitless."

His thumbs found a few straggling tears and wiped them away. "Me too, kid, but maybe we can be scared shitless together."

I nodded.

"I can bring any of my brothers in here and we can ask them whatever questions we want."

"Should we?" I asked.

"I think it might help us a little."

"Okay, that's fine."

"Let me get Cillian." He looked at me. "Don't even think about going anywhere," he said.

"I won't," I told him.

Atticus left the office and I decided to sit down. He returned with Cillian in tow and closed the door behind them.

"Dude, this can't take long. I've got to get back to the bar."

"Cillian, Hazel found out she's pregnant today," Atticus came out and said.

Cillian got really quiet before turning to his brother. "Wait, what?"

"Hazel's pregnant."

Cillian nodded his head and looked at me. "You're pregnant."

"Jesus, this will take all night at this rate!" Atticus shouted. "Yes! Hazel's pregnant."

"Holy shit," he said. "This is crazy to me. I'm sorry *you, Atticus*, got a girl pregnant?"

"What are you trying to say?" I asked, offended.

"No, no! It's not you," Cillian answered me. "It's just not something we ever expected of Atticus."

This is terrible.

"What should we do now?" Atticus asked his brother.

"Well, I mean, are you keeping it?"

"Yes," Atticus and I answered together.

He looked at me, through me, as if to say, *thank you.*

"Okay, you," Cillian said, pointing at me, "need to see a doctor. My girl's got a good one if you want their number."

"Sure, cough it up," Atticus said.

"Fine, let me just text her."

Cillian hit a couple of buttons on his phone then laughed. "She says she thinks this shit is fucking hilarious."

"Tell her thank you so much for the warm congratulations," Atticus spit sarcastically.

"Okay, here's his number," Cillian said, grabbing a sheet of paper and jotting it down.

He handed it over to me and I recorded it in my phone. "Okay, what now?"

"The rest is up to you guys," he said, his hands up as he backed out of the room and escaped through the door.

Atticus stared after his brother, his eyes wide, and focused on the closed door.

"Atticus," I whispered.

He startled, seemingly strung tight, and looked over at me. "You don't have to do anything. I can do this by myself."

"I believe you're strong enough to do this by yourself, but I'd rather do it with you, so can we agree never to bring that up again?" My heart beat in my throat. I nodded as he checked his phone. "I can't believe this," he said.

"What?"

"This band has the most fucked timing." He stuck his phone back in his pocket. "I'm so sorry, Hazel. I have to go to work."

"Oh, okay. Um, I can give you my number and we can meet up later."

He looked at me. "Would you want to come with me? I have a comfortable couch you can lay down on in the studio."

"Would I be in the way?" I asked.

For the first time that night, he smiled at me and I felt my eyes burn. "No, Hazel, you will never be in the way."

"Okay, then, let's go."

He stood up and stared at his feet for a few seconds before looking at me and hesitantly offering his hand. I took it and felt a little relieved. He led me out of the office, down the dark hall to the main part of the busy bar. There was a song playing over the speaker and the crowd loved it, jumping up and down and dancing around. I didn't blame them. It was an incredible song.

"Who is this?" I screamed over the crowd at Atticus.

"What?" he shouted back, moving closer to my ear.

I pointed up. "Whose song is this?"

He stopped and stared at me. "This is my song, Haze."

My mouth dropped open a little bit and he smiled at me before dragging me through the door. Etta was sitting at the table and I ran to her. She threw her arms around my neck.

"He didn't run," I told her, trying to hold back tears.

"That's great, baby," she said.

She let go of me when Atticus came up to us. "Atticus." She smiled.

"Etta," he said, smiling back, "nice to see you again."

She looked at him, and the look sent a clear message. "I'm going home now because I've got to work in the morning." She turned to me and kissed my cheek. "Text me when you get home. I don't care what time it is."

"I will."

"Love you," she said.

"Wait," Atticus said, "did you park in Normandy's lot?"

"Yeah," Etta answered.

"We'll walk you to your car," he said.

Etta's eyes bugged from her head. "Well, damn, Mr. Manners. All right, take me to my car then."

We walked Etta through the lot and made sure she got into her car and drove away before Atticus walked me over to his Impala. My heart started to race.

"The scene of the crime," he teased. I started crying again. "Oh, Hazel, I'm sorry," he said, laughing and wrapping me in a hug.

"I don't know what's wrong with me," my weepy ass sobbed.

"It's a combination of everything, I think. Come on," he said, opening my door for me. I climbed in, glanced in the back for a moment, and noticed my boots were on the seat.

"I left them there just in case I ever ran into you," he told me.

I swallowed. "Thank you."

He started the car and pulled forward. I noticed a pair of fuzzy dice sway back and forth on his rearview mirror. "These are new." I giggled.

Atticus barked out a laugh. "Yeah, I laid a track for a solo artist a few weeks ago and she gave it to me."

"I love anything novelty," I told him.

He tapped his temple. "Noted."

"So you got to see my work, now I get to see yours."

"Yup," he said. He coughed into his hand. "I'm a little nervous, to be honest."

"Don't be. Seriously."

"How can I not be, though? Have you seen your paintings?"

"Flattery will get you everywhere."

"I mean it, Hazel."

"Thank you." I counted to three before I spoke again. "Atticus?"

"Huh?"

"Do you think I could get a copy of that song that was playing at Normandy's?"

"I'll get you anything you want, Hazel."

"I want that song."

"I'll send the track to your phone when I get to the studio."

The Sink was tucked into an old building in Deep Ellum. It was painted a radical green and white in a geometric pattern and had The Sink written in thin metal letters over the top. It looked much smaller than I thought it would be. Atticus parked right out front. I made a move to get out but he grabbed my hand. "Remember?" he asked.

"Yes," I answered, and stayed put while he came to my side of the car and opened the door for me.

He took my hand and helped me out. He approached The Sink's entrance and stuck a key inside the metal door's lock, pushing it open, locking it behind us again, then entered a number combo into a security pad.

"The band recording won't be here for another half hour or so. Follow me," he said, keeping my hand in his.

We walked down a long hall with offices strung along the left side of the building. The right side of the hallway obviously housed the studios because all the walls were covered in expensive-looking acoustic foam. The studio was pretty dark aside from the lights on random equipment. Atticus flipped on a light in an office. I couldn't help the gasp that came from my mouth. There were framed pictures of my first building art piece hung on his walls.

"I've had these for over a year," he confessed.

"That's crazy, Atticus."

He looked at me. "Is it, though?"

I bit my bottom lip and stared at the photos.

"Here," he said, yanking a blanket off an old Chesterfield. "I just came in here to get you this."

He flipped the lights off and led me into a recording studio farthest from the front door. He pointed to a large, plush, leather sofa setting against the farthest wall from the mixing console. I fell into the cushions there and spread the blanket over my legs. Atticus opened up a MacBook and pressed the power button.

His phone chimed, indicating a text, and he checked his last message. "Jamie, Cillian's girlfriend, says you should be eating little things constantly to keep the nausea down in the beginning like this."

"Okay," I said, sitting up, grateful for any advice.

"No sugar, she says."

"All right."

He snapped his fingers. "I've got some almonds in my desk. Do you like almonds?" he asked.

"Yeah, those would be fine."

He sprinted off and returned with a container of almonds and handed them to me. I popped the lid open and ate a few. Atticus went to answer the door when he heard the bell.

"Must be the band. Be right back."

I heard him punch in the security code again and let them in. A jumbled mess of men's voices came trailing down the hall back to the studio and they all piled in one by one. I stood as they entered.

"Guys, this is Hazel," Atticus told them, introducing me.

"Damn, I didn't know Atticus had that much game," one whispered to another.

"Hazel," he continued, "this is the band Thirteen Linen."

"Nice to meet you," I said, waving.

They all smiled or waved and started shrugging off their jackets, setting them on hooks along the wall perpendicular to the one I sat against. Without skipping a beat, they all nestled in, most of the boys on this side of the booth window, one going through to the mic. I sat back down, brought my feet up on the couch crisscross style, and wrapped the blanket around my legs.

Atticus sat at the sounding board, a keyboard to his right and a laptop at his left. He pressed a button on the mixing console. "Ableton crashed for some reason. It's sorting out now. Won't be a minute."

The guy in the booth gave the thumbs up. "Jonathan," Atticus said, turning to his left. "The kick stem is missing something. We're changing it."

"Damn it, Atticus, you always do this."

"I don't give a shit. We're changing it."

He glanced at his computer and messed with a computer program I would bet my life I couldn't navigate through if you paid me a million dollars. He turned to the guy in the booth and gave him two thumbs up. "All right, Alex," Atticus said when he pressed the button that allowed him to talk into the guy in the booth's headphones. "Let's take it from the chorus. Ready whenever you are."

The guy, Alex, started to sing and he was way off pitch, even I could hear it.

"Freaking A, Alex," the guy who Atticus had called Jonathan said. "Can you fix that?" he asked Atticus.

"I can do some pitch blending, yeah, but he needs to get it closer. Alex," he spoke through the mixing console, "one more time."

Alex recorded the same chorus at least twenty times more before Atticus told him to come out of the booth.

"Let me just arrange it," Atticus told them. His fingers glided over his computer as he built layers of something on his screen. He pressed a few buttons on something I would later learn is called a launch pad. As if it was second nature to him, he finessed and arranged their song then turned toward Jonathan.

"This is with the new kick stem," he said, hitting play.

A heavy bass laid out through the overhead speakers, followed by a sick kick drum intro. Even Alex's voice sounded amazing. As the song played, I couldn't believe Atticus had produced it. It had commercial appeal, for sure, but it also had its own flavor, something different, something bigger than I had heard in a very long time, and it gave me butterflies to know he had that kind of talent. It was insane. The song was insane. All of us started swaying in our seats as if we couldn't help ourselves.

Atticus cut it short, disappointing me, and looked at Jonathan. "So?"

"It's the shit," he conceded, making Atticus smile. "You were right."

"You're up," Atticus said, pointing to Jonathan. He went into the booth and sat behind a set of drums then put his headphones on. Atticus leaned over the mixing console. "Warm up with a 6/8 for a minute." Jonathan started playing his drums. "Keep it going," Atticus said, while he put on a pair of headphones himself and started messing around with his laptop.

I started feeling sick again and stood up as quietly as I could, trying to find a bathroom.

Atticus's head whipped my direction and he stood up, his headphones left behind. "You okay?" he asked.

Afraid I might spew all over his carpet if I spoke, I just nodded, gave him a small smile, and made my way out the door into the hall toward the front where I saw a bathroom. Once inside, I closed the door and immediately vomited into the toilet. When I was down to dry-heaving, I took deep breaths to calm my stomach.

I rinsed my mouth out in the sink and wiped my face. Etta, being a nursing student, had the foresight at the store when she got my test to purchase those on-the-go toothbrushes with toothpaste already on them so I could protect my teeth if I was out and got sick. I pulled out the one I'd stuck in my back pocket earlier and with shaking fingers, unwrapped the plastic and brushed my teeth. When I was done, I straightened myself out and emerged, shocked still by Atticus leaning against the wall outside.

"Are you okay?" he asked, concern in his eyes.

"Were you standing there that whole time?" He bit his bottom lip. "Well, that's humiliating."

"No, it's not," he promised, but I didn't believe him. "Do you want to go home?"

"No, it's okay. It's gone now," I told him. *Until the next time, at least.*

Back inside the studio, my face flamed and I almost

laughed when I saw all the worried faces of the boys from Thirteen Linen. I sat down and started to stuff almonds down my throat like the world was ending. The idea of vomiting again was enough for me not to care that I looked like an idiot practically drinking from the canister. Things settled down and they got back to work.

Before I knew it, I'd passed out from exhaustion.

CHAPTER FOUR

"Haze," I heard above me. It was Atticus. He was stroking my hair.

"Hmm?" I asked, turning over. I looked around the studio. It was empty. "Where did everyone go?"

"They left hours ago."

"Hours ago? Why didn't you wake me?"

"Well, you looked comfortable there and I still had some work to do, so I let you sleep." I sat up and stretched. "How are you feeling?"

I still felt full from the almonds. "Good, actually."

He looked relieved. "Are you tired?"

I laughed a little. "Not now."

"Okay," he said, standing up and holding out his hands for me. I took them and he lifted me up.

We stood there, next to each other, breathing in the cool shared air around us. They kept studios almost freezing because the running equipment could get overheated, I guessed. He studied my face. "Does this all feel a little weird?"

"Yes," I told him. "I'm still a little bit in denial."

He bobbed his head up and down but didn't say anything. He peered around the room. I felt like he was unsure of what to say.

"Atticus."

He looked at me, a little bit of a crooked smile on his devastating face. "Hazel."

"Play your drums for me."

His cheeks turned a little pink. He stuck his hands in his pocket and shuffled back and forth like a little boy. My stomach flipped over itself.

"Y-you want to hear me play?" he asked.

"Yes."

He took my hand and butterflies filled my stomach. "Sit right here," he said, setting me in the chair he'd used throughout the night. He tucked my hair behind my ears and set a pair of headphones on my head then touched a button on his mixing console. He leaned over me, his cologne assailing my senses, and messed with his laptop.

He pointed to a button on his screen. "Hit this button when I say so," he said before escaping through the booth door and shutting it behind him.

He sat down at the drums, put on a pair of headphones, and leaned into the microphone. "Give me a thumbs up if you can hear me," his clean, clear voice rang out through my own headphones.

I gave him two thumbs up then began to turn them over to tease him. He gave me a mock sad face, which made me giggle. I flipped them all the way up again and he smiled.

"Okay, Haze," he said, "this shouldn't be too loud, but you should get a good sense of sound. If not, wave at me."

I gave him another thumbs up and waited.

"Now," he said, and I pressed the button he'd told me to.

A song flowed through my headphones. Something that sounded like a plucked string instrument with an echoed accent started it off and it built in layers of accompanying synth, more strings, and a heavy bass beat.

Then all at once, Atticus twirled a stick in his hand, held it briefly in the air, then slammed them down on beat, laying down riffs accompanying the song that sent chills up and down my skin. His hair swung with every down beat. It looked as if he used his entire body while playing, his shoulders gathering and bunching, the muscles in his forearms taut and pulled. His hands. Atticus's hands. Those incredible hands. Memories of the night we had together flooded my memory and I felt hot. The song was beginning to imprint on me, already an automatic association, and I felt inexplicably sad I couldn't live with it on repeat.

It flowed through my veins, and my heart beat pumped heavily every time his drumsticks tapped against the skins of his drums. My hands gripped the edge of the mixing console and, unable to help myself, I stood, leaning closer to the window to watch him more closely, memorize every movement, to learn the way he breathed, the crease in his brow, the set line of his jaw while he played, to know him better.

Atticus was done playing a full two measures before the song breathed its last incredible breath and during those two measures, his chest heaved, his shoulders lifting up and down with each breath. Drumsticks in hands resting on his thighs, his eyes found mine and he stared at my mouth. The fingers of my right hand found my lips, as if I could feel his own on mine again.

Atticus set his headphones on the mic stand near his drums and stood from his stool. He stalked through the room, peering at me from the corner of his eye as he followed me from behind the glass partition. He opened the door and walked back into the room, closing the booth door behind him. His hands found his pockets again and his head bent, cocked to one side.

"Did—" he began then swallowed. "Did you like it?"

I shoved the headphones off my ears and let the headband rest against my neck, my hair caught beneath. "Atticus, that was probably one of the best performances, one of the best songs, I've ever heard."

He toed the ground a little and fought a smile. "So you liked it then?" he fished.

"I didn't just like it, Atticus. I loved it. Did you write that?"

His eyes finally met mine. "Yeah, I wrote that. I have lyrics but I'm still looking for the right person to sing."

"It's so good, Atticus," I told him. "So good."

"Thank you," he quietly replied.

"You don't sing?" I asked him, breaking up the silent room.

"Not even under penalty of death," he teased.

"Good," I told him.

"Good?" he asked, sounding confused.

"Yeah, it's proof you're human after all."

"I'm very human, Hazel," he promised.

"There was a moment, in there," I said, pointing toward his drums, "I wasn't so convinced."

He took his hands out of his pockets and walked forward to stand in front of me. "Well, I am. For instance,

I'm having a very human reaction to your mouth right now."

Butterflies raced just as the nausea renewed, and the moment was doused cold as I doubled over, reached for a small trash bin under the mixing console, and vomited. When I stood, humiliated but feeling relieved, I saw Atticus's face looked sad, like he pitied me.

Without saying anything, I removed the trash liner, cinched it up, and made my way toward the door. Atticus silently followed me, afraid to talk, I thought. I gestured toward the door to have him unlock it for me. I tossed the bag into the dumpster at the side of the building, went back inside, and brushed my teeth yet again.

When I came out of the bathroom, I noticed he'd shut down the studio.

"I guess we need to talk," he said.

"I believe we do," I answered.

"We can go to my place, but my brother will be there with his daughter."

"We need some privacy, I think," I told him.

"Probably."

"Let's go to my apartment."

"Sure. Let me grab a set of clothes at my place, though?"

"Yeah, of course."

"Let's go," he said.

Hesitating a little, he held his hand out for me.

"Atticus?" I asked, his hand hung between us.

"Yes, Hazel?"

"Are you offering that hand because you feel an obligation?"

His eyes softened. "I just want to hold your hand,

Hazel."

I slid my hand into his palm and we threaded our fingers together, making my stomach flip over and over, but in a very good way.

He locked the doors, set the alarm, and led me back out to his car, opening my door for me. We drove uptown to his brother's apartment and parked in the connecting garage. Once inside the posh building, we entered an elevator and I watched his incredible fingers press the button for the twenty-seventh floor. I envied that button.

"So, your brother is banking, huh?"

Atticus laughed. "Have you seen the crowds at Normandy's?"

"Yes," I answered.

It was close to two in the morning when Atticus opened the door. He held a finger over his lips and we tiptoed over smooth concrete floors peppered with random rugs through a quiet house to a bedroom down a long corridor off the open living room and kitchen. When his bedroom door closed, he flipped on the light. The room was organized chaos. Instruments were strewn everywhere, even hung on the walls; random pieces of recording equipment lay along side them. Atticus's bed was big and looked comfortable with its bright white sheets and down comforter. He walked to his closet in the corner, yanked a canvas bag hanging on a hook off the wall, and tossed a few things from his closet inside. He had a connecting bathroom and went to that, grabbing a few essentials along with his toothbrush. He smiled at me as he left the bathroom and held his hand out for me again, so I took it. He flipped off the light and we scaled the hallway once more toward the living room and kitchen.

He stopped short when we saw his brother Aidan in the kitchen wearing a pair of Adidas track pants, shirtless, and hair messy from sleep. I nearly ran into him as we stopped.

"Hello, lovebirds," he greeted us. Aidan turned toward me. "I heard your eggo is preggo."

"Good news travels fast," I whispered.

Atticus looked around. "Where's Molly?"

"In bed, of course," his brother answered.

"Yes," Atticus said, confirming his earlier question.

Aidan looked me over. "Nice to see you again." I smiled at him then he looked over at Atticus. "Never thought this would happen to you."

"Well, it did, Aidan. What of it?"

"I don't know, Atticus. I feel partly responsible for all of you making these kinds of mistakes. I paved the way, so to speak. Maybe you wouldn't have done it if I hadn't taught you all how to do it."

He shrugged. "We're a product of our environment, Aidan."

"That's horseshit. The rest of us may be a product of our environment, but you most certainly are not."

"Well, I think we'll be okay, Aidan. I'm a little bit older than the rest of you when the same thing happened."

"It doesn't matter, though, not really. You're still not in a place to be raising kids."

Atticus tugged on my hand a little and we started walking toward the door until Aidan spoke again.

"You could have had it better than the rest of us, Atticus. You could have made something of yourself."

The wounding declaration saddened and angered me. Angered me because I felt certain Atticus had the potential to make something extraordinary of himself. His talent, his intelligence, was undeniable. Saddened because any chance Atticus had of doing so might have gone right out the door the minute I walked in.

My heart started to beat into my throat when I felt Atticus's hand tighten in mine.

"You're an asshole, Aidan," he gritted.

"You know, for someone so smart, you sure are a fool."

"Keep running your mouth, Aidan, and this won't end well."

"Don't threaten me, Atticus."

"I'm not threatening you, Aidan, but if you're trying to wake up Molly, pissing me off is a good way to do it."

"Fine, we'll talk later."

We made our way to the front door when Aidan threw out, "By the way, Mom and Dad know."

Atticus's hand paused on the door handle. He paused, visibly collecting himself. "Who told them?"

"Cillian."

"That's just great."

"Mom is pretty devastated."

Atticus sighed. "Son of a bitch."

My eyes began to burn.

We left the apartment and didn't say a word as we got into the elevator. Atticus pressed *L* for the lobby and the doors closed. Tears began to fall, so I looked away from him.

"Haze," Atticus said, prodding me with his shoulder.

I tried to compose my voice by clearing it, then answered, "Yeah?"

He wrapped his arms around me and whispered in my ear, "What's wrong?"

"We made a mistake and it's costing you," I spoke into his chest.

"Not any more than it's costing you." He brought me away from him so he could look into my eyes. "I make my own luck, Haze, and I have drive. If nothing else, now I have even *more* reason to find success." He dragged his thumbs across the tops of my cheeks. "Your life. My life. This life. We'll find a way." He smiled at me. "I'm not saying it won't be hard, but we'll do it."

CHAPTER FIVE

When I let him into my studio in Deep Ellum, I watched as he took in all the art on my brick walls.

"Did you do all these?" he asked.

I looked around with him, trying to see them through his eyes. "Yeah, a collection from over the years. I can tell just by looking at them which were my earlier pieces and which weren't. My technique has evolved over the years."

"Always perfecting your craft, yeah?"

"Exactly." I walked over to him and grabbed his canvas bag, taking his hand in mine.

I led him to my bed and tossed his bag on a little reading chair I had in the corner next to it. I crawled on top of my covers and he followed suit. We faced one another on our sides.

"What are we going to do, Atticus?"

"Let's start with the basics before we get into the heavy stuff," he suggested.

"Okay," I agreed.

"Do you have insurance?" he asked. "I can add you to mine if we need to."

"I have pretty good insurance already."

He nodded. "I'll get you Cillian's doctor's number if you want?"

"That would be great, thank you."

We lay there, quiet, neither sure what to say next.

"I have to talk to my parents. Do you want to come with me?" he asked.

"Would you like me to come with you?"

"Hazel, I only want to know what would make you more comfortable."

"I think I'd like to be there. I mean, I think it's important, don't you?" I asked.

"I would prefer for you to be there only because I want my parents to know you." He looked at me. "*I* want to know you," he said.

My eyes burned. Immediately I felt insecure, and doubt seemed to creep in. I wondered if Atticus was as genuine as he seemed or if his generous words were a product of our situation and if it would dissipate with time and the seemingly inevitable growth of bitterness these situations always brought on.

"I want to know you as well," I told him. "Atticus?"

"Yeah."

"A-are you scared?" I asked.

"I'd be lying if I didn't say I wasn't."

"I'm terrified," I admitted.

"That's not abnormal."

"I don't think I'm ready to be a mom yet, Atticus."

Atticus looked stunned. His face read something, but I didn't know what it said. He shook his head as if to clear his thoughts.

"It's a heavy commitment, Haze."

My eyes began to water. “It feels like a cruel joke.”

His brows furrowed. “What does?”

“To get pregnant the first time you have sex.”

The corner of his mouth lifted in a small smile, as if he couldn’t believe it either. “I wish you had said something.”

“It didn’t seem relevant at the time. *Nothing* seemed relevant at the time,” I confessed in a whisper.

“It all happened so fast. I didn’t expect that,” he said.

“There’s something in our chemistry,” I spoke softly, “that is utterly explosive.”

His eyes hooded when I admitted to it. He brought a hand up to my face and slid his fingers gently around my neck; the pad of his thumb followed the line of my jaw. I closed my eyes at his touch and swallowed. When I did this, the skin of my throat pressed deeper into his palm and made my heart race.

“It’s my fault,” he told me. “I should have stopped us.”

“No, it’s not. It’s both our faults. Nothing good ever happens after midnight. We should have called it a night and seen each other the next day or something.”

“You wouldn’t have seen me, Hazel.”

My brows pinched together in earnest. “That’s wrong. We would have seen one another again.”

“If it weren’t for this baby, I wouldn’t have seen you again, Hazel.”

I shook my head against my pillow. “Yes, you would have, Atticus. Before I even found out, I was already starting to feel a little desperate to see you.”

“Why not just come see me before then?”

My face flamed. I was sure my cheeks were painted deep crimson. “Lots of reasons,” I hedged.

“Why, Hazel?”

"Because I was embarrassed, Atticus. You're a virtual stranger. I'd just slept with you in the back of your car, failed to mention that I'd never even done anything before, and left the evidence of as much with you. You're out of my league, dude, and it was all a little hard to wrap my head around. And, to be honest, in the cool light of morning, I felt like you might not be all that real, that who you were was exacerbated by a gorgeous night where the stars aligned just right and perfection was fated.

"But fate had bigger plans for us, it seemed," I continued as he stared into my face. "The pull was tangible." I looked down at my stomach. "And now, so is that night."

Atticus's hand slid down my neck, shoulder, hip, and rounded to settle on the flat of my stomach. His fingers softly bit into the skin there. We stared down at his hand, at the seemingly invisible product of our reckless night. He looked up at me.

"Are you going to tell your grandma soon?" he asked.

My heart started to race at the thought of telling my sweet elderly grandmother news she wouldn't find pleasant at all. "I think I'll wait a few weeks, make sure I'm further along."

He nodded. "That makes sense."

"What are we going to do, Atticus?" I asked him.

"First things first. I think we should get you checked out soon."

"And when I do and it's all confirmed?"

He knew what I was hinting at, and I could tell in his sad expression that he didn't want to consider adoption. He didn't answer. Instead, he breathed deeply, his shoulders rising and falling with his struggling and ever-changing expressions.

"I just want to discuss it, Atticus," I told him, trying to reassure him.

"Of course, let's talk about it, but I just want to preface that with one thing."

"Say it then."

"When Aidan and Ellie told us all they were having a baby, we all fell into a deep depression. It just felt like we were living in a perpetual cycle, and we had expected Aidan to be the first to break that cycle so we could follow suit. Naturally, when it happened, we were distraught. We all perceived their lives as cut short and, frankly, we never got used to the idea of Aidan bringing a baby home with him, not in the entire time Ellie carried Molly.

"But something happened, something profound, when he brought Molly home. There she was, this tiny, insignificant little thing, so fragile, so frightening, but she injected life into all of us and she promised us all a happiness we couldn't have comprehended when we were struggling with the beginning idea of her.

"That's what a child is, Hazel. They're daunting as ideas, but they guarantee happiness beyond measure when they're manifested, looking up at you as if you are the sun and the moon and the stars. That's the look I saw in Molly's eyes and it changed me, changed my perception, changed my mind."

I breathed in his words and let them settle in my chest and head. I knew what he was saying, could hear them, but I couldn't process them. I was still too frightened. "What are you saying, Atticus?"

"I'm saying don't discount it all so quickly, maybe? Let's take some time getting used to the idea of your being pregnant before we start making huge decisions."

"It's too much, though, Atticus. We don't know each other, and you're suggesting we jump into a lifelong commitment with one another."

"We're both rational and seemingly good people, do you agree?"

"Yes," I agreed.

"Then no matter what happens, we know we can act in the best interest of our baby, whether that be at parenting the baby together or deciding to give him or her to a family who deserves them."

I breathed a sigh of relief. I knew I wasn't ready so I was sure adoption was what I wanted at that point. I knew I couldn't be a mom. I didn't know the first thing about it, and I was just starting out my career. I couldn't jeopardize all I'd worked for. I just couldn't.

More than anything, though, I couldn't risk repeating my own mother's history. I refused to let my baby's childhood match mine in any small way.

"Fine, let's just take it one step at a time. Let's get to a doctor," I appeased.

Atticus's shoulders relaxed, which triggered something in me I couldn't quite peg in the moment but later would recognize it as security, something I'd never really felt before on my own. My eyes began to droop closed. Atticus turned me on my side, fitting my back into his chest, and culled me into his body. Sleep overtook the both of us. Me more quickly than him.

CHAPTER SIX

I woke suddenly with violent nausea. Peeling Atticus's hands from around me, I sprinted from the bed toward my bathroom, barely making it to the toilet before spilling bile since there was nothing in my stomach, which turned into dry-heaving. When I no longer felt ill, I stood and brushed my teeth, making my way back toward the bed but stopped short when I noticed Atticus was no longer there.

I looked around and caught him bent over in the fridge. He stood when he heard me pad into the room and turned my direction.

"How are you?" he asked.

"Sick," I mumbled, folding myself onto one of my chic, therefore uncomfortable, metal grated bar stools at my kitchen island.

"I was going to make you some eggs. Does that sound good?" he asked.

"It sounds awful, to be honest, but necessary, so yes, please."

"I can make you anything you have here. I can also go

out really quick and get you something. Just name it, Hazel."

I forced a smile. "Thank you, but eggs are fine. Nothing really sounds good, but I know I need to eat, so it might as well be something with protein."

Atticus whipped up a really tasty omelet, which surprised me. "This is great," I practically yelped.

He laughed. "Are you surprised or something?"

"Well, kinda, I mean, you don't look like someone who can cook."

"Oh yeah?" he asked. "Who do I look like?"

I felt my cheeks heat up. "I don't know."

"Tell me," he urged. He gripped the edge of the countertop on the island, facing me, and leaned in.

"You look like someone who gets their eggs made for *them*. Always."

"Do I?" he asked, the look in his eyes a little dangerous, a little teasing. It made my heart race.

"Yes," I whispered.

"You'd be right, Hazel. I don't make eggs for *anyone*."

"Except for me?"

He nodded once then turned toward my sink and cleaned up after himself. I watched his hands as he worked until he stopped and I looked up. He'd caught me.

"Are you watching me, Hazel?" he asked.

My whole body heated up to an impossible temperature. "Your hands," I told him.

He reached over the island and threaded them through my hair, dragging them through to the tips. "Be right back," he promised, and grabbed his duffel before heading to the bathroom. I heard the shower running and breathed a sigh of relief. He was too much to take in large doses like that. Any more time alone and I knew I'd find myself tumbling on top of my bed, complicating even further an already complicated situation.

When he was done, the door opened and he was showered and dressed, his hair wet. He smelled incredible, so I held my breath as I gathered my own stuff, locking myself in my bathroom if nothing but to catch my breath.

"He's too much," I whispered, turning the water on.

When I was done showering and got dressed, I opened the door to air out the room so I could dry my hair. Atticus was lying on my bed and sat up when he heard me. I smiled at him and got my blow-dryer from underneath the sink, plugging it in. He came into the room, bringing those hands and that scent with him. I felt my stomach flip on itself. He sat at the edge of the tub and faced me, smiling at me, which made my stomach flip once more. I turned on the blow-dryer and began to dry my hair. Atticus folded his arms as he studied me, and I couldn't help but laugh at him.

"What?" I shouted over the din of the dryer.

"You're very pretty, Hazel," he complimented.

"Oh whatever! I don't have any makeup on and my hair is a mess."

He stood and took the dryer from my hands, turning it off. The instant quiet was deafening.

"I'm serious, Hazel," he told me, taking me in his arms. "You are so beautiful."

I lifted my chin to get a better look at him, which brought our mouths dangerously close to one another. He leaned over me and brushed the tip of his nose against mine. "You smell good," he said with hooded eyes. "I wonder if you taste as good as you smell, though."

"There's only one way to find out," I barely got out.

He pressed his lips against my lips; his tongue swept across mine. A small moan escaped his mouth and I felt the vibration of it down my throat. I dropped my brush and heard it click on the tile of the bathroom as I wrapped my arms around his neck. He splayed his hands across my backside and he lifted me, sliding his fingers down to cup the backs of my knees, and sat me on the bathroom counter. We kissed until our lips were raw and time became irrelevant.

When we broke apart, he looked as surprised as I felt. His chest panting, he brought his hands up and ran them through his damp hair. "Damn, Hazel, what is wrong with us?"

I couldn't help the giggle that escaped. "I don't know. Honestly."

"We've got to get out of here unless we want to make yet another mistake. We can't complicate this any more."

I took a deep breath. "Agreed."

I hopped off the counter and finished my hair. He sat at the edge of the tub, looking ready to jump me again. I threw on my makeup and left the bathroom quickly. Atticus following me closely, and we left the apartment in a rush. The clear light of day sobered us a little; I felt as if I could breathe. The reality of what we were about to do brought me all the way back down.

Atticus opened his passenger side door for me and I hopped in. He rounded the front and got in, starting the car and heading toward Oak Cliff to his parents' house. When we pulled up, it looked a lot different than I'd last seen it. There were still toys in the yard but they were organized against the front of the house, and the lawn looked freshly cut and edged. Atticus's dad was outside hand-scraping the peeling paint, readying it to be painted, I assumed. His mom was in the front garden pulling weeds and yanking up its stone border. There were buckets of paint on the porch all stacked on top of each other. Cillian was pulling rickety shutter accents off the window siding and piling them on the walkway.

Butterflies filled my stomach. Atticus looked at me and I at him.

"Here we go," I said.

My hand went to my door handle but Atticus placed his hand on my arm. "Let me get that for you, Hazel."

He got out, jogged to my side of the car, and opened my door for me. By this time, his parents, Cillian, as well as Brendan and Malachi, who I'd discovered were on the sides of the house, all came out front. They all looked hot, and their eyes squinted in the sun as we walked up together. Atticus took my hand, which bolstered me, and we came to a stop in front of the porch. We stayed quiet while Sarah and Casey, sullen faces and all, sat at the top of the porch stairs.

"Aidan said you already know," Atticus began.

Cillian placed his hands on his hips. "I told them," he admitted.

Atticus shook his head. "What the hell, dude? Did it not occur to you that I might want to be the one to break the news?"

Cillian lifted a shoulder.

"It doesn't matter who told me," Sarah said with tears in her eyes. "How could you do this, Atticus?"

I felt my chest tighten.

"Mom, it wasn't planned."

"It never is, Atticus, but here you are now because of it, a waste of intelligence and potential. It just makes me sick to my stomach that this is the path you have chosen for yourself."

Oh shit, I thought, feeling the urge to flee along with an overpowering surge of nausea.

"Intelligence isn't wasted, Mom. It can be misapplied, but it can't ever be wasted."

She looked beyond pissed he'd chosen that moment to contradict her. "What's the difference, Atticus?"

"A misapplication still has room for potential. This won't change anything."

She laughed but it was caustic and made me want to crawl beneath their porch. "Just goes to show you can be as book smart as they come but still be as clueless as the day is long. Atticus, life can't be taught in books, son. It has to be experienced, and I've endured it in droves. Trust me, the dreams you have now are long gone."

"You're being dramatic," he said, looking exasperated.

"Well, you're just going to have to get married," Casey chimed in.

"Whoa, whoa," I said, backing up a little.

"Dad, no," Atticus told him, keeping hold of my hand.

"Do you want to end up like Liam and Malachi? Watching other men play part-time daddy to your kid?" Sarah asked.

"No, of course not, but two wrongs don't make a right. Hazel and I barely know one another."

"Well, get comfortable with each other because you're in this for life. You might as well just marry at this point," Sarah added.

The prospect of marrying Atticus, although someone I

was insanely attracted to and seemingly compatible with, was too daunting an idea. *We'd just met!* "We might give the baby up for adoption," I blurted out, hoping to shift the direction of the conversation.

All of Atticus's family looked at me like they just noticed me.

"Now, this makes sense," Sarah said, a look of relief on her face.

"Wait," Atticus said, facing me, "we said we'd talk about this."

"I know and we will, but I'm more than certain we're going to be giving this baby up, Atticus."

He looked at his feet and shook his head. "I can't have this conversation in front of my family."

"Of course," I agreed, wishing I hadn't said anything.

Etta chose this time to text me, so I stepped aside for a second.

What the hell, Hazel?

shit, sorry. I'm at Atticus's telling the parentals

Oh damn. that shit is so awkward I don't even want to b on text with you

thanks, punk ass

love you

love you too

good luck, she threw in.

thanks

"…and it's none of your fucking business, Liam!" Atticus shouted as he barreled toward me.

My eyes shot wide. "What's going on?"

Atticus shook his head. "Nothing, let's go," he said, grabbing my hand.

"You'll see!" Liam yelled back.

"Just come back for a second," Sarah pleaded.

Atticus shook his head as he led me back to his car and opened my door for me.

"Listen to us!" Casey threw out.

Atticus slid across the hood of his car and piled into the driver's seat, starting the engine, effectively drowning out his family's pleas, and pulled out onto the street.

"Where are we going?" I asked.

"Somewhere we can think," he simply answered.

The entire ride he was quiet. I didn't dare interrupt his thoughts, as he looked too engrossed, like he was trying to remember something. We wound through city streets quickly until we hooked a left on Lemmon. I discovered where he was going.

"The fourth painting," I whispered.

"Yes," he answered.

We pulled into the lot next to my painting and parked. My hand went for the handle again.

"Hazel," he said, "please let me get the door for you."

I nodded.

He let me out of the car and we walked toward the side of the building with my painting.

"Tell me about this one," he said, a tinge of desperation in his tone.

Instead of answering him, I grabbed his hand and placed it palm up on top of mine. I took an index finger and traced the lines in his hand. "Describe it to me," I told him.

He stayed silent for a moment while I ran my finger over the skin of his hand then answered, "It's a woman. She's so realistic I almost find her unbelievable. Isn't that strange?" I smiled at this. "She's wearing a soft pink gown, plush, looks to be late 1700s." He turned toward me. "She's wearing a crown. Is that Marie Antoinette?"

I nodded in confirmation. "Tell me more," I said, still tracing his hand.

"She's falling from somewhere high, but she's reaching for something, a giant diamond necklace."

"Yes," I told him.

"It's The Affair of the Diamond Necklace," he discerned, leaving me impressed. "You've painted an idea."

My hand stopped. "Yes. Which one, though?"

His eyes narrowed as if he was thinking very hard about what it might be.

"You've painted disillusionment."

My palm flattened on his. "That's right," I said, astonished.

"The story says that King Louis XVI commissioned the necklace for one of his mistresses—Madame du Barry—but died before it was completed, which prompted the jewelers to plot to have Marie pick up the tab after failing to sell it outside France. But when she refused, after a much publicized scandal and trial of the real culprits and even though she wasn't involved at all, it was implied that Marie had tried to defraud them, which, unbeknownst to Marie, was the first nail in her coffin as the French used it to confirm their growing disillusionment with the monarchy that eventually led to the French Revolution and poor Marie met the guillotine.

"They had already been slipping from her fingers but that was the first fall, the one that tarnished her irreparably, and the dominos began to topple. She was a scapegoat."

"Let them eat cake," he said.

"Indeed," I answered. I looked at him. "How are you feeling?"

He stared at me. "I'm amazed and a little overwhelmed by your talent right now, why?"

"I meant about our meeting with your parents today."

He offered a small smile. "I know, Hazel."

"Tell me then."

"Can we strike a deal?" he hedged.

"Depends on what it is."

"Let's put the adoption thing on a shelf, just for the time being. Give me three months, give *us* three months. Let's get to know one another, see what happens."

"I don't know, Atticus."

"Just three months, Hazel, and if you still feel as strongly as you do right now, then I'll support you one hundred percent."

I thought about it for a moment then agreed. "Fine, I guess."

His face lit up like the Fourth. "Yes!" he said, throwing me in his arms and swinging me around. He kissed my neck as he set me back down. "Thank you, Hazel."

CHAPTER SEVEN

The following Tuesday, the doctor Atticus's brother recommended agreed to see me before work. Atticus asked if he could pick me up and I said yes. I rushed to the door that morning after I heard him knock, eager to see him. When I swung the door open, he practically tackled me in a hug and kissed my neck, making me giggle. He handed me a bag of something and I peeked inside.

It was a bagel with cream cheese. At first I was excited but after catching a whiff of the cream cheese, I held the bag far from my face, dropping it at my feet and promptly finding the nearest trash bin to catch my vomit.

"Shit, Hazel, I'm sorry," Atticus offered when I returned from brushing my teeth for the fourth time that morning.

"I'm sorry, babe. It was so nice, I promise. I just didn't realize I had an aversion to cream cheese until that moment."

His brows furrowed as he fought a smile. "What did you call me?" he asked.

"Atticus?"

"No, you called me babe."

My face heated up. "I did?"

"Yes, you called me babe."

"I'm sorry. Is that not okay?"

He reached out for me and wrapped his arm around my waist. "It's more than okay, Hazel. I liked it."

"Good," I said, placing the palms of my hands on his cheeks. I brought his face down so I could kiss his lips but pulled away quickly, afraid we'd lose track of time if I let it deepen.

Atticus moaned in complaint, making me laugh. "Can't we just stay here all day?" he asked, then kissed below an ear. "I'll make it worth it," he teased.

I laughed. "We can't, Atticus. The whole reason I even have to see a doctor this morning is because of promises like that."

"Fine," he groaned.

I locked up my apartment and he drove me to my appointment. He held the door open for me and after I checked in, we sat in a waiting room with four other women all in various stages of pregnancy, which weirded me the hell out, let me tell you.

"Fool, I cannot do this," I whispered over my shoulder.

Atticus looked equally freaked. "It'll be okay," he lied. He swallowed, his Adam's apple bobbing up and down.

I stared at him. "You are joking, right?" I gestured to the woman in the room who looked the furthest along and therefore the one who looked the most uncomfortable. "She has her own gravitational pull. If we get too close, we're likely to get sucked in. She is the black hole of pregnancies."

Atticus fought a laugh. "Hazel, come on, man."

"Come on, man? *Come on, man?*" I asked, getting more and more freaked out by the second.

"Hazel Stone," a nurse announced. I stood quickly, ready to bounce the place like a bad habit. "The doctor will see you now."

Atticus stood beside me and took my hand, leading me toward the door. "Don't make me do this, Atticus."

"You have to, Hazel."

"Why? Why do I have to do this? I think this doctor thing is a little overrated. I mean, it's just a giant racket, if you ask me. What did women do before gynos, huh?"

"They died, Hazel. Now, come on," he said, practically dragging me toward the back.

The nurse watched me like I was a rabid dog. I plastered a fake smile on my face and bucked up.

"Can I get your weight?" she asked.

"Oh my God, why?" I asked, turning toward Atticus.

The nurse laughed. "We just need to monitor your weight gain as you progress, honey. It's no big deal."

"Turn around," I ordered Atticus, and he obeyed.

I dropped my bag on the floor and stepped on the scale.

"One twenty-five," the nurse announced to the whole gosh-damn world. Atticus's shoulders began to shake.

Come on, lady! I screamed in my head.

She took my temperature then handed me a plastic specimen cup and two alcohol wipes. "Follow the directions on the packet, sweetheart, and catch a clean specimen mid-stream, slide it into that little door in the room then meet me back here."

I took it all into the bathroom with me and did as she asked. When I was done, I left the bathroom, meeting

Atticus and the nurse outside again. She led me into the room with the dreaded table and handed me a paper gown. "Dress down to nothing, please, and put this on for us. The doctor will be in in just a minute."

"Thank you," I told her as she left the room, though I didn't really mean it.

Atticus watched me. "Well?" he asked as I stood there waiting for him to turn around.

"What do you mean *well*?"

"Do your stuff. Let me see that sweet—" he began, but I cut him off.

"Atticus."

He laughed. "What?"

I tried not to laugh. "Face the wall."

"What? Why? It's not like I haven't already seen—"

"Oh my God, Atticus, please."

He huffed like he was put out but turned around. I quickly took off my clothes, bra, and panties and threw them over his shoulder. I chucked my shoes to the side and slipped on the paper gown, sitting on the table. Atticus lifted my bra and panties as he turned around toward me again. He shifted his brows up and down suggestively.

"Oh my God," I said, snatching them from his hands and folding them in my clothing. I handed them over again and ordered he set them on the table by the only other chair in the room beside the doctor's rolling stool.

"This isn't how I imagined your getting naked in front of me again."

I snorted. "Please."

"Exactly," he flirted.

I coughed into a hand. "You're impossible," I told him.

It was freezing on the table, and I began to shiver.

Atticus followed the movement. "You're cold," he stated.

"Yeah, these things don't give you much coverage, and they keep these rooms just above freezing."

"Sadists," he said just as the doctor came in the room.

I didn't let him explain himself and spoke to the doctor right away.

"Dr. Kagan?"

"Yes," he said, eyeing tattoo-covered Atticus briefly before offering his hand to me and smiling. "Hazel Stone?"

"Yes, nice to meet you." Dr. Kagan's eyes swung to Atticus. "Excuse me, how rude, this is my baby daddy," I told Dr. Kagan as Atticus held out his hand. Atticus choked on nothing.

Dr. Kagan smiled, unsure of what to make of us, it seemed, then took Atticus's hand. "Nice to meet you."

"Nice to meet you as well," Atticus replied before giving me a death glare and making me laugh.

"So you believe you're pregnant?" the doctor asked.

"Yes, I believe that is my current predicament."

"What kind of symptoms are you having?" he asked.

"Let's see, I believe I first noticed when I started ralphing fifteen times a day. That was a pretty good indicator, but that coupled with the fact that I missed the inclination to buy fifteen pounds of chocolate and inhaling it all while drunk dialing men listed as Justin Bieber in the phone book was the clincher."

"So you haven't taken a test?" he asked.

"Yes, I took a test."

"And it was positive? Iffy?" he asked, marking a chart.

"It was, like, positive with a capital P."

He nodded and rolled his stool toward a box of gloves

set in a wire shelf on the wall. He took two out and started to put them on.

"Okay, lie back for me?" he asked.

I obeyed but snapped my fingers for Atticus to come meet me at my head. He jumped up and met my side, taking my hand. Dr. Kagan pulled out the stirrups and placed my heels inside.

He flipped on an exam lamp and brought it closer to his head. "Scoot all the way to the edge for me?" I slid my body toward him. He grabbed a bottle of gel in a warming tray and squirted some on his glove. "Just relax for me," he said, which is the exact opposite thing a body wants to do in that situation. Why do doctors always ask you to relax, like that's even an option?

He felt around in there, which was uber-uncomfortable, then slid his hand out and tossed his gloves. "Well, congratulations, you two," he said kindly. "You're pregnant."

Atticus's hand squeezed mine and I squeezed back. "I'm going to write you a couple of prescriptions for some vitamins. You can get dressed here in a minute and the both of you can come into my office and I'll go over birthing procedures and what you can expect during your pregnancy, and I'll answer any questions you have." He rolled his chair toward his sink, stood, and began to wash his hands. "Does that sound good?" he asked.

I swallowed, still reeling from the fact that he confirmed I was indeed pregnant. It wasn't as if I didn't know, but to hear it from a doctor's mouth felt surreal for some reason.

"That's great," Atticus answered for me.

Dr. Kagan turned around after he dried his hands and smiled. "All right, once you're done, come meet me in my office. It's right next door." Dr. Kagan didn't wait for a response and left the room.

"Too bad they don't have a *currently knocked up* option on social media," I teased Atticus.

Atticus fell into the armchair, gathered all my clothing, and handed them to me. I pulled on my underwear and jeans underneath my gown as Atticus stared into space. I turned my back toward him, put my bra on, as well as pulled on my shirt. I straightened it all out and stood in front of him.

"My womb is definitely *ocupado*," I stated, hoping to alleviate some of the tension.

Atticus looked up into my face. "No vacancy."

I smiled at him. "My egg is so taken Liam Neeson will be starring in the film version."

Atticus laughed, the shock in his eyes dissipating a little. "A high-occupancy vehicle."

This gave me an idea. "Does this mean I can drive in the HOV lane now?" I asked.

Atticus shook his head. "I think it only applies to individuals breathing air."

"Oh, I see."

"Should we go to his office?" he asked.

I swallowed the nervous butterflies desperate to escape. "Yeah," I breathed.

Inside, we sat and listened to twenty minutes of information I definitely didn't remember being taught in sex ed. All I kept thinking while he spouted fact after fact after procedure after procedure after process after process was the fact that if *he* had taught my sex ed, I wouldn't have been in his office that very moment.

When he was all done scaring the shit out of me, we

stood and walked toward reception, both of us looking shell shocked. We stood at the desk then sat silently when the receptionist indicated for us to sit.

"You there, honey?" the receptionist asked, tapping the top of her desk.

I shook my head to clear my thoughts. "Yes, I'm sorry."

"I said, is next month at the same time okay?"

I took a deep breath. "What day?"

"The twenty-second at seven a.m.?" she asked.

I thought for a moment. "Uh, yeah, that's fine."

She took a card from a little tray and wrote my appointment time on it then handed it to me. I stuffed it in my bag and I meandered my way through the waiting room, out the doors, into the morning sun. Atticus met my side and we stared into the parking lot.

"I can't believe I have to go to work right now," I barely eked out.

Atticus turned toward me. "Can you call in?"

I sighed. "It would be a bad idea. Tim is kind of a tyrant."

"I've never met the guy and yet I want to kick his ass."

I laughed then sighed. "It's the thought."

"Come on," he said, grabbing my hand and leading me to his car.

He let me inside and shut the door after me. We rode in silence, not even music on his stereo, all the way to my work. I waited for him to open my door for me; this time he didn't have to prompt me. He leaned in to grab my hand and I went to kiss his cheek as I stood. He turned his face toward mine quickly and caught my mouth with his.

"I'm going to walk you to the door," he spoke against my lips.

I didn't argue with him, despite the fact there was a chance that Tim could see him and it might make my day even worse than it already was going to be fighting morning sickness and Tim's odd obsession with me. I couldn't bring myself to care. Not even a little bit. Atticus's hand went to the back of my neck and I fought the urge to roll my head back.

Five steps from the door. Four. Three. Two. One.

Atticus swung me against him, his other hand biting into the bone of my hip, something desperate in the touch that made me want to melt in a puddle at his feet.

"What time should I pick you up?" he asked.

"Don't worry about it," I said. "I have class tonight at six. I'll just catch the bus to my studio and pick up my car."

He smiled at me. "What time, Hazel?"

"Five."

"I'll be right here waiting."

"But it's not necessary. I—"

"Hazel," he interrupted, "I'll be right here."

"Okay," I agreed as his lips swept over mine.

He took a deep breath against my skin as if he was inhaling everything in the moment and when his tongue found mine, I knew he was tasting it as well. He pulled away too soon and started to walk backward away from me.

"Five o'clock, Hazel Stone."

"Five o'clock, Atticus Kelly."

I turned away from him and swung open the door to the artist's studio. Madison wasn't there yet but Tim was. He stood by my desk, his arms crossed against his chest, facing the window and looking out into the courtyard

Atticus and I were just in.

"So you must be the Hazel on all those flyers," Tim spit out, disbelief in his tone.

I cleared my throat and hung my bag on the side hook of my workstation. "Uh, yeah, that's me."

Tim pointed into the empty courtyard. "And that's the guy who put them up," he stated more than asked.

"Yes," I confirmed, sitting at my desk and tossing my apron over my shoulders.

I began to open my watercolors and inspect all my brushes.

"Did you sleep with him last night? Is that why he dropped you off today?" he asked.

The questions caught me off guard and I spilled blue watercolor all over the top of my desk. "Damn it!"

Instead of helping me, Tim turned toward me, a look of pure disgust on his face. I fought the urge to slap him so I didn't have to look at it anymore. I grabbed a bunch of rags from my rag pile and tried to sop up all the expensive paint.

"That's coming out of your paycheck," he said.

I shot daggers at him. "The hell it will," I told him.

He leaned over me, his palms on the flat of my worktable. "Excuse me?"

"I said *the hell it will*, Tim. You are going to replace the paint out of *your* pocket, actually. Or I could go to Terry and tell him about your interest in my personal sex life. Which would you prefer?"

He looked incensed, but he didn't argue with me. He stood, stomped over to the paint cabinet, and grabbed a replacement of the blue paint I'd spilled. He walked back over to me and slammed the bottle in front of me, making me jump.

"Did you spend the night with him or not?" Tim insisted.

I snorted, tired of his shit and starting to feel nauseated; I couldn't care less about anything else. "You think because you set that bottle there," I said, gesturing to the paint, "that it entitles you to an answer?"

"I don't know why you just don't tell me already. I mean, just confirm it. I know you did. Why else would he be driving you to work?"

"Well, if you know that I did, I wonder why you ask," I sarcastically bit.

"Because I have to know!" he practically shouted. His chest panted. "I have to know, Hazel. Did you sleep with that guy?"

I stood in a rush, knocking my chair over. "No, Tim! No, you don't have to know. The only thing you need to know about me is if I can or can't do the job I'm being paid to do. Other than that, you don't have to know anything! Do I make myself clear?" I asked.

Flashes of emotion crossed his face over and over like a flipping Rolodex. He opened his mouth to speak but I interrupted him.

I doubled over the trash bin near my desk and vomited over and over. I tried to leave the workroom, but Madison chose that exact moment to walk through the door. She rushed over to me.

"Oh my God, are you okay?" she asked, pulling my hair back for me.

I couldn't respond, too busy getting sick.

She led me toward the bathroom. I caught a glimpse of Tim from the corner of my eye. There was a look of pure astonishment and incredulity on his face.

Once in the bathroom, Madison helped me get cleaned up and I rinsed my bin out. I washed my face, brushed my teeth, and blotted a tissue underneath my eyes. Madison leaned against the tiled wall.

"Hazel," she said, a worried look in her eyes.

I couldn't look directly at her. "Yeah?"

"What's going on?"

I let out a frustrated breath. "Tim was harassing me again this morning and I let him have it."

"*Hazel*," she said with inflection.

This time my eyes met hers. "It wasn't the flu, Mads."

All the blood drained from her face. "It's that boy's?"

I nodded. "Atticus's, yeah."

"What are you going to do?" she asked in a concerned tone.

I tugged out the headscarf I kept in my back pocket and wrapped it around my head, pulling pieces of hair out for aesthetic reasons.

"I haven't decided yet," I told her.

"That's understandable," she replied. "Does he know?"

"Yes, he knows. He's been pretty chill about it, actually. He took me to the doctor this morning then dropped me off here." I pointed at the bathroom door toward the workroom. "Thus the freak-out."

Madison studied me.

"*What?*" I asked her.

"Well, I mean, I hope you're not relying on him or anything?"

"Who? Tim?" I asked. "I rely on him freaking the hell out on a daily basis, yeah."

"No," Madison prodded with a finger at my shoulder,

"on Atticus. You don't know him. I just hope you're doing what's best for you."

I nodded and leaned a hip into the sink. "I get what you're saying."

"Do you?" she asked.

"I get you." I hesitated but eventually said, "He feels different, though, Madison."

She smiled sadly at me and bumped her bum against the door to swing it open. As she left, she said, "They always do, Hazel."

CHAPTER EIGHT

Over the next few weeks, Atticus picked me up every morning to drive me to work and every night at five to take me to my car for school. When I would get home from class, he was always there waiting for me with a bag of something protein rich. Eventually the constant morning sickness subsided and I entered my second trimester feeling a little bit more comfortable about presenting my senior exit project without ralphing on the shoes of the judging professors.

I was set to graduate Saturday, December 10, at ten a.m. and come hell or high water I was going to be there. I was too close to the finish line to back out so I powered through some pretty tough times to attend class. I was determined for it to pay off. Atticus worked insane hours. I'd discovered during those weeks that most musicians didn't like work during the day. I once asked him how he could work all night only to be able to show up at my door every morning for doctor's appointments or just to drive me to work. "I'm fine," he'd always say with a smile.

"What are we going to do for Thanksgiving?" Atticus

asked me early November.

I was approaching fourteen weeks and two days. Before Thanksgiving we were set to find out the sex of the baby. We were both so busy getting to know one another and dealing with the logistics of seeing each other that we had yet to discuss our plans in any way. I sometimes had the feeling Atticus was only prolonging the inevitable, knowing time would steer me one direction over another and by one direction, I meant his direction.

"Listen," he said, falling onto my couch, "you're far enough along that I think it's time to tell your grandma, Haze."

"What are you talking about? I'm barely showing."

"*Haze*," he said with a smile, "it's time." He held his arms out and I tumbled on top of him. He wrapped his hands around my body, one hand on the back of my neck, the other at the small of my back. "God, I love the way you feel," he promised in my ear, making me smile and my stomach flip.

His perfect teeth bit into my shoulder and I giggled. "I can't tell her," I told him.

He sighed. "Yes, you can, Haze. Just call her up. I'll be right here with you." He cleared his throat. "Uh, my mom said you can invite her over to our house for Thanksgiving if you want."

I was touched and surprised Sarah offered. She hadn't necessarily warmed up to the idea of our baby, and she was having trouble hiding it. She was a sweet woman but had serious reservations.

"I can't believe I'm saying this, but let me up so I can get my phone."

He slapped my butt as I walked away. "Yeah, baby," I

teased over my shoulder.

It was strange because although we were insanely attracted to one another and despite our sleeping together the one night, we hadn't yet repeated the act. It just didn't feel right yet. We didn't love each other. We weren't married. It wasn't time.

But I *was* falling in love with him. And fast.

I set my phone on the coffee table and pressed *Gram* on my phone. I put it on speaker and sat with shaking hands.

"Am I introducing you? Pretending you're not here?" I asked in a rush as it rang.

"Whatever you want," he said.

"Hello, darlin'!" Gram answered.

"Hey, Gram. How are you?" I asked.

"Oh, you know, same old, same old, honey. About to head out to bingo with my new beau. Name's Carl. Real nice gentleman. You'd like him."

I smiled at Atticus, who smiled back. "That's amazing, Gram. Hey, uh, do you have a quick second, though?"

"For you, baby, always."

I let out a shaky breath. "Well, I have something to tell you."

"Are you okay? Are you hurt? Were you in an accident? Do you need money?" she asked excitedly.

"No, no, no, Gram," I reassured her. "I'm all right. I just have a bit of news to share with you is all."

She sighed on her side of the phone. "Okay, spit it out, child."

"Well, I met a boy," I began.

"Ohhhh," she sang teasingly, "you've got yourself a little boyfriend, have ya?"

"Yes, ma'am." I cleared my throat and Atticus held my

hand. "He's here actually. On speaker."

"Well, hot dog!" she said. "Nice to speak to you, son. What's your name?" she asked.

Atticus sat up as if she was in the room. "Nice to speak to you as well, Hazel. I'm Atticus."

"My word, listen to that voice! A nice, deep voice, Hazel. And a nice old-fashioned name. I like it."

"Thank you," he said, smiling.

"Listen, Gram, before we go any further," I began, "Atticus and I need to tell you something." Gram got quiet, really quiet. "Gram?"

"Yes," I barely heard.

My biggest fear was that I would shock her and from the sound of her voice, it sounded like she'd already figured it out and that's exactly what had happened.

"Well, I'm expecting a baby, Gram," I said.

The other end of the line went dead silent. Atticus and I looked at one another, worried.

"Gram?" I asked.

"I'm here," she said, her voice a jumbled mess, like she'd started crying.

"Oh, Gram, are you okay?"

She cleared her throat. "I'm, well, I just don't know how that could happen, Hazel. You had a plan, darlin'! You had plans."

I started to tear up. "I know, Gram, and I'm going to finish my classes. I'm set to graduate in early December. I promise I'll finish."

"But what about your plans to travel? To apprentice? You had plans, baby," she said, her voice sounding dejected.

My hand went to my mouth to prevent the sobs that

threatened. I sucked in a deep breath to compose myself.

"I know, Grams, and it wasn't planned but it is what it is."

Big fat tears fell down my face and Atticus's worried expression made them worse. His hands caught as many as he could but there weren't enough fingers to dispel them all.

"Let me just wrap my head around this, honey, okay? Can I call you back? I've got Carl ringing at my door anyway."

I nodded like she could see me. "Of course, Grams. Call me as soon as you can?"

"Yes, baby. I will."

"Okay, talk to you soon," I said, trying to keep it together.

The line went dead and I slid my phone off. I looked at Atticus and burst into tears. He wrapped his arms around me.

"It was a bad idea," I cried into his T-shirt.

"She had to find out, Haze."

I nodded against his shoulder as his phone went off. He kept an arm around me as he slid it from his jeans pocket.

"It's work. I have to take it."

I made like I was going to get up, but he pulled me back into his embrace.

"Hey, River, what's up?" he asked another producer from The Sink.

I heard mumbling from the other end but couldn't make out what River was saying.

My ear was pressed against Atticus's chest and his deep voice rumbled through. "No kidding." Pause. "No kidding. Dude, that is amazing." Another long pause and Atticus started to laugh. "Get the hell out of here, River. You are lying through your teeth." Yet another pause. "Okay, yeah. I'll see you tonight then," he finished, ending his call and tossing the phone on my coffee table.

Without warning, Atticus started to kiss me deeply. I could feel his smile against my salted cheeks.

"What is this?" I asked, pulling away briefly before he brought me back in.

It was a twenty-minute make-out session before I could get him to tell me anything.

"There's this artist in LA," he said when he finally pulled away. "She's just signed with High Fidelity and her only requirement? She requested that none of their in-house producers work on her stuff, insisting she knew of a producer she wanted and wouldn't sign unless they agreed."

I sat on my ankles on the sofa cushion. "Get out, Atticus. Is it you?"

He shook his head in disbelief and laughed. "Me, Haze."

"Shut the front door, Atticus Kelly! Oh my God!" I screamed, throwing myself on him and peppering his face with kisses. "This is so amazing."

"I know," he said, his hands wandering over my shoulders, hair, and neck. "I'm in shock."

I laughed. "God, this day."

He sighed and kissed my neck. "Call your Gram back in a few hours, let it settle, and it'll be all right. Invite her to Thanksgiving."

I nodded then a thought occurred to me. "Does this mean you have to go to LA?"

He shook his head. "She's coming here."

I breathed a sigh of relief. "Wow."

"Wow is right."

"What's her name?" I asked.

"Delilah Calvin," he answered.

I grabbed my phone and looked her up. We listened to two songs and agreed she had real talent. I looked up images of her and was blown away.

"Oh my word," I said, showing them to him. "She's gorgeous."

"Yeah," he said, glancing at the photo I held up, then went back to texting River.

"When will she be here?" I asked.

"Next week. Apparently I've met her before but I don't remember it."

I had a hard time believing that. If the girl looked anything remotely close to her picture, it was an impossibility.

"Yeah?" I asked, feeling insecure.

There was one thing about being pregnant while single no one had warned me about. The constant insecurities. Madison wasn't helping either. Though she meant well, she kept encouraging me to consider my options and playing over and over again stories of girls she knew whose men left them after a few months and so on and so on. I told her I couldn't even think about options when Atticus and I were just getting to know one another. It was too soon to consider anything, despite my private reservations and plans for adoption.

Etta was much more practical in her advice compared to Madison's passionate guidance. One, because Etta is smart as hell and thinks everything through with intelligent intensity, and two, because she's just naturally more methodical. Once Etta knows of a problem, she takes down the variables, inevitably works out all the contributing factors, and puzzles out results. She's a scientist, without a doubt. She was much more encouraging than Madison, but she didn't sugarcoat anything to me either. I loved and hated her for this. If she wasn't like a sister to me, I would have written off her advice with a grain of salt, but since she loved me so well, I knew everything she did was from a place of love and took her much more seriously.

Personally, I let my heart guide me too often. A product of being an artist, I thought. I liked to think I was somewhere in the middle of Madison and Etta, though. A balance between the two.

The following week, Atticus had his first recording session with Delilah Calvin.

"You nervous?" I asked him the evening he was set to start.

His fingers trickled over the skin of my forearm, up and down, making me sleepy.

"A little," he admitted.

"You don't have to be," I told him, kissing him at the temple. "Talent doesn't come along like yours every day, you know. It's rare, Atticus. You're ready for this."

He smiled at me. "Thank you, Hazel."

"You're welcome."

"Hey, Hazel?"

"Yeah?"

"I'm almost in love with you," he spoke into the air.

I couldn't fight the smile on my lips. "I'm almost in love with you too, Atticus."

"I can't wait for the fall," he said.

"If I could paint it, it would be aquamarine, with bits of Tiffany blue, turquoise, and powder blue. It'd be moving, constantly changing, evolving, shaping the world around us, influencing it, and swaying it this way and that. It would be infinite."

Atticus kissed me and I kissed him back.

"And if it were song," he told me, "it would be in A major. One hundred thirty-seven beats per minute. It would be haunting. It would be beautiful. It would swim through your skin, raise your heart rate, make your hair stand on end. It would match the rise and fall of the sun. It would be inexhaustible."

"Sounds like a world I could live in."

He looked at me, stared through me, into me. "We will exist there one day, Hazel."

Atticus stared at his phone and noted the time.

"I've got to go, Haze."

He stood and held his hands out for me. I took them and he lifted me beside him. "Go get 'em. Lock that shit down. Blow their minds," I ordered, before pressing a kiss against his mouth.

He took a deep, shaky breath. "I'll text you."

I nodded. "I can drive myself to work tomorrow. Just keep those down."

He shook his head. "I don't care if I have to leave, I'm coming in the morning to take you to work."

I rolled my eyes playfully at him. He kissed my cheek quickly and headed for the door, remembered something, and turned back around. He got down on his knees in front of me and slid his palm over my belly before kissing it.

CHAPTER NINE

The next morning, my alarm went off and I felt the butterflies in my stomach flutter at the thought of seeing Atticus. I hopped in the shower, got dressed, and did my hair and makeup. I ate something, watched a little TV, and about twenty 'til, Atticus still hadn't arrived. I checked my phone but there were no messages.

"Must still be working," I told no one. I looked around the room. "Who am I talking to?" I glanced at my belly. "How about you?" I asked the little mutant Kelly/Stone. "Am I talking to you?"

I decided not to text Atticus in case he was busy. I didn't want to give him any further anxiety. I grabbed my keys, locked my studio, and rang Etta while I drove myself to work.

"Yo, baby cakes!" she answered. "Where you at?"

"Headed to freaking work."

"Say hi to Atticus for me," she said.

"Oh, I'm driving myself. It was his first day with Delilah Calvin."

"Oh, cool," she said.

"Yeah, so it feels like I haven't seen you in ages and ages. Why don't you come over later or something?"

"'Cause Etta has herself a hot date, Hazel, that's why."

"Damn, Etta, what's his name?"

"Simon. He's in med school."

"Oooh." I sang, "Docta! Docta! Give me the news!"

Etta laughed. "Girl, you are so dumb."

I giggled. "Whatever. You love me."

"Lord knows I do." I heard mumbling in the background. "Listen, I have to go. My professor is giving me the stink eye."

"You answered this call during class?"

"Hazel, I do what I want. "

I laughed. "Go, you dork."

"Love you."

"Love you too. Bye."

I hung up the phone as I pulled up to work, parked, and headed for the artist loft I worked in. I walked through the courtyard and began to open the door when I heard my name. I turned around to find a winded Atticus.

"Damn, Hazel," he panted, "I'm sorry. I lost track of time."

I smiled at him. "Not a big deal, babe."

"It is a big deal, though. We only get an allotted time together every day while you're in school, and I look forward to hanging with you."

My hand found his cheek. "Atticus, don't kick yourself for this." I kissed his mouth. "How did the session go?"

"It's still going," he said. "I just ran out real quick to catch you before you went in. Hazel, the stuff we're creating is insane."

My heart beat quickly. "That's fantastic. So freaking

happy for you!"

"For us. I'm happy for us. I'm doing this for you. For us." He kissed me again; this time it held an edge to it that made me weak in the knees. "I gotta go."

"Go," I said, swatting his butt, "kick ass. Take names."

He saluted me. "Yes, ma'am." He started to walk off but yelled over his shoulder. "See you after work!"

But Atticus didn't come by after work because I texted him it wasn't necessary since I had my car. He said he needed sleep anyway and I agreed. He said he'd call me when I got home from class, though.

Tuesday, the next day, he didn't come by to take me to work. Neither did he come by on Wednesday. It wasn't until Thursday, after my last class for the week, did he end up coming by at nine p.m.

"I missed you," he said, kissing my temple as we settled on my couch together.

"I missed you too," I said, yawning. "It was a crazy week."

"No kidding," he agreed. "Hopefully this will all pan out and the album will sell well."

"I hope so. What's Delilah like?" I asked.

"She's cool. Kind of eccentric, kind of out there, but she's cool."

I nodded. "Cool."

"How's Tim been treating you?" he asked.

"I think he knows I'm preggers."

"How?"

"Maybe because I'm wearing a little baggier clothing? Or maybe it's because I've vomited in the bathroom for weeks straight every day?"

Atticus laughed. "That might do it. Has he asked about

it?"

"Not directly." I shifted, unsure if I should admit to the truth.

If I was being honest, Tim had started treating me even worse. It was obvious he was struggling with his personal feelings for me. He'd often quip I was making a huge mistake with Atticus, that he was probably as useless as he looked, and that he was going to leave me once he grew tired of me. Totally inappropriate things. The problem was I wasn't pretending what he was saying bothered me anymore, and the negative attention he was getting from me was only spurring him on. He knew I'd never turn him in because I wasn't exactly in a situation to risk my job, and I knew he'd never fire me because he was in love with me. So this growing hate-filled tension was building in the workshop. Even Madison was starting to intervene during our shouting matches, something she never did.

"Hazel," Atticus said, watching me. "Did Tim say something?

"Uh, no," I hedged.

"Did he touch you?" he asked, sitting up.

"No," I said, dragging him back down to me. "He's just the same asshole as always."

"Just quit that shit, Hazel."

I sighed. "I need the job and I enjoy the work, despite Tim."

"There's got to be something else you could do that will utilize your talent in this godforsaken city."

"Possibly, but the idea of shifting to a new place while pregnant is a little bit daunting."

Atticus nodded but didn't look convinced.

I decided to change the subject. "Do you work

tonight?"

"Yeah, at eleven."

I checked how annoying I found that. "What about the weekend?" I asked.

"Yeah, I've got an all-day Saturday session with Delilah."

"Okay," I crisply replied.

"I'd rather be with you, Hazel, trust me."

My heart softened. "I know, Atticus," I said, wrapping my arms around his neck. I sat up a little. "Will you at least be able to make the sonogram on Tuesday morning? We find out the gender."

He smiled. "I wouldn't miss it for anything in the world."

CHAPTER TEN

The following Tuesday, I drove myself to the hospital for a 3D sonogram with plans of meeting Atticus there. I waited outside the entrance for a few minutes, even texted him, but I didn't get a response.

Hey, I texted Etta.

You there? she texted back.

Yeah, Atticus hasn't shown yet

Maybe he's just late

I ignored the pit growing in my stomach. **I don't think so E**

Hazel, chill. Text him the address and go up. Good luck! I better be your first call!

Ok love you

Love you

I texted him the address and went upstairs to the sonogram clinic Dr. Kagan referred me to.

"Just sign in, baby," the receptionist said, sliding a clipboard my direction. "How many weeks?" she asked.

"Fifteen," I told her.

"Exciting stuff!" she said with a giant smile.

I was too nervous to be excited. "Yeah, thanks," I offered.

"Just take a seat. We'll call you in a minute."

I did as she said and sat in the chair nearest the door. Every time it opened, I would peek over to see if it was Atticus. I kept checking my phone over and over but got no response.

"Hazel Stone," a technician called out, making me feel sick.

I nodded and dialed Atticus. It went straight to voicemail.

"Atticus, it's Hazel. Uh, they've called me back for the 3D sono. I was hoping you would have been here by now. If you're close, try to hurry a little so you don't miss it. Uh, well, bye."

I hung up and stuck my phone in my bag.

"Right this way," she said, leading me to a dark, cavernous room. It was plush, though, full of rich fabrics and nice furnishings.

She signaled for me slide on top of the medical chair. "How are you today?" she asked.

"I'm well, thank you," I lied.

She peered over her shoulder. "You alone today?" she asked casually.

"Uh, yeah," I answered, feeling a little humiliated.

She had me pull my shirt up and unbutton my jeans. She pulled the tabs down and slid them a little down my hips before tucking towels over the waistband.

"Still fitting in regular clothes," she commented with a smile. "Won't be long before you'll need something with some stretch," she added conversationally.

"Yeah," I answered, afraid to talk anymore. The room

felt like it was closing in on me.

"Let's find out who we've got here," she said, taking warmed gel and squirting it over my small pot belly.

I kept looking at the door hoping Atticus would walk in but he didn't, and my heart began to ache. I fought tears. She placed the ultrasound probe on my belly and began shifting the gel over the surface of my skin. I could see the baby's small form on screen; it kept kicking its little legs and shifting its tiny arms.

"Oh my God," I said, staring at it. "It's so sweet looking."

The tech smiled at me as she took measurements with her machine and shifted the probe to check out all its little parts.

"Do you want to know the sex?" she asked me.

I swallowed. "Uh, yes, I think so."

"I can keep it a secret if you prefer."

"No," I told her, "please. I'd like to know."

She slid the probe so she could get a good shot, took several pictures, then turned to me. "You're having a little girl, Miss Stone." For some reason, tears started falling and I couldn't stop them. The tech leaned over and took several tissues from a nearby box. "Congratulations," she said softly.

I swiped at my eyes with the tissue. "Thank you."

She untucked the towels from my waistband and wiped my stomach for me. "You're all done, babe. I'll give you a minute. Just see the receptionist on your way out." She stood, handed me a disc and a few sonogram pictures, then walked toward the door. "Congrats again," she said, and left the room.

I stood up, situated my clothing, and visited reception. I

walked out of that hospital and removed my phone from my bag. No missed calls. No missed texts. I dialed and waited.

"Etta, it's me," I said when it went to voicemail. "Just wanted you to know it's a girl. Call me when you can. Love you."

I hung up and rang my grandma but it too went to voicemail. "Grams, it's Hazel. I know you're still kind of processing everything, but I thought you'd want to know it's a girl. I'll try you again later. Love you."

I hung up and went to my car, sat in the driver's seat, and cried into the steering wheel.

CHAPTER ELEVEN

I decided to go up to The Sink just to make sure Atticus wasn't hurt or dead or whatever. He knew how important it was to me that he showed, and he let me down. This time I wasn't afraid to tell him how I felt.

The Sink's doors were locked so I knocked. The receptionist buzzed me in, smiled, and pointed toward Atticus's studio. I mustered up a smile for her and walked with purpose down the hall. His door was cracked open and there was an entire team of people in there, which intimidated me, but what really got to me was the fact that Atticus and Delilah were laughing together, their heads close, her hand on his shoulder. I pushed the door open some and leaned my shoulder against the jamb of the door, watching in horror at their body language.

Eventually the room started to notice me and people turned around one by one. It wasn't until Atticus and the gorgeous Delilah took note of the quiet that they bothered to look up from their private revelry.

Atticus looked shocked to see me. "Hazel!" His head swung toward the wall clock and I watched as his expression fell when he saw the time. "Oh my God," he said, his shoulders sagging. "I can't believe it. I lost track of time."

I gave him a caustic smile. "It's fine," I said, tossing the disc and the pictures at his feet. "You're obviously busy." Everyone looked confused but a few who knew who I was looked at me with a little bit of pity, which really irritated me. "You must be Delilah," I said, walking forward and reaching my hand out toward the brunette goddess. Atticus could tell I was pissed. His breaths sped up and his mouth went slack. "I'm Hazel," I introduced myself.

Delilah looked secure in herself. She eyed me with her cat eyes and the look spoke volumes. She knew exactly who I was and she did not care, not even a little bit. "Nice to meet you," she purred.

"Likewise," I told her.

I waved at all the boys and started to back out of the room. Atticus started to stand. "Catch you on the flip, fellas," I said, a fake plastic smile on my face.

I practically sprinted down the hall toward the doors, determined to get out before Atticus could catch me. I threw open the doors and ran to my car, shoved the driver's side door open, and fell inside. My hands fumbled with the keys as they tried to find the ignition. That's when I noticed Atticus come out the doors. He looked the opposite direction from me, followed the line of the street, then spotted me. My keys finally found their purchase and turned, the engine rumbling to life. Atticus ran at me, coming full speed. I reached out to close my door but he caught it with his hands.

"No, you don't, Hazel."

"Fuck you, Atticus Kelly!" I shouted, the tears already

pouring.

"Hazel, Hazel, wait!" he pleaded, pulling my door open as I tried to pull it shut.

"Let go!" I demanded.

"Hazel! I'm sorry, okay? I lost track of time. We were just making a lot of progress. I had an alarm set, but I guess I put the phone on silent or something and missed it."

"Yeah, lost track of time with that friggin' chick."

"What the hell are you talking about?"

"Your body language told me everything I need to know." I looked at the ceiling of my car. "This is why I don't date musicians. This is why."

He looked like a deer caught in headlights. "I literally have no clue what you're talking about."

"Come on, Atticus! She had her hand on your shoulder. Your heads were close. Those are boundaries crossed."

He looked pensive for a moment. "I didn't even realize, Hazel. I swear to God."

I shook my head. "I don't care anymore, Atticus." A fresh burst of emotion flooded forth. "You let me down. You don't know what it was like sitting in that room by myself at what was supposed to be a cool thing. It was the first glimpse I got into what will probably be my future, and my eyes opened. I can't do that. I won't do that to my kid."

"What are you saying?" he asked, an edge to his tone.

"I'm saying I'm going to look for an adoption agency, Atticus."

I tried to close the door but his hands were firmly planted on the frame and he wouldn't budge. "You're being too hasty, Hazel. This isn't a permanent thing, okay?

Can't you see I'm doing this for us? I'm doing this for our future!" he desperately argued.

"How can there be a future, Atticus, when we're not even in the present? Huh?"

"We just have to sacrifice a little bit now is all," he reasoned.

"If we were an established couple, this would make sense, Atticus, but we're not. We're still getting to know one another. We don't even know if we're meant to be."

"Bullshit!" he shouted. "That's bullshit, Hazel, and you know it. I knew the second we laid on the ground staring up into the sky that night. I knew it the second your hand found mine. I knew it the second I tasted your lips with mine. I knew it during those *unbelievable* hours in my car. I knew it that horrifying morning. I know you know it too. It's fate."

I started crying harder and hit my steering wheel in frustration. "Stop it, Atticus!"

He shook his head back and forth. "I'm not ever going to stop, Hazel. I know it seems stupid. I know how insane the notion that two people can, in fact, be divinely designed sounds, but I know it's true. I know this now. Because I can tell you with absolute certainty that you are meant to be with me, Hazel Stone."

"Please," I begged, not sure if my heart could take any more. "Please."

He took a deep breath. "We did things a little backwards, but I'm going to make them right. Just stick this out with me."

He pulled at the door and I no longer had the strength to prevent him from opening it. When he wrested it away from me, he fell on his knees, yanked me toward him, and held me harder than I'd ever been held.

I bawled into his neck. "I don't know if I can do this," I confessed.

"Let's take it one day at a time, Hazel," he soothed.

I cried over his beautiful skin while he ran a hand over my hair, neck, and face. He pushed his arm underneath my legs and slid me out of the car, shut the door, and walked with me toward his car, placing me inside. He walked back to my car, got my keys and my bag, then climbed into the driver's side of his own. He started it and took his phone out.

"River," he said, "I'm calling it. No more sessions until after Thanksgiving."

He hung up then grabbed my hand; we rode in silence all the way to my studio. Without saying a word still, we walked up to my apartment. He took my keys and opened the door, shut it behind us, picked me up again and took us both to my bed. He kicked the covers off as we fell into it but found them again and brought them over us, completely over us. It was dark and quiet. Soothing. He pressed my body against his, ran his hand down my leg, and cupped the back of my knee before bringing it between his legs. We sat there intertwined like that for at least half an hour, enough for my body to calm down, my heart rate to slow.

I shifted and his body stiffened. "Stay with me like this, Hazel."

I relaxed my muscles and settled into him. Only then did he calm down himself.

"Can your grandma come for Thanksgiving?" he asked.

I shook my head. "She can't come."

Atticus's hands tensed on my shoulders. "Why not?"

"Apparently my mom surprised her. She asked if she could bring her but I said I wasn't comfortable with my mom knowing where I lived."

He sighed. "I see." He kissed my forehead. "I'm sorry, Hazel."

"It's okay, Atticus."

"You'll come home with me. We'll eat well. We'll talk. We'll kiss. We'll touch." I smiled up at him. "I love it when you smile, Hazel. It makes me happy."

A little bit of the afternoon sun seeped through the comforter over our heads. He climbed down my body, his mouth against my stomach, and kissed me there over and over. "Hazel," he spoke into my skin.

"Yeah."

"What are we having?" he asked, stopping and looking up at me.

I smiled at him. "What do you want it to be?"

"Healthy," he answered.

"You don't have a preference?" I asked.

His chin rested on the bone of my hip and he shook his head from side to side. "Not at all."

"How do you feel about the color pink?" I asked him.

Atticus's eyes turned glassy and his grin grew so wide I was afraid it would burst off his face. "It's a girl?"

I nodded and he brought his face up to mine, kissing me deeply. "What about a name?" he asked.

"I have one," I told him.

"What is it?" he asked.

"The night we met you named the little girl in my first painting."

He stared at me. "Juniper," he whispered.

"Juniper," I repeated.

"Juniper Kelly," he said, making me smile.
"Juniper Kelly," I tested on my tongue.
"No, Juniper *Hazel* Kelly," he corrected.

CHAPTER TWELVE

Thanksgiving Day, Atticus picked me up at my apartment and took me over to his parents' house. We had to park the length of a football field from their home since the street was so congested with cars. As we waltzed up the porch, I was blasted by noise through the closed door.

"How many people are here?" I asked him.

"I think just my parents, my brothers, their kids and girlfriends."

"How many is that?"

"Probably about twenty," he explained as the door burst open and kids came rushing through, screaming and laughing.

"Whoa," Atticus said, swooping a little boy about four. "Careful, Jeremiah," he said, kissing his cheek.

"Uncle Atticus, who is this?" Jeremiah asked, pointing at me.

"This is Hazel."

"Hi!" Jeremiah greeted, squirming out of his uncle's arms and running off to join the others.

I followed Atticus into the house. The TV was blaring

and there were people all over laughing and shouting. Children were running everywhere. It was a little louder than I was used to, growing up with no siblings in a house with my quiet grams.

"Hey!" they all shouted in unison as we came through.

Six little kids ran up to Atticus and jumped on him. They all fell to the floor laughing. I watched one little girl, probably about two, parading around him in some sort of princess gown, little plastic heels slapping on the wood floor around him.

"Well, if it isn't Princess Eva!" Atticus shouted.

She picked up the skirt of her gown and lifted it. "Pretty!" she said.

Atticus, with little boys hanging off each arm, kneeled before her. "Your Majesty," he teased, making her giggle.

All three tackled him back to the ground and he started laughing. "Guys! Guys! Please."

But they were unrelenting and only doubled their efforts on bringing him down.

"You must be Hazel," said a pretty woman to my right.

"Yes," I said with a smile.

"I'm Ellie," she introduced herself. "Aidan's girlfriend and Molly's mom?"

"Nice to meet you," I told her.

"Nice to meet you as well," she replied. She hooked her arm with mine and started walking.

I turned around to see Atticus staring after me with a smile.

"He'll be around, babe," she said, reassuring me. "I just want to introduce you to all the girls." She brought me into the kitchen where Sarah and a few other girls were hanging out. "You guys, this is Hazel." They all waved and said hi. "This is Brendan's girlfriend, Jennifer," she said, gesturing to a pretty girl with bright blonde hair.

"Nice to finally meet you," Jennifer said with a smile.

"I'm Jamie," another beautiful introduced herself. "Cillian's girlfriend."

She was of Asian ancestry and breathtaking.

"Maggie." A beautiful redhead waved. "I'm Liam's ex."

"I'm Isla, Malachi's ex-girlfriend," the last girl said. She was tall and had long black hair.

"Nice to meet you all," I said, feeling a bit intimidated.

There was no question about it, these women were quite the collection of beautiful. The Kelly boys dug the aesthetic. I turned toward Atticus's mom and she came forward, quick to give me a hug.

"Hello, baby," she greeted. "How have you been?"

"I'm fine, thank you."

All the girls sat down. Jennifer offered me an empty chair and I sat.

"We heard you're expecting?" Jamie asked.

"Uh, yes," I answered. "Have you all known long?" I asked.

"We all found out today," Maggie answered.

Sarah turned toward the stove to stir something.

I smiled a them. "Shocked?" I asked.

They all stayed quiet for a moment before Isla said, "I won't lie; we were a little surprised. Atticus— well, I mean, it's not really like Atticus." She cleared her throat. "But that's not to say unwelcome," she added warmly.

I didn't know how to respond to them. It was obvious Atticus was their golden boy, whom they all relied on, and I was a giant wrench thrown into their plans.

"Atticus says you paint?" Jennifer asked.

I nodded. "I do."

"Two artists," Sarah commented. "A pretty hard life," she added.

"True," I agreed. "I don't think it's impossible to be successful, though. We're both incredibly hard workers. Sweat equity and all that."

"Mmm," Sarah responded.

I felt like I had to qualify myself, us. "Atticus will be something, Sarah," I promised her. "I won't let him be anything else."

She turned toward me, her eyes wet. "Kelly men do whatever they want to do, darlin'."

"Then it's a good thing Atticus wants to be someone. I won't stop him. I won't get in the way."

Sarah turned toward me. "That's not Atticus, though, Hazel. He'll put you in the way. You'll become his way."

I turned and looked toward the other women but they all had their heads down, pretending to be working or on their phones.

I looked at Sarah again. "What are you saying, Sarah? Speak plainly."

"I'm not saying anything, really. I'm only trying to express how hard this whole thing is going to be if he starts to love you, because Atticus doesn't do anything without real passion. He won't love you without that same passion. You are going to be his whole world. He will shift his entire life, even to his own detriment.

"Ever since he was little, he's been that way. He has an obsessive need to please the people he loves. I'm j-just, please, be careful with him."

I swallowed. "I'll be careful."

Dinner was strange. I mostly kept quiet and observed

Atticus with his brothers. They were happy, playful, and teasing. They all loved one another very much. They exuded loyalty as well. It was refreshing. They were definitely different and very interesting.

Atticus's phone rang and he kissed my temple as he stood to answer it.

"Hey, River," he said, walking toward the front door, probably so he could hear his conversation over his loud family.

A few minutes later he returned, running the palms of his hands over his arms to get them warm since he left without his jacket. "I've got to go," he told them all.

They whined and complained. I looked at him, a little taken aback.

"Where?" I asked.

"The Sink. Delilah is desperate to record, hit with inspiration."

My blood started boiling. I stood and turned toward his family and plastered a fake smile on my face. "It was nice to meet you girls," I told them. "Boys, always a pleasure."

Each of the girls stood and kissed my cheek. As we made our way to the door, each of the brothers gave me a bear hug. Sarah and Casey kissed my forehead.

Atticus ran a little ahead and opened my door for me. I got in without saying a word.

"You're pissed," he said when he got in himself, started it up, and took off.

"Most definitely," I admitted.

"I'm taking you with me, Hazel."

I turned toward him. "I'm not going."

He laughed. "The fuck you aren't."

I laughed back. "You can't make me."

He stopped the car in the middle of his parents' street, took off his seatbelt, reached over, unclicked mine, then dragged me by the top of my jeans closer to him.

"Atticus!"

His lips found mine and then his tongue. He broke away and kissed up my neck. "I bet I can."

I fought the urge to give in. "No," I told him.

He dragged his lips down my neck and bit my collarbone softly. "Please, Hazel," he begged.

"No," I insisted, but felt myself wavering.

He slid his hands around my jaw and his teeth found my earlobe. "Please," he whispered.

I let out a shaky breath in answer.

With his lips still at my ear, he brought my seatbelt around and clicked me in before pulling away and buckling in himself again. We eyed one another but neither of us said anything. When we arrived at The Sink, I grabbed the sketchpad I always kept in his car. I waited for him to open my door for me and we walked to the studio. Once inside, I hit the bathroom because preggos gotta pee! A lot.

When I was done, I washed my hands and picked up my pad I'd set on the receptionist's desk before waltzing back to Atticus's studio. I rounded the corner and it was just Atticus and Delilah.

I began to smile but the shocked look on her face made it falter. "What is she doing here?" she asked him.

I was too surprised to say anything. Atticus eyed her strangely then said, "It's Thanksgiving. I was with my family when River called. I thought I'd bring her along for this session."

Delilah checked herself and tried to laugh but didn't

pull it off. "Oh, yeah, of course," she said.

"Don't mind me," I told them, lifting up the pad.

I sat on the couch, pulled my legs up, and began to sketch. I felt Delilah's eyes on me constantly, though, and kept looking up to find her openly staring at me. At one point I got up to use the restroom just to get out of the studio. I was starting not to trust Delilah. Hard pressed, I had to admit she had a killer voice and a talent for writing lyrics. And as much as I also hated to have admitted it, they were an incredible writing team. From what I heard, I knew it was going to do well. There was no way their collaborations weren't going to hit charts. This made me excited for Atticus but also extremely nervous because, despite it all, I could tell she was into him, really into him. She saw me as an obstacle, and she didn't strike me as the type to let little things like girlfriends get in her way. She was just gorgeous enough that competition would be rare, and she looked like she was used to winning.

"Damn," Atticus said, standing up. "I'll be right back. I'm missing a pedal. I think it's in River's studio."

He walked out but not before bending over and kissing the top of my head. I'd set my pencil back on paper but felt Delilah's eyes once more. This time when I looked up, she spoke to me.

She swung back and forth in her rolling chair casually. "How long have you been together?" she asked.

"Fifteen weeks," I answered.

She snorted. "That's an odd way of putting it. Why not just say three or four months or something?"

"Oh, I don't now," I replied. "It could be because I'm just an odd girl or maybe it's because Atticus got me pregnant the first day we met and that's how far along our baby is."

Delilah choked on nothing, her body rocking forward as she sat upright. "You're pregnant?"

I shifted so my legs and feet were tucked beside me. "Yeah."

She turned quiet, reflective, then asked, "So it was, like, a one-night stand gone wrong or something?"

"No," I explained, "more like fate on fast forward."

She didn't respond to that. Instead, she stated, "So it hasn't been very long then."

"Long enough," I assured her. I studied her and leaned forward. "Do you think I'm so stupid that I don't see what you're doing?"

"What am I doing?" she asked, feigning innocence.

"You're gleaning information about us, trying to find your angle, and to add insult to injury, you're actually asking *me* of all people!"

"That's just not true. He's my producer. I'm going to be spending *lots* of time with him," she said, "and I'm just trying to get to know him is all."

"Sure, sure," I bit sarcastically. "See, the thing is, Delilah, I'm not an idiot. I know your kind. Girls like you are crawling all over Deep Ellum, so I'm quite familiar with them already."

"Girls like me?" she asked.

"Yes, girls exactly like you."

"And what kind of girl do you think I am?" she asked, crossing her long legs.

"You're the I-want-what-I-want-and-I-get-what-I-want girl, the spoiled, beautiful girl who clicks her heels loudly and demands attention kind. You're one of the ones who sees something pretty and has to have it for her own, even if it belongs to someone else."

She smiled at me, all pretense leaving her face. "Speaking of. *You're* very pretty, do you know that?" she asked.

"What does that have any—?" I began, but she cut me off.

She breathed in through her nose and looked me up and down, clicking her tongue once. "I just like a challenge is all."

My blood began to boil. "If I wasn't knocked up, Delilah," I left hanging.

"What? You'd tackle me or something?"

"Maybe."

"Classy."

I shook my head at her. "Oh, and hunting someone down who's taken is? I've never understood how so many drones in this world think that violence is the epitome of wrong. Sometimes a violent offense deserves a violent reaction. How else will the offender ever learn?" My feet hit the floor and I stared directly at her. "See, that's the problem with you. You probably grew up in a big house with a rich daddy who let you get away with murder because corporal punishment was considered taboo, but I didn't. I grew up poor, surrounded by druggies and prostitutes, and when someone fucked with you, you popped them the fuck back. Pacifism is a characteristic for the civilized, but civilized you are not. So listen up, *Delilah*, come after him and I'm coming after you."

"You know what's funny to me?" she asked, but I didn't deign to take the bait. She continued anyway. "You can bluster and rant all you want, but the only thing I have to do is wait."

"For?" I couldn't help myself.

"You're going to get bigger and bigger, fatter and fatter, and more hormonal and more insecure, and eventually you're going to sink your own ship and when that happens, I'll be there with a life raft big enough for me and Atticus. And trust me when I say that he will *enjoy the ride.*"

I threw my pad on the floor and stood up in a rush just as Atticus came in. He startled and stopped short, reading the room.

"Is everything okay?" he asked, looking unsure.

"We're great," Delilah answered, her voice plastic.

Atticus watched me. "Hazel?" he asked. "You okay?"

All the fight I had in me deflated and I fell onto the couch. "I'm great, babe," I lied.

He sat in his chair. "Well, that pedal is gone," he went on, unaware of the shitstorm he interrupted. "I think River took it home or put it somewhere weird. Whatever. Anyway, I think I've got an idea," he droned on.

I tuned him out as I picked up my pad and pencil again but not before staring daggers into the back of Delilah's neck.

Atticus and Delilah didn't get done until after two a.m., which was a problem because I had to work early in the morning. Delilah offered to drive him back home if I wanted to take Atticus's car. I refused, of course, and ended up crashing on the sofa. When I woke, she was gone.

"Atticus, I have to talk to you," I said as we meandered the dark streets back to my studio.

"What, babe?" he asked.

His face, lit by the light of his dash, looked tired and I

knew it was the wrong moment to bring anything up.

"Never mind," I said, "let's just get home and get some rest. I have to work tomorrow."

Atticus's hand went to his forehead. "Son of a bitch!" he exclaimed. "I can't believe you have to work tomorrow. I'm so sorry we were out so late."

"It's okay," I told him.

"No, it's not. Tomorrow is going to suck for you." He looked at me. "Is there no way you could call in?" he asked for the millionth time since we found out I was pregnant.

I shook my head. "I really can't. We're behind on orders as it is with Christmas coming up."

He nodded. "Okay, then let's just get you home. I'll crash with you so we can wake up at the last possible minute."

"Okay," I agreed.

When we got back to my house, we toppled into bed, still dressed. We fell asleep quickly, my back at his chest. He pulled me close and kissed the back of my neck. I tried to calm my heart, but it wouldn't settle, too busy worrying over the things Delilah threatened. I was definitely going to have to talk to Atticus.

CHAPTER THIRTEEN

The Friday after Thanksgiving, I woke early, still unable to sleep, and showered, getting ready for my day. When I came out of the bathroom, Atticus was sprawled over my small full mattress, his long legs hanging off the edge, his beautiful hands clutched at the sheets. I leaned over him and kissed his cheek with every intention of getting to work on my own but when I lifted off the bed, his hand caught my arm and he pulled me into him.

"Let me take you," his deep morning voice requested.

He stood up and went to the bathroom to brush his teeth. I grabbed a protein bar and an apple from the kitchen and ate them fast.

"Let's go, sweet pea," he said.

We locked the door and as we went to his car, he held my hand. I brought our joined fingers up and studied them. My own were starting to *swell.*

"Atticus," I said nervously.

"Yeah?"

"I need to tell you something and I don't think you're going to like it."

He stopped in his tracks. "What's going on?"

"Well, when you left the room last night, Delilah and I had a chat."

He kept walking. "I figured as much. Something felt weird."

"Yeah, well, she essentially admitted to being into you."

He looked at me like I was crazy. "Are you sure it's not just—?" he began before thinking twice and holding his tongue.

"What?" I asked. "Just say it."

"Well, hormones or whatever. Are you sure it's not just an insecurity or something?" he stupidly asked.

I shook my head, desperate to keep my cool so it didn't fuel his accusation, although I was seething inside. "It's a good thing you're pretty," I threatened. "I assure you, Atticus Kelly, that it is not *hormones*, as you say."

We reached the car and he opened my door for me so I climbed in.

"What did she say exactly?" he asked, his tone skeptical.

"You know what?" I said, pissed. "Never mind."

"*Hazel*," he said. "Are you okay?"

I laughed at the window. "Peachy."

"Hazel," he said, as we pulled up to my work.

I jumped out before he had a chance to open it for me and walked briskly toward the courtyard.

"Hazel!" he said, racing to catch up. "Hazel," he said again, reaching me and grabbing my arm.

I pulled it away. "Listen, I'm just going to say this once and it's not hormones or insecurities or whatever you're looking for it to be. She told me she was going to try and get you. I'm just relaying the message."

He shook his head. "This blows my mind because last

night she told me you guys just talked about your paintings or whatever."

I looked at him, annoyed. "She's lying."

"You didn't talk about your work at all?" he asked.

"My answer isn't going to change, Atticus!" I shouted.

"I'm just trying to piece it all together," he defended.

"What's to piece together? I'm telling you exactly what happened. You left the room, she pounced, asking all these questions about us, how long we've been together, and I told her I wasn't stupid, that I knew what she was doing!"

"Wait, she asked how long we've been together and you just blurt out accusations?"

I was seething at this point. "If you had been there, you would have seen what I saw!"

The workroom door opened and Tim peeked out his stupid head. "Hazel, is this guy bothering you?"

I watched Atticus. His hands formed fists when he saw Tim, his jaw gritted.

"No, Tim, go back inside. I'll be in in a second," I told him.

"Come inside, Hazel. I'll take care of him," Tim said, overstepping yet again.

"Go back inside!" Atticus shouted at him.

Tim came through the door all the way into the courtyard. "Watch the way you talk to me!" he yelled.

"Oh my God, Tim! Please! I'll be there in a second!" I pleaded.

Atticus advanced on Tim. "Yeah, *Tim,* go back inside."

Tim squared off against Atticus, which looked ridiculous since Atticus had at least a foot and probably twenty-five pounds on him.

"Get the fuck off this property," Tim demanded.

"Make me, old man," Atticus spit out.

I started to get worried and pulled at Atticus's arm. "Atticus, just go. I'll call you later."

He stared at me, a hurt look on his face. "You want me gone? Fine."

He started to walk away but Tim, being the asshole he was, had to get the last word. "And don't cross property lines again or I'll be forced to call security."

Without missing a beat, Atticus whipped back around and reeled back, socking Tim in the face. Tim fell back and landed on his back, his hand going to his eye.

"Oh my God!" I shouted. "Atticus!"

Atticus leaned over him. "That's for making Hazel's life miserable, you prick. She's mine, asshole. Go near her, look at her, make her uncomfortable, say *anything* other than shop talk to her, and I'll hunt you down."

My hands went to my mouth when Tim stood and looked at me. "You're fired. Get the hell out of here or I'll press charges."

Atticus stood tall but looked as shocked as I felt, whether it was at himself for blowing his top or at what Tim said, I didn't know.

"Tim, I—" I began.

"No, get out of here. I'm done with this bullshit. Take your slut ass out of here."

I saw it. Saw the moment Tim called me a slut and Atticus lost it but could do nothing about it. Atticus advanced again with yet another uppercut and I screamed. This time when Tim went down, he stayed down, groaning.

"Oh my God," I said, my hands going to my forehead. "What is happening?"

"Come on," Atticus quieted, reaching for me.

I refused his hand and started to walk toward his car.

"Don't come back, skank!" Tim yelled after me.

Atticus turned back but I grasped at him, held him back, desperate to get out of there. "Atticus, ignore him! Come on!"

Atticus shook his head, his eyes filled with anger, but he obeyed me. When we got into his car, he peeled out. We rode in absolute silence all the way back to my apartment.

Once inside, though, I unleashed.

"I can't believe what just happened!" I shouted at him.

"Whatever, that guy deserved it."

He fell on my couch, nursing a bruised and bleeding hand. I grabbed a washcloth from the bathroom and went to the freezer for ice, wetting the cloth in the kitchen sink. I sat next to him and placed the washcloth full of ice on his hand. He sucked in a breath.

"I needed that job, Atticus. Now I'm going to have to pay Cobra coverage."

"What is that?" he asked.

"When you're fired from a job, you lose your insurance rate. If you want to continue with coverage, you have to pay the rate the insurance company requires. I can't afford to lose my insurance for obvious reasons. Now I'll be forced to pay more. How am I going to pay for that, huh? I have no savings. I have nothing."

Atticus gulped. "I can just add you to mine then," he said.

"How? You can't just add people to your plan, Atticus. I can't believe this," I said, examining his hand. "What if Tim presses charges?"

"He won't," he said.

"How do you know?"

"Because then he'd have to answer to all the sexual harassment shit he pulled on you and he knows he'd lose because Madison saw it all with her own eyes. He knows she'd testify on your behalf."

I shook my head. "I loved the work, Atticus."

"For that, I'm really sorry, Hazel."

My eyes burned. "I feel so lost now. That job was a bit of stability for me."

"Hey," he said, sitting up and resting his good hand on my neck. "You can rely on me, Hazel."

I shook my head. "What are you talking about? What happened back there?"

"I told you, he deserved it. He's a sexist perv and he took advantage of the fact that you needed the job. He knew what he was doing. He's a bastard."

"I need cash," I told him. "I live paycheck to paycheck, and I'm only one away from being kicked out of this place."

"I told you I've got you."

"I'm not going to rely on you like that, Atticus. I need to stand on my own two feet."

"Let me just do my thing, Hazel."

"Well, what do you have in mind?"

"I bet Aidan could use you at Normandy's."

"Oh jeez, like what?" I asked.

"I don't know. I'll ask him."

"I'm not so sure about that," I said.

"Just let me do this. At least let it tide you over? I feel like shit for getting you fired."

"You should," I needled.

Atticus looked wounded. "I really am sorry," he said.

I sighed. "I know, Atticus. Let's just put this fire out and see where it takes us."

He nodded.

CHAPTER FOURTEEN

The following Friday I started at Normandy's. I bar-backed and it was a baptism by fire, let me tell you. Hundreds of people crowded around and my only job was to pop bottles and hand them over, making sure to add it to people's tabs or run cards or give change. Because of this, I had to try and keep track of people's faces and their names. It was work I wasn't used to and I screwed up a few receipts. Aidan was cool about it, but I could tell he was a little annoyed.

I already missed my watercolors. I found myself daydreaming about my stupid cels. It was assembly-line work, I know, but it was still *painting*. I found my eyes growing teary and had to check myself several times. To top it off, Atticus was at The Sink with Delilah and imagining them working together made me emotionally drained.

"Yo!" a yuppy punk yelled, snapping his fingers in my face. "I asked for a beer. Are you deaf?"

"Sorry," I apologized, trying to remember what he had been drinking all night.

The jerk looked over my shoulder at Cillian and shouted, "You need a new beer girl, Cillian! She's worthless." He started laughing, but Cillian wasn't giving him the reaction he wanted and his smile fell.

Cillian marched up behind me, the palm of his hand landing on the bar top beside me, his chest against my back protectively. "This is Hazel. She's family and you will treat her as much. Apologize."

The popped-collar douche raised his hands as if surrendering. "Hey, man, sorry."

"Not to me, dillweed. To her."

He looked at me. "I'm sorry."

"Now," Cillian said, "you're gonna walk out of here, catch a cab, go home, and when you get there, you're going to think about what it's like to be a woman working in a bar with drunk idiots surrounding her."

"You're banning me?" the guy asked.

"I didn't say I was banning you. I said you're gone for the night. Now go."

The guy walked out. Cillian turned to me and winked. He held his fist out for me and I bumped my own with his. We went back to work and I felt better knowing Cillian was right there to back me up. The rest of the shift went pretty smoothly. I didn't know if it was because I had more confidence or if it was because I figured out a routine, but I didn't screw up any more tabs and we closed the bar out successfully, not a penny out of place.

Aidan eyed me. "It was sort of hairy in the beginning there but you held your own, which is pretty hard to do your first shift. You did well, Hazel."

"Thanks," I said. "And thanks for the job."

"Don't mention it," he said, reaching over and grabbing

my tip bucket. "Count it."

I pulled the cash out, matched the bills, and added them all up. "Two hundred thirty," I told him.

"Good," he said, laying another fifty on the stack. "If you ever make under two fifty on the weekends, tell me," he said, stalking off before I had the chance to thank him. I think he planned it that way. Aidan didn't strike me as the kind who liked that kind of attention.

The Saturday after, I made more than three hundred, which was nice considering my rent was due soon. I felt more secure and decided to drive over to The Sink to see Atticus after my shift. I texted him but instead of texting back, he sent a video.

Weird, I thought. When I pulled up to a stoplight, I pressed play. Loud, booming music rang through and the room was dark. There were a ton of people but only two stuck out to me. Delilah. And Atticus. It was hard to see his face but it was definitely his jacket, and I could see the tattoos on his hands. She sat on his lap, his hands on her thighs as she sang along with her own track.

I laughed something dry, something caustic, and looked out onto the empty street before me.

"This is why I don't date musicians," I said out loud.

CHAPTER FIFTEEN

The next morning Etta came over when I called her crying unintelligibly.

"I'll be right there!" she said, hanging up.

Trying to see through the unceasing tears, I texted Aidan and apologized that I wouldn't be working there anymore and if he needed further explanation, to ask Atticus.

Within fifteen minutes, my phone blew up with calls from not only Atticus, but Aidan, Cillian, Liam, Malachi, *and* Brendan. Atticus texted me over and over, but I didn't bother to look at them, erasing each one as they came in.

When Etta walked in I basically tackled her in a hug.

"Oh my God, babe, what is going on?" she asked.

She walked me over to my couch and we sat down. I laid my head on her lap, and she covered me with the knitted throw I kept nearby.

"I wish I'd never met him," I spoke.

"Oh, come on, Hazel. It couldn't have been that bad," she said, smoothing back my hair.

I took out my phone, opened it, and handed it to her.

She pressed play on the video; the tears renewed as I listened. "Son of a gun," she whispered, making my heart ache. "I just can't believe this."

"Well, it's all right there."

She shook her head. "No, I mean, it's all a little convenient, don't you think?"

"I know this was one of her ploys," I agreed. "I figured that all out pretty quickly but what I want to know is, ploy or not, how did she land on his lap and why are his hands on her legs?"

"Who took the video?" she asked. I could practically see the wheels turning in her head.

"Probably her assistant."

"She has an assistant?" she asked.

"Yes, Etta, she's the type of person who needs an assistant. She's got a record deal. She's important. She's beautiful," I lamented.

"She is scandalous," Etta added.

"You *think*?"

Etta replayed the video, wounding me without knowing it, and looked closely as it played.

"This just doesn't add up," she said.

"Etta! That's his jacket. Those are his tattoos."

"Well, you can't really see his tattoos all that well."

"Etta, for Chrissakes!"

She sighed. "I'm just trying to give him the benefit of the doubt is all."

"The evidence is all right there."

"It's not like him to do that," Etta said.

"I thought that too, but that's what happens when you've only known someone for fifteen weeks."

"Fifteen weeks can be long enough to know someone if

that someone is as open as Atticus."

I sat up and swiped the palms of my hands under my eyes. "Why are you defending him? Did you not see the video?"

She grabbed my hand. "I saw a video of a boy who looked similar to Atticus, wearing his jacket, and had tattoos. I don't know if it was him for sure, though. You yourself told me she said she was going to do what she could to get him. For that reason alone, I think we should talk to him."

I scoffed. "Oh my God, Etta! I'm *not* going to talk to him. It is what it is! You can't argue with video!"

"Blurry video!"

I shook my head at her and walked to my dresser, taking out a pair of shorts and a tank top. I undressed and tossed all my stuff on the floor. I stood in front of my mirror, my hand going to my stomach. Etta looked at me through the reflection of the mirror.

"Oh my God," she said. "I know what this is."

"What?" I asked, yanking my hand off my stomach and throwing on my shorts and tank.

"This is about the baby."

"Of course this is about the baby!"

"No," she argued, "this is your fear coming through. You see an opportunity to bail and you're bailing. You don't really care if that was him or not. You're going to convince yourself it was and you aren't going to entertain any other idea."

My heart sped into my throat and I tried to swallow it down. "I-I don't know what you're talking about."

"You know *exactly* what I'm talking about, Hazel."

"No more, Etta."

"Oh no!" she said, raising up off the couch. "I'm not going to let you screw this up! Just because your mom was a screwup does not mean you are going to be! You are a completely different person, Hazel."

Tears began to slip down my cheeks. "Enough, Etta."

"Hazel, you will be a different kind of mom. Trust me."

"How can that be?' I asked, falling to my knees, my face buried in my hands. "Look at where I come from," I sobbed. "Look at the stock. I can't do that to my kid. I can't put her through that."

Etta stomped over to me and picked up my head, my cheeks in her hands. "You are not your mom, Hazel."

"I am," I battled.

"You aren't!" she insisted.

"Etta, I can't do this alone, and I don't know him well enough."

"You do, Hazel. You know him. I-I think you love him."

My stomach plummeted to my feet, refusing to acknowledge what I suspected as well. "I can't do this."

"You can," she comforted.

I shook my head. "I know what I saw in that video," I told her.

Her hands fell at her side. "You are determined to ruin things, aren't you?"

"Enough, Etta."

"No!" she countered. "Enough from *you*, Hazel." She walked toward the door, yanked her keys from the bar top, and headed for the door. "I'm going to class. Call me when you get your head out of your ass!" she yelled, slamming my door.

I crawled into bed and pulled the covers over my head. My phone kept going off but I left it on the coffee table where it was. I passed the time praying, something I hadn't done in a long time, eventually calming down enough to fall asleep.

Bang! Bang! Bang! Someone pounded on my door. I woke, my chest feeling heavy.

"Hazel!" Atticus's voice echoed through the door. Adrenaline pumped through my body at an alarming rate. "Hazel, it's me. Please open up."

"Go away, Atticus."

"What the hell is going on?" he asked, his tone desperate.

I ignored the impulse to run and open the door for him. I stood up instead and practically crawled to the door. I placed the palms of my hands on its face. "I texted you last night," I said through the door.

"Hazel, open up, babe."

Tears spilled down my cheeks. "I was coming to see you and, uh, my phone went off. It was a message from you, a video, actually."

"I don't know what you're talking about," he said.

"Oh, I know that. Someone, probably Delilah's assistant, sent it from your phone. I expected sabotage from her, but what I didn't expect was what was on that video."

He got really quiet. "What was on it?" he asked.

"It was you. Delilah was on your lap." I hesitated at the next bit. "Your hands were on her legs."

"Hazel, you've got to believe me, it wasn't me," he insisted. "Please, open the door."

"See, the thing is, I think it was you. It was your jacket, your tattoos on your hands."

"Hazel," he pleaded, "I swear to God, Hazel. That was

not me."

"The eyes don't deceive, Atticus."

"I don't have a fucking video on my phone. They must have deleted it. Can you send it to me?"

"Ask Delilah for it. I'm sure she has the original."

"Hazel," he begged, making my heart hurt. "I swear, Hazel." I didn't answer him. I heard what sounded like his back sliding down my front door then a sharp bang at what I thought was his head hitting the surface. "I can't believe this shit," I heard.

I sat on my ankles and cried into my hands.

"Hazel, are you still there?"

"Y-yes," I answered.

"I'm going to find out what the fuck happened, and I'm going to prove to you I didn't do this." He sucked in a breath. "I'm deflated, disheartened."

"Why?" I asked, unable to help myself.

"Because you don't trust me."

"How does it feel?" I asked.

I heard him stand up and walk away.

"Goodbye, Atticus Kelly."

CHAPTER SIXTEEN

December Third

I didn't hear from Atticus for four days, not even a text, not that I had a lot of time to think about it, because December third was my senior exhibit, my final project, my final grade. I'd spent months working hard, practically bleeding onto my canvases, and the third was the day of my gallery. I tried on about a million outfits but my small belly was throwing me off. I ended up wearing something so funky it felt borderline psychotic. I was so tired of second-guessing myself, tired of feeling insecure, tired of being tired.

"Miss Stone?" Professor Danes asked.

"Yes, sir?"

"Can you walk us through?" he asked.

"Oh! Of course," I said, shaking off my thoughts. "I thought we could start at this end. Each piece progresses. The theme is madness."

"As in demented?" Professor Danes asked.

Atticus came into my line of sight then. Our eyes

caught. My stomach plummeted.

"As in fanatical love," I answered. It was a theme I'd chosen long before I'd ever met Atticus. It was surreal.

Atticus stood a few feet back from the judging professors so he wouldn't disturb us, but his presence sent me to a place I wasn't prepared to be.

I fumbled over my practiced presentation. "I, um, I'm —"

"It's okay, Hazel," my theory professor, Dr. Lombard, appeased. "Just speak from your heart." He gestured to my first piece. "Who is this?" he asked.

I swallowed and then, as if a damn opened, it all came pouring out. "I am her, but she is all of us," I began.

I described each piece with more passion than I thought I held, explained ideas I was aware of when I painted but decided against revealing. They were too vulnerable, too tender, too delicate, but that day I exposed myself, opened up my chest and out spilled every hurt, every agony, every emotional laceration that ever existed. And with each painting you saw the progression of healing, the dogged determination to be revived, all fueled by the deepest love that at the time I threw it on canvas was nothing but an intellection. That is, until my last painting. The one I started painting when I met Atticus.

"Ah, now this," Professor Lombard exclaimed. "This was your last?" he asked.

"Yes," I confirmed.

The third professor, Dr. Torres, slapped his hands to his chest. "*¡Qué linda!* Hazel, this is your masterpiece."

"Dr. Danes," Dr. Lombard said, "did she work on this in your class?"

"Yes," he confirmed. "It was one of her quickest. I've

never seen her work so diligently."

"This is the piece that healed you, Hazel," Dr. Lombard mentioned. This caught me by surprise. "Whatever motivated this piece healed you," he said.

All the breath in my chest rushed out at once. "No, sir," I implored. "It's still a work in progress."

Dr. Danes shook his head back and forth. "No, Miss Stone, it is not."

My eyes started to burn and I sucked in a breath to compose myself.

All three men looked at one another. "I think we can all agree, gentlemen, that this is probably one of the best pieces to come out of this school in many years?" Dr. Danes asked. They nodded in agreement and Dr. Danes turned toward me. "Congratulations, Miss Stone. You've more than passed. In fact, I'm going to take this piece in for consideration at the DMA."

"Oh my God," I said, my hands starting to shake.

Each shook my hand and Dr. Danes hugged me. "You're going to do wonderful things, Miss Stone."

They left me standing there and exited the university gallery, leaving me alone with Atticus. I looked at him as he meandered around another student's sculpture, his hands clasped behind his back, his shoulders leaning forward a bit. His body language looked humbled, which saddened me.

"You came," I said, fighting tears.

"I had to see for myself," he said.

I swept my hands out and presented my pieces as if they weren't hundreds of hours of my time and blood and sweat and tears.

"Hazel," he pledged like a vow.

"Please not here," I said. "Not after one of the best moments of my life."

"When?" he asked.

"Let's get something to eat," I offered.

The invitation shocked him. I could see it in his face. "Anywhere you want to go," he said. I walked forward through the doors and he kept close to me. "You're stunning, Hazel."

"Beautiful words from a beautiful mouth," I countered.

"They aren't words, Hazel. They're the gospel truth."

It'd begun to rain and there was an all-night diner that housed a lot of local students across the street so I sprinted toward it. Inside, we took off our coats and hung them on the rack near the door. The inside of the diner was all dark wood, easily a hundred years old, and cozy. I chose a booth in the back corner and slid in. Atticus sat beside me. We watched the rain trickle down the cloudy glass windows.

"I saw the video," he said.

My eyes found his. "Did you now?"

His hand found the back of his neck. "It looks incriminating, I'll admit." I laughed. "But it wasn't me, Hazel."

"Okay," I bit.

"I swear, Hazel. It— you were right that she, uh, Delilah, has some sort of strange fascination with me. I kind of don't know why, and I hate it but whatever."

"Oh, you can admit that now, can you? I told you and you didn't believe me."

"No, it's not that I didn't believe you. I was only trying to break the thing down, find out exactly what happened."

"The second I told you her intentions, you should have

believed me." I shook my head and stared out the window.

"I'm sorry. Really."

I shrugged my shoulder.

"It was River in that video."

I looked at him. "You must think I'm a gosh-damn fool."

He shook his head slowly. "I definitely don't think that."

He took out his phone and showed me a picture of River's hands. I looked closely. They did resemble Atticus's.

"And the jacket?"

"This feels so fucking stupid to explain, but I let him borrow it when he went out to his car for that damn missing pedal and I guess he never took it off. I think Delilah took advantage of the situation." I sighed. "If you look closer in the video you can also see River's boots, the ones he always wears."

I took out my phone and played the video again, this time focusing on the shoes and hands. I laid the phone down. "Okay," I breathed, "I believe you."

He scooted over in the booth and I watched as he slowly laid his arm across my shoulders. "I'm sorry I didn't believe you when you said she was up to no good."

I nodded. "I'm sorry I didn't believe you when you said it wasn't you in the video."

He kissed my temple. "I'll be glad when she's gone," he spoke into my hair.

"She's still going to be working at The Sink?"

"Yeah, Hazel. The label doesn't want to break their contract any more than we do."

"That sucks, " I mentioned absently. "Who is her producer now? Let me guess," I joked, "River?"

Atticus shifted so he could get a better look at me. "*I'm* still her producer, Hazel."

My mouth dropped open. "You aren't serious."

"Hazel, the contract specifically states my name. I can't back out. The Sink would lose hundreds of thousands of dollars. I'd be liable, probably sued." I grabbed my bag and started to exit the booth. "Hazel!" he shouted, chasing after me. "Hazel, stop!"

I broke through the diner doors into the pouring rain. Briefly, I raised my face and palms toward the sky. "Help me," I whispered into the wind.

I started walking toward the university's parking lots in search of my car.

"Hazel," Atticus begged, catching up with me. He walked sideways beside me as I trudged ahead.

"Atticus, I think it'd be best if we just called this shit what it was and go our separate ways."

He bit out an unbelieving laugh. "There is no fucking way I'm doing that."

I stopped short and he followed suit. "Why?" I asked.

"Because I'm falling in love with you, Hazel, and you're carrying our daughter."

Tears fell and mixed with the rain. "And yet you'll still work with her?"

"I don't have a choice, Hazel!"

"You do!"

"I don't, though! I signed a contract. I had a lawyer look at it two days ago and there is no way out of it without it costing me a fortune, not to mention what breaking it would mean for my career. That kind of news travels. I can't support a family on what I make now, but if I can get through this contract, who knows the possibilities? I don't have a choice, Hazel." I kept walking. "You have to see this from my angle," he said.

I reached my car. "That's the thing, Atticus. I know you can't break your contract but looking at it from your angle means a world of hurt *for me.* Imagining you working closely with her every day would kill me. You'd come to my house every night, kiss my lips, hold my hand, and all the while I'd know you sat all day beside her, her working her magic, and not knowing for sure if it was affecting you until it was too late, until I was already in love with you, stuck with a newborn and totally alone. I can't—won't—do that."

"I can't believe this," Atticus said, his hair plastered to his neck, rain dripping down his face and nose. "What do I have to do to prove to you that you're *it* for me, Hazel Stone? You're the gosh-damn *one*! The world can throw a thousand Delilahs in front of you and I'll stomp every fucking one of them to get to you." He leaned over me, his eyes searching mine. They lit with an understanding I didn't anticipate. "But you don't care, do you? You want an out. You're scared and you want an out." He shook his head. "I can't fucking believe I didn't see it before." He stepped back. "Fine, you want out?" He lifted his hands in surrender. "You got it."

He turned and walked away. Words rested on the tip of my tongue, a desperate "wait," a panicked "hold on," but they didn't or couldn't come, and I felt ill to my stomach when he turned the corner of the giant stone building that housed the university art gallery. He was out of sight but not, could never be, out of my mind.

Why am I like this, Atticus?

CHAPTER SEVENTEEN

December Tenth

Graduation day. I hadn't any intentions of attending, but Dr. Danes requested I be there so he could introduce me to his Dallas Museum of Art rep friend and I felt like if I didn't show I'd be committing career suicide. I'd been trying for days to look for a day job but pickings were slim, and the only places hiring were food service related. I wasn't above it, but I needed something with a bit more stability and better hours. I was getting tired more easily and fell asleep at the foot of my canvas more than once.

Before our blowout, Etta and I had mailed invites to my graduation, including some to all of Atticus's family. For some reason, despite that day in the rain, I was hoping he would show. He was all I thought about. I wanted him. I wasn't afraid to admit he was right about my being afraid. Etta was right as well. I just didn't know how to find a place between hating his working with Delilah and knowing he was contractually obligated to do so. I reasoned out while lying in my bed for days on end, that if he would just show graduation day, I could apologize, regain time lost, because the world had stopped spinning without him. I needed him to pick me up and start the rotation again.

I wanted to find my okay place, and I didn't think I could find it without his help. My imagination was my own worst enemy. I always did that to myself. I sabotaged myself, created problems for myself. It was as if I invited pain, and I didn't know why I did it. As much as I was loath to concede to it, I believed it all stemmed from my mother. She was a terrible mom. There was no other way to put it. One day, without warning, she left me on my Grams's doorstep, which devastated me. Although my Gram was great and she loved me so well, there was no getting over sitting on the porch for hours on end waiting for my mom to come home, wondering what I did to make her leave.

Which is why it was so hard for me to be in the situation I was in. As much I wanted to hope I could create the stability a little kid needed, I was afraid I couldn't do it alone. My mom couldn't. What made me think I could? I didn't know Atticus long enough to make the leap. Notice I said *long enough*. I believed then I knew him well enough, just not *long enough*. I thought there was a difference. I couldn't imagine falling in love with my baby only to realize she deserved more than I could give to her because I couldn't give her a dad. I grew up without a dad. It messes with you. You constantly wonder whether you're worth anything. You constantly seek out people who can give you what he was supposed to give you, but they'll never be able to fulfill that for you because they aren't your dad. It's a vicious cycle. You keep repeating the same mistakes over and over hoping for different results, yet you're not shocked when you get more of the same.

I hopped in the shower and cried into the downpour.

"How do I know what to do?" I asked out loud, sobbing. "God, please, tell me what I'm supposed to do." I leaned over to grab my shampoo bottle and felt something in my stomach. My hand flew to my belly. "Oh my God," I whispered when I felt tiny little kicks against my skin. "Oh my God," I said over and over.

Without thinking about it, I jumped out of the shower and ran for my phone. My hands hovered over a text to Atticus.

Atticus, I began to type, **I thought you should know that I felt our daughter kick today.**

Then I erased it all.

Thought you would want to know that I felt her today

Again, I erased it.

I'm sorry. Can we talk? p.s. I felt her today.

My eyes burned as I erased it all again and locked the phone.

Atticus

I stared at my phone, trying to gather the courage to tell her that I knew her graduation was that day and I wanted to ask her how she was doing. I wanted to tell her I missed her. That if I could, I would do everything over again so differently. As I did this, the typing indicator popped up under my last text to Haze and my heart flew into my throat.

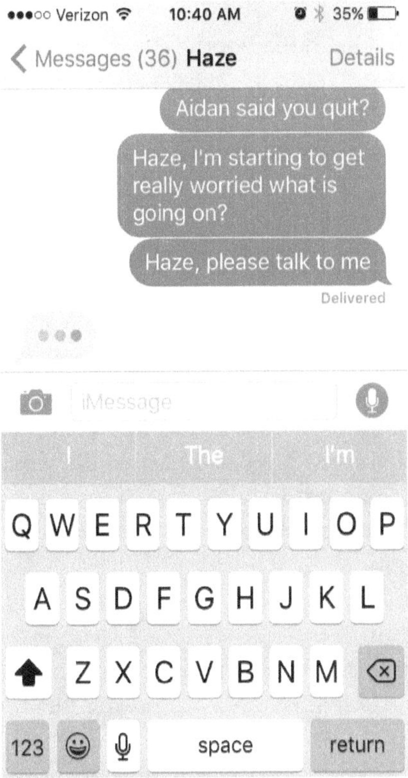

"Gosh-damn it, Hazel, what are you doing?" I said.

I sat up and watched that bubble disappear then reappear, disappear then reappear, disappear then reappear. My knee bounced as I watched the screen, waiting for the bubble to appear again. But it didn't.

"You ready to keep going?" Delilah asked me, a plastic smile on her fucking face.

"Yeah," I groaned.

"You okay?" she asked, leaning closer to me. I

automatically leaned away.

"I'm fine, Delilah. Get in the booth."

Her eyes narrowed. "You don't have to be a dick about it."

"I do, actually. You're fucked up and it's caused me a lot of problems."

"Listen, my label is paying a lot of money—" she started to threaten.

"Stop right there," I interrupted her. "I'm here, aren't I? I'm fulfilling my end of the contract, but you know what *wasn't* in there? My being your little bitch wasn't in there. My tolerating your scandalous ass wasn't in there. So I'm gonna create your music and it's going to be fucking fresh, but that doesn't mean I have to like doing it. Now get in the gosh-damn booth."

She swallowed and stood, opening the door to the booth and settling inside.

When the door closed, River turned to me. "Dude, don't fuck this up for us."

"I'm doing my job, River. You know what she did, yet I'm still here, right? Consider that not fucking this up for you."

I closed out my day with about half an hour to spare, threw on my jacket, and rushed out of the studio. I was going to Hazel's graduation, even if she didn't want me to be there. I thought back to the disappearing texts and wondered if she actually did. I jumped in the Impala, my heart racing, and headed to the auditorium she'd listed on her invite to my mom. I drove into the lot and threw the car in park, practically sprinting to the auditorium. My hands shook as I reached for the door and pulled it open. I wound through the packed lobby, my chest tight with anticipation. My eyes meandered over the crowd when I spotted her, across the room, near the bar concession.

God, she is beautiful. And so fucking smart. And so fucking creative. She's a fucking genius.

Her long chestnut hair swung forward when she looked down at her phone. Her finger hung over the screen's face. Her hand formed a fist then she put the phone in the pocket of her graduation gown.

She didn't realize it, but her pregnancy made her insanely hot to me. I couldn't describe it out loud without sounding like a fucking caveman, but knowing she was carrying our daughter did something to my insides. It woke something in me I didn't know laid dormant, something primal. I saw her face and I thought *protect.* I touched her skin and I thought *mine.* I kissed her lips and I thought *want.* And I did, *so fucking much.* I hadn't met anyone like her, and I knew I never would. She was made for me. And I was made to worship her.

She started to search the crowd for someone and I deluded myself into thinking it might be me. I ducked behind a group of people so she wouldn't see me and start demanding I leave, in case I *wasn't* who she was searching for. When her hazel eyes had seen all they wanted to see, she turned toward a door heading into the auditorium and broke through. It was only then I felt as if I could breathe again.

I leaned against a marble column, tucked my hands in my pockets, and closed my eyes to catch my breath. *I want her. I want her. I want her.*

"If you'll all please take a seat, the ceremony will begin shortly," a woman's voice rang through the room. I absently noted the acoustics in there were killer.

I joined the herd into the theater and chose a seat in the back, in the dark, where she wouldn't be able to see me.

I couldn't even tell you who gave the commencement speech or what was said. All I knew was Hazel. She stood out to me in sea of graduation caps, her long hair, the way she carried herself, her secret smiles. She laughed with someone beside her, I didn't know who, and it made me jealous as hell that she had friendships with others, friends she could laugh and joke with, friends I didn't even know yet.

Since it was a fall graduation, there weren't many graduates, so they got to Hazel's row fairly quickly. I stood when she did and started filming on my phone. When she walked up the stage, I hit the photo option while I recorded. The flash went off when they said her name and I hadn't expected it to.

"Shit," I whispered, and fumbled to turn it off.

Hazel

"Hazel Stone," the coordinator spoke into the microphone.

There was a flash of light from someone's camera somewhere in the back of the theater. *Must be a mistake*, I thought.

"Congratulations," Dr. Danes said, handing me my diploma holder.

"Thank you, Professor Danes."

I descended the stage and took my seat again. It was all such a whirlwind. I didn't even have an opportunity to think about how alone I was until I sat down and looked around to see if he was there. *He's not here. How could he not come?* I bit my bottom lip to prevent myself from crying. *I caused this. I should have tried to work it out. I should have tried harder.*

Just then, my baby started moving around and the tears I fought so hard to keep back came pouring out.

"You okay?" my friend Donivan asked.

"Yeah, dude, fine. Just a little emotional."

He smiled and nodded. "No doubt."

I sucked in a breath to distract myself, which worked. I wiped the tears away and felt relief when my face dried.

After the ceremony, I sat in the lobby waiting for Professor Danes as he requested. I took off my cap and unzipped my gown to get some air. Polyester is no bueno for ventilation, muchachos.

"Miss Stone," Dr. Danes called out.

I turned toward him and smiled. "Professor Danes."

He brought a little woman forward. She was, maybe sixty, with the most chic haircut I'd ever seen, and clothes that would rival Coco Chanel.

"Hazel Stone, this is Cordelia Clements. She's curator for the DMA."

She held out her hand and I took it. "Miss Clements, so nice to meet you."

"And you as well, my darling."

"I showed her your piece, Hazel, and she was very impressed," Professor Danes said.

"Very impressed, " Miss Clements confirmed. "I was wondering if you would be interested in exhibiting?"

I was floored, almost speechless. "Uh, uh, uh," I stuttered. "I mean, of course. That is a dream come true for me, actually."

Cordelia Clements smiled. "It would be an honor." She

looked over her shoulder. "Listen, I'm sorry to lay that on you and run," she teased, "but I've got a fellow over there looking to get home. I'll have an appraiser run by the school and have your piece appraised. We'll get the piece in about six weeks or so for exhibition?"

"Uh, yes, of course," I stammered, a little out of breath.

She kissed both my cheeks and squeezed my hands. "Quite the talent, Miss Stone."

She started to walk away but before I had an opportunity to register what happened, she turned around. "Oh, also, so sorry. I've got a local artist needing an apprentice while he opens a gallery sponsored by the museum. I think you'd be perfect for the role. Are you attached anywhere?"

"No, ma'am."

She looked at Dr. Danes and winked. "I'll look past that ma'am business," she playfully dug. "I'll give him your contact information. Do you have a card?" she asked.

"Oh, yes!" I exclaimed, reaching into my pocket and taking out the cards Dr. Danes insisted I bring. I gave her three.

"Eager," she teased when she took in the number. "I like that. Goodbye, darling. We'll be in touch."

She turned and people parted for her naturally. She was a force to be reckoned with.

"Well." I sighed.

Professor Danes smiled. "That was Cordelia."

"She's magnificent," I said.

"That she is," he agreed. "Now, if you'll excuse me?"

I gave him a hug. "Thank you for everything."

"You're a rarity, Miss Stone. It's not often I have a

student with a talent as natural as yours. I can't wait to see what you do with it."

"Thank you, sir."

He nodded and smiled then disappeared within the crowd.

I turned, hoping to miraculously find Atticus there. No one was there, of course.

"Time to get home, I guess," I told no one.

My hand went to my stomach. Well, not *no one.*

CHAPTER EIGHTEEN

Atticus

December 10th

Well, I went to your graduation today. You looked beautiful, as always. I wanted to grab you, hug you, kiss you, but I didn't. I'm a coward, apparently. Never thought of myself as such but I'm scared of you.

I know you won't want to read this but I have to lay it out there. I only have two more weeks on the contract. I'm counting down the days, the hours, the minutes, the seconds, the nanoseconds.

I think about you constantly.

I wonder how you're feeling, what you're doing with your days. I've been trying to put cash in your bank account but they won't let me because I don't know the account number. I think I'm pissing off the tellers going in there every day but I don't care. I tried to pay your December rent but apparently you already did. I'll try January, I guess.

I miss you, Haze. I feel like we're stuck in quicksand. Move an inch and we'll sink deeper but we want out, we want free. Damned if we do, damned if we don't. I don't want it to be like this anymore. I crave your skin, miss your hands on me. I feel the loss, Haze. It set up in my chest and won't move out. It refuses to move out.

I won't send you this letter. I don't think you'll read it. Maybe you would. I don't know. I'll hold on to it for a while anyway.

Miss you, Haze.

-Atticus

***

December 13th

Eleven days left on the contract.

I drove by your studio today but your car wasn't there. I know that's stalker-type shit but I can't help it. You must have gotten a job or something. I hope you're eating. You get so sick when you don't and I worry about you. My mom asked about you today. She doesn't know. Only my brothers know and they're keeping quiet. I asked them to. I keep hoping things will change. Is that delusional?

Want you, Haze.

-Atticus

***

* * *

December 17th

Seven days left on the contract.

Today the label heads heard most of the remaining tracks and liked them. One of them called me personally, but it felt bittersweet not being able to call you immediately after and tell you about it. They've been marketing like crazy in select markets. They released a single organically and it went viral, so they're putting it on the radio. It feels surreal. There's this unspoken pressure to finish the album with a bang, but I'm finding it hard to be creative since you've been gone, and I've literally started to hate the artist. I've visited all your paintings over and over but they've lost their potency now that I know and need the artist more than I want the muse they supplied.

Need you, Haze.

-Atticus

***

December 21st

Three days left on the contract.

The single is sitting at number twelve and rising. I can't believe you're not around to celebrate this with me.

The label heads offered me a job. They prefer I move to LA but say they'll let me work from anywhere. It feels like a dream come true but it won't register. I won't say why. You should know by now.

I wonder if you suffer as much as I do.

Does your heart feel ripped to shreds?
Can you feel mine at your feet?
It beats. I know it beats because I can feel it pounding, an agonizing cadence that counts your fucking name.
Just finish me off, Hazel. One careful step and you'd give me relief.
Put me out of my misery.

I'm starting to hate you.

-Atticus

***

December 23rd

One day left on the contract.

I texted you. I had to. I needed to know if you felt anything anymore as I do. You didn't respond, though.

I wonder how you could just leave us like this? I can't believe how you've done me.

I can't believe it.

I can't fucking believe it.

You're cruel.

* * *

-Atticus

*****

December 24th

Ding, dong. The witch is dead.

It sucks my first number-one hit was with her, but it is what it is. Anyway, I'm done. I fulfilled my contract and I got a number-one hit out of it. The album drops in March. I've already got a label position and the power to veto exclusivity so the million other offers on the table can still be considered or worked in tandem. Whatever I want, basically. It's ideal. I'd tell you about them but I don't think you'd care.

Malachi told Mom about us. The family is pissed at me now. Like I'm the one who is hardheaded and won't realize the truth. Like I'm the one who could somehow change your mind. Like I had a fucking choice.

Go to hell, Hazel Stone.

- *The one who wanted you but doesn't anymore*

CHAPTER NINETEEN

Hazel

Etta and I are talking again but she's busy with school and her new boyfriend. We text a lot more than we used to, but it's better than nothing.

I'm sick. My doctor doesn't know what's going on, but he's monitoring me closely. It's nothing he's seen before. They called a few specialists in but they're all stumped. It's not cancer. It's not any sort of disease they're familiar with. I'm starting to reject pregnancy. It feels like a cruel joke. Just as I'm falling in love with her, my body wants to get rid of her. My hands go to my belly and hold there.

I'm scared to tell Atticus. There feels like too much to throw on him at once. I was an idiot. I am a *huge* idiot. His single went number one. I was sure he was living it up. Why wouldn't he be? And I didn't want to put a damper on all that. He was thrown into the spotlight he was made for. I couldn't even keep up with the number of women who threw themselves at his metaphorical feet on social.

He had an interview on the Edge. I heard it. He sounded happy. He sounded as if he was having the time of his life.

Was I going to show up and douse his life with cold water then? *I* couldn't do it. I was hoping it would all turn out well anyway and when I went into labor just let him know he was welcome to come up to the hospital.

I drove by The Sink all the time. His car was there almost all the time. It was some stalker-type shit but I didn't care.

"Hazel, are you ready?" James asked.

James was the artist Cordelia Clements said was looking for an apprentice. He was insanely talented; I had learned so much in the short time I had already been working with him.

Since word had gotten out in the community that my finals art piece was going to be featured, I'd gotten some notoriety and was able to sell a few commissions as well as a few of my existing pieces. James added me as an artist to the gallery's website and I'd gotten a few hits from there as well. I was starting to make a name for myself. It was ideal.

Christmas came and went and I spent the day crying in bed wishing I could see Atticus. Etta tried to drag me out but I just couldn't go to her aunt's house in the state I was in. Her family would worry about me; I couldn't do that to them. Later that night, though, she came back with a plate of food and we watched *Elf*.

"Yes, James," I answered, and smiled at him.

"How are you feeling, honey?" he asked, his hand going to my little belly.

"Okay," I lied, patting his hand sweetly.

He pushed some of my hair behind my ear and patted

my cheek. "Hazel, you are a terrible liar."

"I'll be okay," I tried to reassure him, not entirely convinced I would be, but hoping for the best.

He studied me and decided my answer was okay. "How was your New Year's?" he asked, changing the subject, taking out his keys, and unlocking the large glass door to the new gallery attached to the DMA.

"It was fine." I smiled. "Uneventful. Not a lot I can do in my condition and all that."

A few construction workers came in after us and waved. We waved back and headed for James's office. I sat down in a big comfy chair he'd had brought in for me across from his desk. He fell into his own swivel chair and rocked back and forth.

"How can I be so tired? I just got here."

I giggled. "It's our first day back after break. We're straight not up to par."

"My excuse is booze, though," he joshed.

"A valid excuse as any."

"I knew I hired you for a reason," he teased. "You help justify all my bad decisions."

I bowed in my chair and extended an arm dramatically. "I'm the master enabler."

"The best kind." He sighed. "Well, I guess we should get started." He groaned.

"I guess so." I winked.

He sat up and powered on his laptop. "In a few minutes," he said. "Let my machine warm up a little."

"A good idea."

"Thank you, Master Enabler."

"You're welcome."

"I would kill for for an espresso," he said, his hands

folded on his chest. "I don't think I could go another second without one."

"I wouldn't mind a chai tea."

"Well, if you need a chai, who am I to stand in your way? Jeez, you're so demanding, Hazel."

"I know," I conceded.

"I'll run down to the corner then." He walked over to me and stood beside me, grabbing my hand. "I have my cell. Let me know if you need me."

"I will, James. Thank you."

He left me on my own and I pulled out my phone, glancing at Atticus's social pages.

Just back from LA. Killed another session with artist Young Jock. Keep your eyes open for this talent. Single in six weeks.

It had a picture of him and, I assumed, Young Jock. Atticus looked so good it was insane. The post had just under seventy thousand likes and at least twenty thousand comments. He had more than two hundred thousand followers in less than a few weeks. It must have been a whirlwind for him. I was so happy for him, but his rapid success made him feel that much further from me. He felt so far away. He felt unreachable.

A few minutes later, I heard James come through the door and got up to help him. I opened the glass door to his office and began to meet him in the unfinished gallery when an extraordinary pain ripped through my abdomen. I screamed at the top of my lungs and fell to my knees.

That was when time seemed to crawl at a snail's pace.

James's face contorted in horror. The drinks he carried spilled to the floor in slow motion, the liquid forming an arch as they spun to the concrete. Men from the construction teams ran for me as I began to fall.

"Hazel!" James shouted, sounding low and muffled to my ears. His eyes widened; his mouth hung in obvious despair.

My shoulder met concrete, a sharp crack sounded as my skull met ground. My head heavy, I brought it forward to take in my body. Blood seeped through my slacks so heavily it had already started to pool around my hips. Several men reached me, their eyes exuded horror.

I'm going to die, I thought as my lids begged to droop closed.

"Juniper," I whispered as a tear fell. "Atticus," I agonized.

James hovered over me and cradled my head, his face wet with tears. "Hazel, baby, stay with me."

"I'll dial 911," a man's voice echoed through me.

I heard footsteps running around me. One man ran into the street hollering for help. Another yelled to give me some room. They were all yelling. Deep, prolonged syllables spun around my head.

I felt my life slipping, could feel the tired, drugged pull to darkness.

"*Atticus*," I whispered.

James picked up my hand and felt my pulse. "Where is the ambulance?" He looked in my eyes. "Focus, Hazel. Stay aware," his panicked voice pleaded.

"Atticus," I begged.

"I'll call him," James promised. "Just stay with me, Hazel."

"Atticus," I slurred as the black overtook me.

***

***

"Tell me what the *fuck* is going on!" I heard around me. Unable to open my eyes, I had no clue where I was, but I knew it was him. *Atticus*. Atticus's beautiful voice. *At least I got to hear him one last time*, I thought.

Black. Sound. Black. Sound.

I faded in and out.

"Placental abruption."

"Severe bleeding."

"C-section."

"Surgery."

"Hysterectomy."

"Pray."

"Hard."

Atticus's hands found my face. I knew it was him. I knew his skin. "Hazel," his broken voice begged, "Hazel, fight. Do you hear me? Fucking fight, Hazel."

His hands were ripped from me and I faded to black again but not before the broken roar of Atticus Kelly swam through my equally broken heart.

CHAPTER TWENTY

There were beeps. Some sort of pump. There were muffled voices over a speaker. My throat killed.

Juniper.

I tried to bring my hands up to check my stomach but they wouldn't cooperate.

"*Ungh*," was all I was able to say.

"Hazel," I quickly heard beside me. He leaned forward and took up my hand between his own.

I dragged my eyes open as my head lolled Atticus's direction.

"Atticus," a hoarse voice, mine, sounded.

He squeezed my hand and broke down in a groan. He cleared his throat. "You're alive," he told me. I swallowed.

His hand met my forehead and he dragged his thumb across, tucking pieces of hair away.

"Juniper," I barely got out.

"She's alive but in the NICU. She's," he cleared his throat of emotion, "very tiny. So tiny, Hazel. She's fighting, though."

Tears ran down the sides of my face.

"You did good, Haze," he said. My eyes squeezed tight as more tears spilled. He absorbed them into his own skin. "Sleep, Haze," he encouraged.

So I did.

***

"I can't make these kinds of decisions without Hazel," I heard Atticus say. His voice sounded exhausted.

My eyes struggled to open. "What decisions?" I asked.

Atticus, his mom, Grams, Etta, a doctor, and two nurses looked my direction. Atticus and Etta came to my side quickly.

"Tell her," Etta ordered Atticus.

Atticus let out a breath. "Um, Hazel, Juniper needs medicine."

"Sodium citrate," Etta offered, like I knew what the hell she was talking about.

"Her, uh, kidneys are shutting down," he explained.

"Oh my God," I whispered.

"The medicine is necessary," he said.

"Give it to her. Whatever she needs, give it to her," I told them.

Atticus looked at the doctor and nodded then the doctor left the room.

"Is she going to be okay?" I asked him. He looked at Etta and Etta returned the look. "Tell me what is going on," I panicked. Atticus's eyes glassed over. "Oh my God," I whispered.

"Hazel," Etta assuaged.

"Don't. Cut the bullshit, Etta, and give me it to me

straight."

Etta began to cry. Etta never cried. Ever. "She's just come a little too early for the best results, babe."

"What does that mean?" I asked.

"The odds of her surviving—" Atticus laid out, stabbing me through the heart.

The sound that came out of me was otherworldly, the immediate pain was acute.

"Move," I demanded, sliding my legs over the side of the bed. "Take me to her."

"Wait," Atticus pleaded. "Let me get your doctor."

Everyone in the room stood, their faces looked shocked.

"Absolutely not," I said, grabbing the bedrail.

"Let me help you," Etta said, lifting me by my elbow. "But take your time."

The pain in my abdomen was insane but I didn't care. I stood as tall as my body would let me and took a step. Etta gathered all my IVs and the IV pole near me. Atticus found me then and wrapped his arm around my back, his hand under my arm.

"I don't think this is a good idea," Grams said, speaking for the first time. "She shouldn't be walking."

"I promise, Grams, she'll be fine. Walking is encouraged after surgery. She'll be fine," Etta told her.

Sarah sat back down, her face buried in her hands.

I looked up at Atticus. "Take me to our daughter."

I walked as well as I could toward the NICU, which was situated near the recovery ward.

"In here," Atticus said, shoving open the outer doors. He pressed a button and a nurse buzzed us in when she saw him.

The walls were lined with dramatic incubators full of

tiny babies. There were three women surrounding one incubator, their hands working. A nurse greeted us.

"Hey, guys," she said. "You must be Juniper's mom."

All the breath left my chest. "Yes," I answered.

"I know you're recovering from surgery," she soothed, "but I need you to wash your hands, please. Dad, you too," she said, walking us over to a wash station. "Have you had a fever in the last twenty-four hours?" she asked.

"I don't believe so," I told her.

"Hold on, I'll call down to your room."

She called down to my nurse and confirmed I hadn't.

"Before we wash your hands," she said, "toss your phones in these anti-microbial envelopes. You'll still be able to use them but it will prevent cross contamination. Don't touch the bag, just toss the phone in and I'll seal it."

"Okay," we both said.

She sealed the bags and laid them aside.

She taught me how to wash my hands with the antiseptic soap they had in individually wrapped packs. There were two sinks and Atticus, having obviously done it before, washed his as well under her supervision.

"Would you like to meet your daughter?" she asked me.

"Yes," I said, my voice sounding broken.

She gathered my IVs and IV pole and Etta blew me a kiss goodbye.

"I'll see you out here," she said, and I nodded.

The woman took Atticus and me to the incubator with all the nurses standing around, which made my stomach fall to my feet. They parted, forced smiles on their faces, and I leaned over the glass.

"*Oh my God,*" I whispered.

She was so tiny. The little hair she had was my color.

She could fit in the palm of Atticus's hand, probably. Her skin was red and looked paper thin. Her little chest pulled in and out through a mechanical ventilator. There was tape and tubes all over her small figure. Rolled blankets supported her tiny bones.

I had trouble breathing when I took in her fragile state. "Oh my God," I gasped this time, so overcome I lost my balance, forcing Atticus to catch me. When I righted, I tried to control the sobs that ached to come out. Atticus squeezed his body against mine. "She can't die," I told him. "I won't let her."

"We're going to fight," he said. "She's a fighter too, Haze." But his face looked lost, panicked, negating his words.

I turned to one of the nurses. "Can I hold her?"

"Yes," she answered, and began pulling a comfortable-looking glider my way.

Atticus lowered me down and helped me sit.

"We'll do some skin to skin," she said, gesturing to the top of my gown.

I pulled at the snaps at my shoulder and folded the flap back. The nurse opened the incubator door and carefully slid Juniper out. She made a soft sigh and I memorized the sound immediately. Very carefully she laid Juniper's naked body against mine. She was warm but her feet felt cold.

"Can I have a blanket?" I asked.

"I'll get a warm one," one of the nurses told me and scampered off.

My hand went to Juniper's head. My fingers ran along her downy soft hair and velvety-but-too-thin skin. I kissed her at the temple and she sighed again. Atticus moved near me, his arms folded across his chest as he watched me.

"You're both so beautiful," he told us. He took out his phone and snapped a shot of us together.

"This is surreal," I told him. Tears poured down my face. "It wasn't supposed to be like this. She wasn't supposed to come yet."

"I know, Haze."

I looked at him, fighting the tears. "I'm scared, Atticus."

He nodded. "So am I."

I took a deep breath and focused on touching her skin, keeping her warm. "Put your palm on her back," I told him.

He reached forward and placed his hand on her skin. It covered her entire body. Juniper sighed again, making my heart skip a beat.

The nurse came in with the blanket and laid it across us. Atticus began to move his hand away but I shook my head. He kept it there but sat on his haunches beside us. Juniper's breathing steadied.

"I love you, Juniper," I told her. Atticus's eyes met mine. "Keep going, baby."

He watched me. "How do you feel?" he asked.

I took a moment to answer. I didn't know how, really. I went with honesty. "Scared shitless. Overwhelmed. In pain. Happy to see you. " I paused. "*Nervous* to see you. I'm a lot of things all at once. H-how are you?"

"The same. *Exactly* the same."

I looked down at our baby. "This is our *daughter*, Atticus."

I heard him swallow. "I'm a dad."

I smiled at him. "I'm a mom."

"You said surreal."

"Yeah."

"That's perfect," he said.

"*She's* perfect."

"No doubt," he agreed.

"She's so fragile, though."

"I'm scared for her," he admitted.

"So am I, Atticus."

He fought the emotion in his voice. "She *has* to stick around. I have too many plans for her. Too many things we need to do. I'm looking forward to a life with her, to first days of school, and worrying over first dates, to sending her off to college, to walking her down the aisle."

My chin shook and my face grew wet. "She has to," I desperately agreed.

I felt his hand rub Juniper's back. I hoped she was absorbing my heat, my skin, my love. I hoped she was absorbing Atticus's as well. I peered down at her face when the nurse came to check on her.

"She's asleep," I told her.

The nurse nodded. She looked over at Juniper's monitor. "That's the best her blood pressure has been since they brought her in."

The nurse walked away with a pat on my shoulder.

"Are you okay?" Atticus asked.

My incision was stinging so bad, but I refused to admit to it. "I'm fine," I told him.

He looked at me. "You're lying. You're in pain."

"I'm not moving. An inch."

He nodded. "A guy called from your cell for me. That's how I knew you were here."

"That was James," I told him.

He avoided eye contact. "Is that a guy you're seeing or

something?" he asked.

"Atticus." His eyes finally met mine. "James is my boss. I was at work w-when it happened."

He said nothing. His body language gave nothing away.

"Where do you work?" he asked.

"One of my senior art pieces is being exhibited at the DMA and—"

"One of your pieces is in the museum?" he asked.

"Yes."

"It was that last piece," he stated more than asked.

I nodded.

"Go on," he said after checking on Juniper.

"So the curator suggested I apprentice with James. He's another local artist and is in charge of creating their first gallery. I'm helping him acquire art as well as arrange relationships with artists and preparing to cater to the public. Its main focus is to supply art to those who may not have ever considered the investment or might not be able to. It's a gallery for the masses."

"That's sounds perfect for you, Haze."

"It is," I agreed. "I have you to thank for it."

"That was all you."

"I wouldn't have put myself out there, though, if you hadn't inspired me."

He smiled. It was small but it was there. "Or punched your ex-boss."

"Or that," I teased. I kissed Juniper's head once more. I couldn't stop myself. "Atticus, I have to tell you something."

"I'm listening."

"That last piece, the one in the museum, I painted it for you. You were the reason. It's why it's my best piece.

That's what I mean by you inspiring me. I never would have been considered for exhibition if it hadn't been for you."

He shook his head, the expression on his face looked strained, his brows furrowed. "I can't talk about this right now."

The pain in my stomach intensified somehow. "I'm sorry. Of course."

There was a long, silent pause between us before he said, "Do you know you almost died, Hazel?" I shook my head, then lightly rested my cheek on Juniper's head. "You lost so much blood. *So much blood.* They had to give you three transfusions."

"Did they get her out quickly?" I asked.

"As quickly as they could." He rested his forehead on my shoulder. I wanted to kiss his temple but I held back. He stared at Juniper. "I thought horrible things, ran through scenarios over and over and none of them good. I was sick to my stomach when you were in surgery."

A memory came to the front of my mind.

"Atticus?"

"Yes, Hazel."

I took a deep breath. "I'm barren now, aren't I?"

He looked into my eyes. "*Hazel,*" he breathed.

I bit my bottom lip and squeezed my eyes shut. Yet another hit. "Oh my God," I whispered.

"I'm so sorry," he told me, and I could tell he meant it. No matter how he felt about me, I could tell he meant what he said.

"What happened?" I asked, bracing myself.

"There was too much blood loss, too severe a hemorrhage. They could only focus on keeping you and

Juniper alive."

I swallowed the lump in my throat. "I can't hear any more."

"Of course," he said.

I leaned as far back in the chair as possible to alleviate some of the pain in my belly. It helped but not by much.

"You've gone pale," he said, sitting up. His hand left Juniper's back and she whimpered, breaking my heart a little. I cuddled her closer and she settled down. "You need pain meds," he said, standing.

"No, Atticus, please. They'll make me go back. I can't leave her. Please, Atticus," I begged.

He looked down at me with pity in his eyes. "I hate to see you in pain, though."

"There isn't a pain worse than the idea of leaving her right now. Please. Sit."

He reluctantly sat. "Can I text Etta? See if the nurses there will bring you a pill or something?"

"As long as they don't make me go back. I won't go back."

"Okay," he said, picking up his phone and typing out a message.

He laid the phone on the arm of my chair and looked around. There was a single stool with rolling wheels in a corner. He asked to borrow it and they gave him the okay. He slid it beside me and sat. His phone indicated a text and we both looked down.

They're bringing her something now, Etta texted.

Already I felt relief. My personal nurse came through and gave a small plastic pill cup and water cup to a NICU nurse.

"She said they can hook you back up to your morphine

drip if you want to go back to your room?" the nurse asked.

"No," I rushed. "I'll just take the pill, thank you. I'll be okay."

She nodded and gave me an understanding smile. "Here you are," she said, tipping the pill cup into my mouth then bringing the water cup to my lips. I drank and swallowed the pill.

"Thank you," I told her.

"No problem, sweetheart."

Atticus let out a shaky breath. "I hope those kick in soon."

I felt overwhelmed with emotion for some reason. Tears started spilling out without notice. "You're being so nice to me."

His brows furrowed again. "Hazel," he soothed. "Don't cry, Haze. Breathe for me. Focus on Juniper."

I took a deep breath through my nose and cuddled my daughter closer. I breathed deeply for at least a minute. "I don't know what's wrong with me."

"You're hormones are probably all over the place. You're scared for our daughter; you're recovering from a serious surgery. It's too much for one person to take."

I met his eyes. "And I'm seeing you for the first time since that wretched day." He nodded. I looked down at Juniper's face. "She's so small but so beautiful," I told him.

"I think being with you again has soothed her."

"I think being with her again has soothed me too."

"I read somewhere once that skin to skin was so important, but I hadn't ever put much stock in it until this moment."

"It's the only power I have right now," I told him.

He shook his head back and forth and stared at the ground, his hands on his knees. "You have no idea the power you have," he spoke, his message purposely vague.

His slender fingers threaded through his hair then down the back of his neck. His knuckles went white.

"Tense?" I whispered.

His hands dropped to his thighs. "This has been the craziest day of my life, Hazel."

"For me too, but I had the advantage of being passed out for most of it while you had to endure every second. I'm sorry for that."

He cocked his head to the side and stared at me. "I can't imagine what you've suffered. Don't downplay what you've been through."

"I would suffer a hundred, a thousand, an infinite amount more if it meant she could have had a little more time inside with me, though."

"Hazel, it happened. It wasn't your fault."

"What if it was, though?" I asked in a whisper. "What if I did something?"

"Short of drinking or drugs or something equally dangerous, there's nothing that would have caused this except fate, and I know you wouldn't have done those things. Fate is just a cruel bitch."

I stared deep into his eyes, could see the deeper meaning there, and my heart raced. "Sometimes she can be kind, though," I countered.

"Sure," he conceded, but I could tell he didn't actually believe it.

"I'm giving her your last name," I told him.

His face turned into something resembling shock. "I didn't think you would want that."

"I do want that. Of course I want that," I told him.

"Thank you."

He slid his hand beneath the blanket again but didn't put his hand on Juniper's back right away.

"Want my hand to get warm first," he made clear.

"You can place it on my skin if you want," I offered.

He slid his hand to the broad of my back and let it sit there, getting warm. I fought the burn of tears the feel of his skin on mine brought forth. It felt right on mine, beautiful on mine, perfect on mine. I felt him extend his fingers, stretching the width of his hand as far as it would go. He slid his hand down to the small of my back, let it linger there for a moment, sending familiar chills through to my soul, then shifted around under the blanket to Juniper's sweet little body.

"I didn't think it was possible," he spoke low.

"What?" I asked.

"To love someone as violently as I love her," he told me, his eyes on mine, looking straight through me it seemed.

"Suddenly the world is so much smaller," I said. "She's *become* my new world."

He rolled his stool even closer, his legs straddled me. "An instantaneous enlightenment," he stated. "Nothing could possibly compare."

"And yet I've never been more frightened in my life. Like that world teeters on a knife's edge, ready to tip to either side with the slightest gust," I whispered.

"It's brittle, breakable," he agreed.

"It's not fair that someone you love could be so insubstantial, so fine, so vulnerable. I don't want this test," I said, terrified. "We're too wide open, too susceptible."

"We don't have a choice, though, do we?"

"No," I said.

His free hand found the back of my neck. "Can you fight?" he asked.

"Until my dying breath," I confided.

We sat still, quiet, absorbing our daughter and praying silently.

The medicine kicked in and I felt like I could sit as I was for days if they would have let me, but a nurse asked if I wanted to try pumping to stimulate milk, so Atticus removed his shirt and took my place. The nurse covered them in the blanket and I felt my heart skip a beat once more.I stole his phone and took a picture of him with her.

"Need something to blow up at her wedding," I whispered to him.

He audibly swallowed. "Thank you," he said.

The nurse took me to a pumping station they had all set up. It was painful and no milk came, but they promised it would in a few days and that the colostrum I was producing was good for her. She wasn't yet strong enough to latch on, so I had a feeling I would be living at that pump station. They planned on feeding her intravenously.

When I was done, I joined Atticus again. He sat with her, his cheek at her head. He was talking to her.

"What are you telling her?" I asked after a nurse brought me a more comfortable chair.

He smiled at me. "Her name, how much I love her, that I need her to fight." I smiled back at him but it turned into a quaking chin. His free hand found mine and squeezed. "We can do this, Haze. We're going to pull through this. All *three* of us."

I took a deep breath and found solace in his confidence.

"How are you feeling?" he asked.

"Much better," I told him.

The nurses came over and fed my colostrum through her IV. It felt good to watch her get what I was producing. Just one more thing I could do to help her.

Atticus held my hand for several minutes before he asked, "Hazel, several weeks ago, I was looking at my phone, at our texts, and a text indicator popped up from you." My heart sank. "It disappeared."

I knew exactly what he was talking about. "I had just been in the shower and reached for my shampoo bottle. When I did, I felt her move." His eyes squeezed shut. "I wanted to tell you but I didn't know how."

He let go of my hand and it killed me, but I understood.

Loud, shrill beeping came from our station and I stood in a panic. The nurses ran over and without hesitation took Juniper off Atticus's chest and placed her flat in her incubator. They worked so quickly I didn't have a chance to understand what was going on. Hands went everywhere and Atticus stood, his hands on his head.

"What's happening?" I asked, my tone panicked.

One of the nurses calmly answered, without glancing up, her hands still working. "She's not breathing."

I started to lose my balance but Atticus's hands caught me. We both stood there, unable to speak, as they worked on our daughter.

One minute.

Two minutes.

Three minutes.

Four minutes.

Suddenly the nurses' shoulders relaxed and one shut off the alarms. They turned, their faces reflecting none of the drama I'd just witnessed.

"Oh my God." I sighed, leaning into Atticus.

"She's fine now, babe," the nurse said, patting my arm. "This happens a lot with the little ones like this."

"It does?" I asked, my heart still pounding in my chest, adrenaline surging through my body.

Atticus and I leaned over her incubator. Her little chest rose and fell consistently. She was sleeping. I swayed on my feet and Atticus held me up.

"You need sleep, Hazel."

"I can't leave her," I said, shaking my head.

"Hazel, let me take you to the room. Get some rest. I'll come right back. I'll hold her the entire night until you're ready to take back over. She'll never be without one of us."

"I can't," I said.

"Hazel, you can't take care of her if you're falling over with exhaustion. You're recovering."

"Atticus," I said, looking up at him.

"Please, Hazel," he begged. "I can't worry about both of you. It's killing me."

I swallowed, wanting to refuse, but eventually nodded and reached over, caressing her tiny hands and feet then kissed her head. Atticus pulled his shirt on and helped me back to my room. It was empty. I glanced up at the clock. It was close to four a.m. My own nurse saw Atticus coming down the hall with me and helped me sit at the edge of the bed. I bit my bottom lip to prevent shouting out in pain when I rolled back onto the mattress. Atticus reached his hand out toward my hair, hesitated, thought better of it, and let his hand drop. He looked like he wanted to say something but he stayed quiet. I nodded at him and he lifted his shoulders as if in defeat then left the room to return to Juniper.

The nurse tucked me in. "You need anything?" she asked.

"No, thank you," I said, already drifting to sleep the exhaustion was so deep.

Thank God for Atticus, I thought.

CHAPTER TWENTY-ONE

Atticus

Juniper laid against my bare chest. She felt warm, relaxed. That was my main focus. I couldn't do anything else but hold her and pray, so that's what I did. She was scary tiny. Too fragile. My gut ached for her.

The hate that had taken up residence in my chest for Hazel was starting to dissipate. When I saw her covered in her own blood, her hands cradling her small belly even though she wasn't conscious, it knifed me in the chest. All the disappointment in her, the bitter detest I'd built came seeping out. I had no time to worry about anything else but her and Juniper's survival.

I imagined the doctors coming out and telling me Hazel didn't make it and, despite having only known her for twenty-three weeks, the idea stopped me cold, threatened to rip me to shreds. Keeping her alive was just as much about self-preservation because if she did die, I knew I would be altered permanently. While she was in surgery, it clawed at me from the inside out and I almost lost it. I broke down right there on the cold floor, an unholy sound erupted from my chest and my brothers had to hold me back from running after her and our daughter.

I took a deep breath and kissed the top of Juniper's head.

The doctor came out. I remembered noting his face looked relaxed, relieved, and I held my breath as he explained they had both made it, that both were alive. I fell to my knees, my hands going to my head. Everyone around me started sobbing. I felt like I could finally breathe.

He revealed what happened. How the placenta carrying our daughter had detached and caused severe bleeding, how if she had come in even a few minutes later neither would have survived. Hazel would never have children again, though, and my heart bled for her. He told me our daughter was hanging on for dear life. He didn't sugarcoat it, didn't give us any false hope, but he did promise they would do everything in their power to keep her here.

My palm found Juniper's small back and laid there.

And here she was. My little Juniper with her sad eyes and tiny fingers. My little Juniper with her mother's hair. My wee baby Juniper. One pound, four ounces, less than a foot long, Juniper. I cleared my throat of emotion when a nurse approached.

"You all right?" she asked. "Can I get you some water? I can order up a breakfast tray? You've been sitting there for four hours now."

"I'm fine," I told her, rocking Juniper. "Thank you."

She smiled kindly. "Nice to see a daddy so dedicated," she said.

"I don't know what I'm doing, though," I told her.

She pulled back the blanket a little to see Juniper's face then peered back at her monitors. "If it brings you any comfort," she spoke softly, "I've seen hundreds of dads come through here and you seem to be as capable as any of the seasoned fathers." She smiled.

"Thank you," I said, actually feeling a little bit more reassured. "I've got a few nieces and nephews. Maybe that helped."

She smiled. "A bit of baby training then," she teased, then walked toward the next incubator and checked on the baby there.

My phone rang. It was River. I had left a message earlier but had yet to speak with him. I needed to pee really badly anyway so I thought I'd put Juniper down for a second while I relieved myself and called River back. One of the nurses came over to help me put her in the incubator.

"Just going to the restroom. Check on Hazel," I said, putting my shirt back on. "Be right back."

"No problem," she said, tucking Juniper in.

I stared at her for at least half a minute as she slept before I could conjure up the courage to leave. I hauled ass to the restroom, peed, washed my hands, and picked up my cell to call River as I walked toward Hazel's room.

"Yo, dude, what's up?" River asked. "How are you?"

"Fine. I'm fine."

"How is— how is Hazel?"

"She'll recover. Juniper is, well, she's the wild card. River, she is the smallest baby I have ever seen in my fucking life and I'm scared shitless but she can fight like a punk, I just know it."

"Good, man. That's great. Well, we're all pulling for

you. I let the label know what happened. They should be contacting you soon."

"Cool, thanks. Yeah, I won't be making it back to LA next week.

"They understand, dude."

"Thanks, River."

"Yeah, let me know if anything changes."

"Yeah, no problem."

"Talk to you later," he said.

"Bye."

I hung up as I approached Hazel's door and knocked once.

"Come in," Hazel's tired voice called out.

When I came through, tucked back the door's privacy curtain, and stepped into the room, she was just beginning to sit up with the help of a nurse.

"Good morning," her scratchy voice told me. "How is Juniper?" she asked.

"She's perfect," I said. "Didn't have any problems at all. She just slept on my chest all night."

Hazel sighed. "I'm getting ready to see her," she said. "They took out all my yucky tubes and stuff and said I can shower. I didn't want to hold her without washing up." I nodded, wishing I could do the same. "Your mom dropped off a bag of your stuff about five this morning while I was pumping for Juniper," she informed me, like she could read my mind.

"That's great. That way I don't have to leave."

"You wanna go first?" she asked.

My brows furrowed, hating how nice she was being. I didn't want her to be nice.

"No, thank you, Hazel."

"I had the nurse bring in towels and bedding for you." She pointed at the built-in sofa in the corner of the room. "That converts to a bed. I even had her bring an extra pillow."

I swallowed. "Thank you."

I watched as she struggled to get to the restroom, and it made my gut ache for her too. She was obviously in tremendous pain but she was trying to hide it, trudging through for Juniper, and possibly me. She broke my heart. *In so many different ways.*

Hazel

Showering felt wonderful. The simple acts of cleaning my hair and brushing my teeth really lifted my spirits, and I was starting to get a little bit of movement back, though I was still experiencing a great deal of pain. The nurses were impressed with my recovery, remarking that I must have had great genes. I think it was Juniper. I needed to recover as quickly as possible for her. I needed to be useful to Atticus too. He looked to be in pain himself. The bags beneath his eyes were purple and swollen. When I emerged, dressed in a pair of yoga pants and a T-shirt Grams had bought and left in the room for me, along with a long note telling me she loved me, while I was with Juniper and Atticus, I sat on the edge of the bed to blow-dry my hair so I didn't get Juniper wet.

Atticus was sitting in a chair against the wall, his legs extended and crossed at the ankles, his eyes closed.

"Atticus," I whispered.

His eyes sluggishly opened. "Yeah?"

"Do you want me to get the nurse to make your bed for

you?"

He took a deep breath through his nose and sat up. "No, thank you," he said, standing up. He grabbed his bag and headed for the shower, closing the door behind him. I turned my blow-dryer on and quickly dried my hair. I remembered how I needed to do skin to skin and changed out my T-shirt for a new hospital gown but left my yoga pants on. I almost bolted for the door, I was so excited to see Juniper, but ran into Atticus instead.

"Ungh," I grunted. Shooting pains blasted through my abdomen and I doubled over.

"Hazel!" he said, grabbing for me. He brought me to the bed and helped me sit. I breathed through the pain then met his eyes. "I'm sorry," he told me, concern written all over his face.

"I'm fine," I said, trying to keep my tone steady.

"Are you going to see Juniper?" he asked.

"I was," I told him.

"Let me walk you," he offered.

"You don't have to do that, Atticus," I insisted. "You need rest. Sleep. I can get there—"

"Hazel," he said once, holding me up by the elbow.

Carefully, I shuffled to the NICU. I expected him to leave me there but he came in, unable to be this close to her, I guessed, without looking at her. We washed our hands like we were taught then Atticus took me to her station. We leaned over her incubator.

"Oh my God, she is so beautiful," I said, overwhelmed by the very sight of her.

"Prettiest girl ever," he said.

My eyes filled with tears. "Thank you," I said, placing my hand on her back.

"For what, Hazel?"

"For her," I said. "No matter what goes on between us, I can't thank you enough."

He shook his head. "I'm the only one who should be doing the thanking."

He stuck his arm in and put his hand next to mine.

"We could go around and around, so let's just agree she is everything and call it."

"She's everything."

We watched her, felt her little back rise and fall with the mechanical ventilator.

"I'll be happy when she has more meat on her," I said.

"And can breathe on her own."

"Let's take solace in small victories then. What do you think?"

"Agreed. What should we aim for today?"

"Just going the day without some sort of breathing intervention?" I asked.

He nodded and I snuck my hand out. I attempted to sit down but was having trouble. Atticus grabbed me by the elbows and lowered me onto the glider. He moved to grab Juniper for me so I peeled back the tabs of my gown. He laid her little body on mine, her tubes and IVs running across my shoulders. He situated them so I wouldn't pinch any then headed to the nurse's station for a blanket. When he returned, he laid it across us and Juniper sighed, making my head swim with happiness. I kissed the top of her little head.

Atticus sat beside us in that same stool from the day before.

"You have to be so tired, Atticus."

"The shower gave me a second wind," he said,

watching her face.

I didn't argue with him. I knew he was exhausted but I didn't blame him for wanting to stay.

"How did she do overnight and this morning?" I asked him.

"She was perfect. No incidents."

I breathed a sigh of relief and brushed her little cheek with the outside of my index finger.

"Hey," he said, his eyes drooping a little.

"Yeah," I answered.

"One of my songs went number one."

I nodded. "I know. Congratulations, Atticus. I heard your interview on the Edge. You sounded good, happy."

"You listened to my interview?"

"I've been keeping up with you," I admitted.

He looked shocked then his eyes softened. "I wasn't happy, Hazel."

"You'd just hit number one. You should have been on top of the world."

"I should have been, yeah, but I was f—," he began to curse, then looked down at Juniper as if she could understand him. It made my heart melt. "I was in bad shape, Hazel."

"I'm so sorry," I said. "I know it's too late. I can't tell you how many times my fingers hovered over your name in my phone. I had always intended to apologize."

Atticus shook his head. "What is an apology now, Hazel?"

I swallowed. "It can be whatever you want it to be. It's weeks too late, I agree, but I want you to know that I *am* sorry. I had legit reasons for feeling the way I did, but I should have handled it differently.

"Then I got sick," I began.

He sat up, his eyes opened. "You got sick?" he asked.

"They couldn't figure out what was going on but my liver started malfunctioning and my body started to reject the pregnancy. They were monitoring us weekly when it happened."

"Jesus, Hazel," he whispered, "why didn't you tell me?"

"You were on top of the world, Atticus. I couldn't be the one to bring you back down. You would have quit and rushed back, and I couldn't let you risk everything when we didn't know what was going on yet."

"That wasn't your decision to make, Hazel."

"In hindsight, it looks bad, but you have to understand, my doctors, the specialists they sent me to, they all told me they were being the absolute most cautious they could be by monitoring me as frequently as they were. There is no way they could have anticipated this."

"You should have called."

"I was striking up the nerve."

"You should have called."

"I know."

He paused. "I would have taken the call, Hazel."

I took a deep breath to steady my heart. "You would have."

"I would have taken care of you."

"I know, Atticus." He sat up and ran his hands down his face then through his hair. "Get some sleep."

He shook his head. "I can't leave you guys."

"Yes, you can, Atticus. I'm tube free, showered, rested. I'm feeling a lot better. We'll be right down the hall."

He shook his head again. Instead of arguing with him, I asked a passing nurse if I could have another glider for him as well as a pillow and a blanket. She was more than happy to help and we got him set up beside us, his feet propped. He hugged the pillow and the nurse draped the blanket over his legs. He was asleep within a minute. I looked over at his sleeping form then down at Juniper's.

I breathed easily. They came freely for the first time in months.

CHAPTER TWENTY-TWO

I'd been sitting for three hours straight and decided to stand with Juniper. A nurse helped me up so we wouldn't wake Atticus. I needed to relieve myself so she helped me put our daughter in the incubator and I scurried off to the toilet and to grab another pain pill from my nurse. I was doing as well as you possibly could under the circumstances, and I was proud of how I was handling myself.

"I need to take your vitals, babe," the day nurse informed me before giving me my pain pill. I looked longingly in the direction of the NICU. "Won't take long. Promise."

I nodded and shuffled into the room behind her. I sat at the edge of the bed as she took my temperature and checked my blood pressure.

A loud, blaring siren sounded through the floor. A robotic voice came over the loud speaker announcing a code. My heart beat into my throat. The nurse's eyes widened.

"Where is that code at?" I asked.

"Uh," she said.

"Is it for the NICU?" I asked, panicked.

"Miss Stone," she calmly began.

I ripped the cuff off my arm and stood, already heading for the door. I moved so quickly I could feel my incision pulling, but I didn't care. I only wanted to get to the NICU. I pushed through the doors only to see ten people standing around Juniper's incubator. The blanket and pillow Atticus had been using were piled on the floor next to his glider. He paced back and forth near her, his hands on his head, tears in his eyes.

"What's going on?" I demanded, my eyes already burning.

He came to me quickly and helped me stand near them. "Something's wrong."

"She's not breathing?" I asked, adrenaline pumping through my body at an alarming rate.

"Not breathing and something else. I can't tell what it is."

I dared not disturb the doctors and nurses around her, but I wanted to shout for an explanation.

Her doctor yelled for something and we watched as a nurse methodically retrieved something from their station and returned quickly.

"Please, God," I whispered. "*Please*, God. *Please*, God," I begged over and over.

Every time I'd ask for God's help, Atticus would squeeze my hands a little harder as if to emphasize the prayer. Her heart kept flatlining, coming back, flatlining, coming back, flatlining. I swayed on my feet.

"She won't stabilize!" her doctor yelled in frustration, making me sick to my stomach.

She flatlined again. My body reeled waiting for it to start again.

"*One,*" I whispered. "*Two, three, four, five, six, seven.*" No sound. Nothing. Just the desperate shuffles of the doctors and nurses, their voices low but determined. "*Eight, nine, ten, eleven, twelve.*" I counted two minutes, three minutes, four, five. Several nurses stepped back and I sucked in a violent breath. "What are they doing?" I asked. "What are you doing!" I yelled. "Help her!" A couple wouldn't meet my eyes, which incensed me. "Help her!" I shouted, pushing forward. Her doctor's shoulders sagged, his hand stilled over her little body. I started to break down. "What are you doing! Why are you stopping!" My hands gripped at the glass of her incubator. "Please. Please. You have to keep going. She's my baby," I gasped. I sobbed, my arms cradling the glass, my cheek pressed against the surface.

A blur of activity occurred around me but it didn't register. They called time of death and I almost vomited, dry-heaving. I felt my incision start to bleed.

"No, no, no, no, no. No. No, no," I kept saying over and over, refusing to accept it. I looked at Atticus, desperate. "Do something, Atticus," I demanded. "Do something. Make them bring her back. Please, Atticus." He stood still, all the color drained from his face. "Atticus," I sobbed. "Fix this, Atticus. Please. I can't live without her."

He burst into action, grabbing the doctor by his coat. All the nurses screamed but the doctor held up his hands for them to calm. Atticus dragged him over to Juniper. "Try harder," he said, his voice eerily controlled.

The doctor placed his hands on Atticus's, his face sorrowful. "I'm sorry, son."

"Don't tell me sorry. Don't. Bring her back," he insisted, his face growing wet.

"She's gone, son."

"I'll pay you whatever you want," he begged. "Everything I have, I'll give it to you. Just… *please.*"

But the doctor didn't respond. He had nothing to say.

Atticus studied his face. I saw it. Saw when he graduated from agonizing despair to instant incredible heartache. I could barely look at him. I wasn't where he was. I would never be there. He dropped his grip and staggered backward, he bent back, fell to his knees and sat on his ankles, his hands suspended at his sides, his head hung and his back hunched.

"*No!*" he bellowed. It was soul deep, desolate. It vibrated from the tips of my toes to the tips of my hair and I felt his misery. It permeated my skin and mixed with my own sorrow, burrowing into me, and I didn't think I could survive it.

I wouldn't accept it. Couldn't.

I scrambled to the side of her incubator and ripped it open. Carefully, I removed Juniper and sat down with her. I spoke to her, touched her still warm skin. "Juniper," I pleaded. I rocked her back and forth. It was unhinged. I knew it but I didn't care. I *had* to try. What kind of mother would I be if I didn't try? "Juniper," I whispered, caressing her tiny baby head. "Please, honey," I incoherently mumbled, bathing her in my tears.

Atticus brought his feet forward, his knees bent, his arms sat on top. He watched me, his eyes bloodshot red.

"She's gone, Haze," his scratchy voice informed me.

"No, Atticus," I denied.

The nurses were huddled and crying and I hated it.

Their crying meant the unthinkable.

Atticus stood, gingerly picked me up, folded me against his chest, settled in the glider, and sat me sideways on his lap. We stared at our daughter. At her peaceful face. At her still chest.

The world had ended.

CHAPTER TWENTY-THREE

"Get up, baby," Grams woke me, sitting on the edge of the bed.

I sank a little into her side. "I can't, Grams."

"You can, Hazel. Be strong."

She leaned over me and kissed my forehead.

I was already crying but I stood. On autopilot, I took a shower, washed and dried my hair, put on the black dress Etta had laid out for me. The black Mary Janes. The black wide-brim hat. The black sunglasses. The black wrap cardigan. The black thoughts.

They piled me into a car. I wasn't sure whose. Etta had made all the arrangements for her. I couldn't do it, couldn't choose a casket or music or anything else. The only thing I contributed was the baptismal gown I had bought months before because I saw it at a store and it spoke to me. Little did I know what it was saying.

They were talking to me. Grams and Etta were. I didn't hear what they were saying. I didn't particularly want to know. Everything anyone ever said to me since Juniper's passing was a knife to the heart. It didn't matter what they said. It could have been something completely harmless but I would still tie it back to my baby. I learned to tune people out.

The only person I didn't want to tune out was Atticus but he never contacted me. Not once. Not a single time. Another knife to my shredded heart.

They withdrew me from the car and walked me to the church, through the atrium, the narthex. I was aware enough to recognize the church was packed. They shuffled me up the aisle, sheltering me on both sides, and sat me in the front pew on the right. I looked up and saw Juniper's infinitesimal wood casket.

"Oh my God," I whispered, toppling forward. Etta caught me and set me back up. She sat beside me and held on tightly.

"Come on, babe," she said. "Lean on me."

I avoided looking at it, at her. I couldn't. My head turned to the left and I saw Atticus's brothers and mom and dad line in the first row as well across the aisle. He was there, his head hung. Aidan had his arm in a death grip. It made me feel ill to imagine him there in pain.

The whole thing was my fault. *If I had just told him I was sick. If I could have anticipated what was going to happen. Maybe I could have prevented it.* I blamed myself. I was to blame.

I bent forward, sobbing. Atticus's family stared. I could feel their eyes, which made me cry even harder. Etta and Grams wrapped their arms around me, whispering in an attempt to soothe. The priest, who had been at the altar preparing, came down to me.

"Hazel," he said, laying his hand on my shoulder, "I won't start until you're ready."

I pulled myself together as much as possible. "Go on,

Father," I whispered. "I'll never be ready."

He looked at me with sorrow in his eyes and it nearly killed me. He ascended the altar steps again and turned toward the packed church.

"All rise," he said.

CHAPTER TWENTY-FOUR

"Hazel," Etta said, reaching for my arm. She pulled me out of a car I didn't remember getting into and out into a gray, cold, foggy morning. It began to mist light rain. Etta had a big black umbrella she opened and held over the two of us. Grams came around to my other side and wrapped her arm around my back.

They led me down a gravel walkway under the cover of hundred-year-old trees. We approached a beautiful garden full of tiny headstones. *A children's graveyard. What a pitiable, awful thing*, I thought. I looked down at my shoes, refusing to look at their names. We approached a small plot already dug out. The rain slapped the top of the umbrella in hollow drips and I remembered thinking that rain had always been so beautiful to me before that moment, but it was permanently altered then, a forever agony to be associated with the second worst day of my life.

"Somebody kill me," I said. I turned to Etta. "Kill me, Etta. Please."

Tears strung down her face. "No, Hazel."

"Why?"

"Because I love you, Hazel. Because God loves you."

"I don't care, Etta."

"You will," she explained, holding me tighter.

"I won't care. Ever. Never again."

"Think that now," she said. "Think it now and I will hold you until you no longer think it anymore."

"I don't want to be held. I want death."

She didn't respond. Instead, she kissed my cheek, my temple, and squeezed me tightly.

Someone was sobbing on the other side of the plot and my eyes found him. It was Atticus. Tough Atticus. Deep Atticus. Poor Atticus. He couldn't hold himself up, and it killed me to see him like that. His brothers surrounded him, five pillars of strength.

The casket arrived. They set it on some sort of stand. Without thinking, I ran to her and threw myself over her, sobbing openly against its woodgrain face. Etta helped me up as they rolled her over the plot. My gloved hands tore at the skin of my neck, unable to help themselves.

I don't remember them lowering her, my mind's attempt at self-preservation, I guessed. I don't remember the priest's prayers. I don't remember when they buried her. I don't remember it. All I could remember were her little sighs and how I wanted to hear them again but I couldn't.

When I finally looked up, most everyone had gone. It was only Atticus's brothers, myself, and Etta.

"I'm sorry," I said, looking Atticus in the eye. He didn't respond. "I'm so sorry."

"You should be sorry," Liam told me, gutting me. My eyes clenched shut for a moment as I absorbed what he said.

"Liam!" Aidan shouted.

"If she had told Atticus what was going on, we could have prevented it!" Liam yelled.

Atticus stared at me and I stared back.

"You don't know that!" Cillian yelled.

"She's an awful person!" Malachi chimed in.

"That's enough!" Etta demanded.

We continued to stare at one another, across the grave of our daughter.

"Look at what she's done to Atticus," Brendan told Aidan and Cillian.

"She didn't do anything to him!" Etta defended me.

Atticus blinked once, his mouth slightly ajar, his eyes trained on me and mine on him.

"She left him when all he wanted to do was love her!" Liam added.

"You don't know all the details, obviously," Etta said, disdain in her tone.

"He just wanted to help them," Liam threw back.

"Enough!" Aidan said. "Enough."

It grew quiet for a moment as we looked on one another.

"It's too late now, though," Brendan said. "Now Atticus is fucked in the head and it's all because of her."

His comment cut through me, sliced me in half. All my breath left my lungs.

"Brendan," Cillian said, "Juniper was her daughter too."

I staggered forward at that and fell on top of her wet grave. Etta screamed and tried to grab for me but I shook her off. All the boys sucked in a breath. I grabbed fistfuls of dirt as I wrapped my arms around the small mound of earth.

"Leave me," I told Etta. "Leave, Etta." She bent by my side and our eyes met. "Please, Etta. Please leave me be." She nodded and stood. I watched as she retreated to the main gate and disappeared into the grove of trees where all the cars were.

I heard shuffling and watched Atticus's brothers follow Etta's path to the cars. I looked up as Atticus laid down on the wet dirt beside me. His hand met mine and we regarded the other. We laid there for minutes, possibly hours, I didn't know.

"I'm sorry, too," he finally said, his hair wet against the side of his face.

Thunder rolled above us, tumbling over itself, and the rain came harder.

He stood, grabbed a fistful of dirt, and staggered to the gate. I watched him go. Watched as he disappeared as the others had.

"I'm expected to survive this," I told Juniper. "Can you tell me how I'm supposed to do that, my darling one? Since I took my real first breath the second you took yours? Since you took my last the second you breathed yours?" My hand cascaded over the earth. "You would have been extraordinary. Just look at who your father was. Yes, you would have been extraordinary. And it would have been a beautiful life. Now I have to wait to see you again, my tiny girl. What am I going to do with my time before then, huh? I have no one to love here anymore and no longer belong." Tears poured down my face and mixed with the wet dirt. "Poor Atticus," I told her, "I've ruined his life.

"I'm going to miss you, Juniper Kelly. I guess your soul was just too pretty to stay. I can see how God would want you. I can see that. I can see how. Pray for me, baby girl. Save me while you're there, will you? I'm damaged even more now and need fixing. Pray for your dad, too. He might need it more than I will.

"I love you, Juniper."

CHAPTER TWENTY-FIVE

One month later…

"Do you want something to eat?" Etta asked me.

I pulled the covers around my shoulders. "No," I said.

"You have to eat something, Hazel," she said. "You're still recovering from surgery and you've lost so much weight. I'm starting to worry about you."

"I'm fine, Etta."

Two months later…

"How is she doing?" James asked Etta.

She took a sip from her mug on my bar top. "Not well," she answered, as if I wasn't fifteen feet from her, lying in my bed. "She's still not eating. I can see her ribs now."

James took a deep breath and let it out slowly. "I'm holding her position. Cordelia insists on it as well. She can take all the time she needs."

"Thank you, James," she said.

* * *

Three months later…

"Someone dropped off an envelope with your name on it," Etta said.

I heard the envelope rip and the rustling of paper. "Oh my God," she whispered.

"What?" I barely got out.

"They're letters from Atticus."

I sat up, scared out of my mind. "What do they say?"

Her eyes scanned each one. Her expression changed from worry to shock. "Um, nothing really. They say nothing."

"Etta," I demanded, holding out my hand.

"No," she said, pressing them to her chest, "you're too fragile for these."

"Etta," I insisted.

"They're from before, when you broke up."

I felt my heart beat into my throat. "Why would he send them now?" I asked.

She looked at the top of a legal envelope, the one they'd been delivered in, I assumed. "Atticus wrote them but Aidan's name is on the return address." She opened the envelope farther and a Post-it slipped out. She picked it up. "He says he wants you to know how much Atticus suffers without you, though he won't admit it. He says to read the letters when you are stable enough so you know and come back to him."

I laid back down, my eyes already burning. "Get rid of them," I said, afraid to see his words, afraid I wouldn't be able to handle them.

"I'll put them up in the cabinet," she said.

"Fine," I said.

Four months later…

I'd read the letters that night after Etta had left. I'd read them every day since. Aidan was wrong. Atticus hated me. It was Juniper's original due date. I pulled the covers over my head.

Five months later…

I got out of bed.

Six months later…

I picked up my brushes.

Seven months later…

James and Cordelia welcomed me back to the gallery.

Eight months later….

I spent every waking minute of my day I wasn't at work painting.

Nine months later…

Painting was a therapy.

Ten months later…

The therapy was working.

***

Eleven months later…

I showed my finished pieces to James. He showed them to Cordelia.

Twelve months later…

"Have you thought more about exhibition?" James asked.

"I'm not ready to share them," I said.

"It's your best work, Hazel. Some of the best I've ever seen."

"It's because I bled on those canvases."

"I can tell," he said, sitting down in his swivel chair. "Cordelia has an open block, and she wants to feature you in that shared exhibit."

I took a deep breath. "When is it again?"

"Three weeks," he said.

A range of emotion flooded through me before landing on peace. "How do I move forward?" I asked.

"Just say the word and I'll tell Cordelia. We'll get you added to the event, update the invites ASAP before they're sent out." He looked at me. "What do you say?"

"Call her," I answered.

Two weeks later…

Atticus

"One more time," I told River.

There was a knock on the door. "Come in," River

called out.

"Atticus," I heard behind me. I swung around to see *Etta* standing in my studio.

"Etta," I said, surprised.

"Can I talk to you?" she asked.

I looked down at River, who waved me away. I stood. "Come to my office," I said, walking out into the hall and opening my door for her.

I offered a chair and she sat. I moved behind my desk and did the same. I didn't say anything, didn't know what to say.

She cleared her throat. "How are you?" she asked.

"I'm getting there," I told her truthfully.

"Good." She reached into her purse and pulled out a square, stiff envelope. "I wanted to give this to you. She doesn't know I'm here. In fact, she'd kill me if she knew I was disturbing you, but I thought you should come."

She handed the envelope over and I opened it. It was an invitation to an exhibition featuring Hazel at the DMA.

"Etta," I said, drawing her name out. "I don't know."

Etta stood. "Come, Atticus." She began to walk out but she turned back around and added, "You really need to see it for yourself."

She didn't give me a chance to respond because she left. I scrambled around my desk and watched her leave the building. I looked down at the invite in my hand. It was for the following Saturday. I was due to be in LA the Friday before. I sat back down again and picked up my office phone.

"Hey, it's me. I need to move our Saturday session to Monday."

* * *

One week later…

I pulled the cuff of my shirt out of the sleeve of my tailored suit jacket and straightened my tie and vest. I approached the front of the DMA. People dressed impeccably milled about outside. My heart beat into my throat when an attendant opened the door for me, knowing Hazel was just on the other side.

"Good evening, sir," he greeted.

I smiled, my eyes going to the large, cavernous foyer peppered with tables and chairs. There was a sectioned-off wing of the museum roped with velvet, and I discerned it must be where the exhibit was. I spotted a podium at the head of the tables that were filling up quickly. I picked a table in the back, half the chairs were filled with stiff people who looked so stuck up it was a wonder they could sit at all. I slid into one beside a gentleman who took one look at me and scooted his chair an inch toward his wife. I'd have been offended if I hadn't thought it one of the funniest things I'd ever seen.

A woman approached the podium.

"Good evening," she said. "I'd like to welcome you to the launch of *FifteenTwentyFive*." She winked. "Cleverly titled, as we are showcasing works from fifteen revolutionary artists all under the age of twenty-five. I usually start off with listing our artists' accomplishments but, since our artists have yet to truly embark on their careers, for most this is their freshman exhibit, I've decided to allow them to speak to you all personally. I think it will help you truly understand their works and get into the psyche behind each piece. I've never seen a piece that wasn't altered in my mind's eye once I'd met the artist. So, without further ado, please welcome our first artist, Akio Deshi."

Everyone clapped as Akio stood from her seat and approached the podium. She spoke a little about herself and which art pieces belonged to her, mentioned her inspiration and what she expected the viewer to see. My eyes searched the sea of heads seated, looking for Hazel. There were too many people and I couldn't find her. I had to endure thirteen more artists' speeches, and I thought I would tear my hair out. When the last artist finished, the audience clapped and my stomach plummeted to my feet as the woman who was running the whole shindig approached the microphone.

"Lastly, we have Miss Hazel Stone. Miss Stone is local, ladies and gentlemen. Perhaps you've seen her work around town on the sides of many prominent Dallas buildings or even here in the museum. We have a permanent piece in our collection just acquired from her last week. I believe we're going to see wonderful things from her in the future. Please help me in welcoming Hazel Stone," she said.

People clapped for her more than they had for anyone else, which made me beam with pride for her. Local girl done well to them, but if they'd only known her as I did. They'd have been standing. They'd have never ceased clapping.

She stood and the sight of her stole all the breath in my lungs. Her hair was a little shorter, the bones in her face a bit more defined, but it was Hazel. She wore something that belonged on an eclectic couture catwalk, which I expected, but what I wasn't expecting was the rush of emotion I got once I saw her. My hand went to my chest and stayed there as if it could calm the violent heart that beat beneath my ribs. She stunned me. She was *stunning*.

"Good evening," her velvet voice greeted. "Thank you, Cordelia, and thank you all for such a warm welcome." She smiled but it melted away. "I'm— I joined tonight's event on a whim. I hadn't been ready to show these pieces to anyone. See, they cut deeply for me. I don't think I could ever convey just how far. The theme is devastation. I know this feels melodramatic for someone as young as myself, an artist's prerogative, but I have no hesitation in admitting this is far from the truth. I hope you will see as much in my works, let it speak to you, through you.

"Own what you see, apply it to your world, because the art isn't in the paint, in the strokes, even in the subject matter. The art is in its influence on you, if it can help you. If it invokes a change in you, there lies the art. My pain is on display," she admitted. "If the manifestation of it on canvas can bring you any closer to peace yourselves, then my pain doesn't go to waste.

"Thank you," she spoke softly, then returned to her seat.

The crowd didn't know how to react. There were a few women around me whose faces broke their careful facades. A few held back tears. The first woman who spoke approached the ropes and held them back, inviting everyone in. People piled inside. I stayed behind, not sure if I was afraid to see or if I wanted the opportunity to appreciate them with as little distraction as possible. Or it could have been because I wanted an opportunity to watch Hazel.

She sat in her chair, all the people around her gone. She folded a napkin over and over. The woman, the one who introduced her, called out to her so she stood, meandering through the tables and chairs to reach her. The woman patted her shoulder and they wrapped their arms around one another as they walked through to the exhibition.

I stood quickly and made my way their direction. When I reached the open mouth of the wing, I took in the expanse of people, trying to spot Hazel. Most of them surrounded three large works in the rear of the gallery. Each piece looked to be about ten feet high by ten feet wide. I couldn't see what they were but I knew they were Hazel's immediately. I recognized her style. I knew her brushstrokes so well. That's when I spotted her. She was alone, in a secluded section off to the side of her pieces. Her hands were situated behind her back, which rested against the wall. No one was talking to her. I could tell a few wanted to but she kept her eyes on the floor. She didn't notice them. She was in a world of her own making.

I worked around the people, my eyes focused on her. I weaved my way to the opposite side of her works, refusing to look at them until I was close enough to really take them in. I waited for someone to leave the line marked on the floor and when someone did, I toed the line. I took two deep breaths and brought my face up. All my breaths rushed out at once. My hands involuntarily went to my head.

It was us. It was Hazel and me. We were wrapped in one another, a sea of skin and her hair. Colors bled into one another. They were bold and earthy and jewel toned and beautiful. My hands fell to my chest. My eyes felt scalded, parched, desperate for wet. I sucked in a breath. We were the focus of the canvas yet there was so much going on. I could barely keep up with it as I searched every inch, taking it all in. If it were a song, it would be the most beautiful one ever written.

Without thinking, I moved to the second and stopped cold. It was us but torn apart, our hands reached for each other but we were being pulled to opposite corners of the canvas, our bodies already slipping beyond its limits. Our fingers were so close to one another it looked as though they were touching, but if you looked closely you would see a sliver of space. So small yet such a chasm.

I rushed to the third and almost yelled out in pain. It was us, our backs to one another, floating in black but between us was a bow of a juniper bush, the berries and leaves painted with such intense detail from the right angle you would think it had been nailed to the canvas. It was utterly haunting, utterly beautiful, and utterly agonizing.

My head whipped right. I found Hazel, who had already found me. Her eyes reflected grief. She swallowed; her chin quivered as she fought the emotion inside her.

I shook my head. I had no words. She came to me and faced the painting. My eyes wouldn't leave her.

"Hazel," I said, tasting her name on my tongue. She turned her body toward mine but closed her eyes. "Look at me, Hazel." They fluttered open. A tear from each came spilling down. "I miss her too." Her face contorted in pain and I took her in my arms, squeezing her to my chest. "They're beautiful, Hazel. The paintings, they are evergreen, they will live forever, even when we have not. You have immortalized her, us."

She sobbed into my chest and I let her. I placed my arm beneath her knees and lifted her against my chest. People parted like the Red Sea. The woman who had introduced her nodded at me and I nodded back. I saw Etta crying from the corner of my eye. She was with someone and he was hugging her. I took her through the exhibit, the museum foyer, and out the exterior doors. I walked her through the busy streets of Dallas to the parking lot where we laid that first night. I set her down then brought her over to me as I laid across the paved lot. I tucked her into my side and wrapped my arms around her body.

She stopped crying and her eyes found mine. "I've missed you, Atticus."

"I've missed you, Hazel. You have haunted me, frequented my dreams, my thoughts." I looked down at her. "A year without you has been torture."

"How can we have a future with a past this bloody?" she asked.

"One day at a time," I told her, standing up.

I grabbed her hands and brought her up beside me. "Come with me, Hazel."

She didn't question it when I held out my hand for her. She slipped it into mine and followed me without question. I took her to my car a block away and opened her door for her. She tucked into the passenger's seat and I piled into the driver's. I drove her to my new apartment and as we parked, I ordered Thai from the place downstairs. She held my hand as we got into my elevator and rode it to the twenty-fifth floor. She held my hand when we entered my apartment. She held my hand as I gave her the tour. She held my hand as we sat on the couch.

She sat on one end and I on the other. I picked her legs up by the ankles and laid them on the top of the sofa next to my knee. I removed both her shoes for her and set them on the coffee table. We absorbed one another in that quiet room. She looked out onto the city lights below then back at me. Her eyes caught the enlarged photograph I'd had framed of Juniper and me, the one she'd taken.

She starting breathing really hard and my stomach plummeted. I grabbed her hand and took her over to it. Her fingers traced our outlines. "Oh my God," she said.

"I know."

"I miss her so much."

"She's left a giant hole," I said.

She looked into my eyes, and I found it hard to meet them. "I *love* and *hate* your face," I told her.

She nodded. "I know," she said.

"I can't help it," I confessed.

"Atticus," she said, "I *know*."

The bell rang and I answered the door. I paid the guy, told him to keep the change, and set the food on the table. She helped me set it all out then I grabbed a few plates and some nice chopsticks from my kitchen as well as a few serving spoons. We dished out helpings and sat at opposite sides of the table. We stared at one another, neither touching our dinner.

"Do I remind you of her?" I asked her.

She nodded. "Yes," she answered, "which is how I know."

I stared down at my plate, unable to eat. "Can you talk about her yet?"

"Not yet," she said.

"I can't either. It hurts too much."

"I have a gaping hole. I know everybody says that. I know it sounds stupid, but it's really true. For me, at least," she admitted.

"I can't fill it," I said, acknowledging my own. "I can't

seem to find anything to numb it. I've tried. Kept busy at work, hung with my family. I tried to spend time with my nieces and nephews, but they just made it worse. I drank for a little bit in the beginning," I confessed. "I've found myself thinking about you a lot, Hazel."

"I've thought of you constantly," she told me.

"I miss your skin, crave it, actually. It's like a drug for me."

She brought her hands up and rested them on the surface of the table. "Is it?"

"But I'm afraid to touch you," I told her.

"Because touching me means remembering her?"

"Yes."

"And yet you want me anyway, right? But how can you want someone so much and detest them all in the same breath?" she asked.

"Is that how you feel?" I asked.

She nodded. "I feel sick without you but sitting with you here, now, I can only see her and she brings a pain I don't believe I will ever get over."

"What are we going to do?" I asked her, pushing my plate away.

"I don't know."

"I can't get over you, Hazel Stone. I tried."

"I can't get over *you*, Atticus Kelly. *I* tried."

"We're stuck in this limbo then. A perpetual state of pain and no matter how hard we try, it will never go away?"

She swallowed. "Yes."

She was crying, which made me feel ill.

"Come here, Hazel," I said as I stood.

I met her halfway around the table and scooped her up,

bringing her to my couch again. This time we laid flat beside one another; I wrapped my arms around her.

"Lay with me, touch me," I said, "until we can know each other again without pain."

CHAPTER TWENTY-SIX

Hazel

We'd fallen asleep. I hadn't expected to fall asleep. Carefully I stood, trying not to wake him, but he grabbed my wrist. My heart leapt into my throat.

"Don't ever do that to me again, Hazel. Don't ever leave me to wonder where you went."

I turned and looked down at him. The sun had yet to rise and his face was barely visible, but I saw it, saw the despair there. I swallowed.

"I wasn't leaving," I promised and meant it.

His thumb caressed my wrist. "Are you sure?"

"Very sure, Atticus."

"Stay with me today."

"I don't have anything to wear," I told him, looking down at my ridiculous dress.

"Throw your underwear in the washer. I've got a robe you can wear. I've also got something you can wear for the day. Just stay with me."

I nodded. He sat up, ran his fingers through his hair,

and stood. He grabbed my hand and led me into his cavernous bedroom. He yanked a robe from his closet and handed it to me.

"Can I have a shower?" I asked.

"Of course," he said, and showed me his impressive new bathroom.

He pointed out all his soaps, even produced a gorgeous shampoo and conditioner he pilfered from a hotel he'd stayed at in Japan six months prior. He said he took a couple because they reminded him of me, which made my heart beat harder than it had in a very long time.

"I don't suppose you'd have an extra toothbrush," I asked.

"Use mine," he said, handing me his.

"Thank you," I whispered.

He gave me a towel for my hair and told me to throw my unmentionables to him and he'd wash them for me.

I did as he asked then started the shower. I tried to quiet my nerves but I couldn't. They were live wires on fire and setting off all over. I washed my body and hair then stepped back out onto the carpet outside his shower. I took a few steps onto the tile and discovered he had a floor heater and must have turned it on for me without my noticing. I put on the robe and wrapped my hair in the towel. Before closing the robe, I glanced at my reflection and took in the faded C-section scar across my bikini line. Unable to stare anymore, I closed the robe and cinched it.

I heard the washer beep and the sound of its door opening, so I padded through to the combined living and kitchen and rounded a hidden corner where the laundry was. Atticus, his own hair wet, his clothes changed, was pulling clean, wet clothes from the washer and stuffing them into the dryer. I saw my stuff mixed with his and it made my heart pound a little harder. He threw a dryer sheet in and started it up. He turned around and saw me there. He leaned against the dryer and smiled.

"How was your shower?" he asked.

"Perfect," I told him. "How was yours?"

"I have another room. Never used the shower in there before. Thought this was as good a time as any." He sat up from his leaning position. "I think I've found something that might fit you." He walked past me, so I followed him back into his bedroom to a walk-in closet.

He held up a pair of jeans and handed them over. "I wore those in tenth grade."

I laughed as I held them up to my body. "They might fit if I roll the cuffs," I said.

His tattooed fingers pushed hanger after hanger back until he landed on a V-neck white T-shirt and pulled it free of its home. He handed it over and I took it. The towel around my hair was beginning to fall so I pulled it off my head. He took it and put it in a laundry hamper at the back. We sat in his quiet closet, staring at one another for a brief moment before we headed out. He grabbed my hand before he walked back to the bathroom then dropped it. He reached into the shower for his toothbrush and the toothpaste. He went to the sink and started to brush his teeth. I pulled myself up on to the counter next to him, piling the clothes he'd given me on top of my lap. He tried to smile around his toothbrush, which made me laugh without thinking, something I hadn't done in a very long time. His free hand found my face; an index finger brushed against my cheek. He spit and rinsed then wiped his mouth. The way he did it reminded me of something a little boy would do, which made me smile.

"Let's eat," he said. "You didn't have any dinner last night."

"Neither did you, Atticus."

"You're so much smaller than I am, though. Smaller people can't skip meals."

I shook my head. "You're funny, Atticus."

He took my hand and ran the tip of his thumb across the lines of my palm. "I wanna be your friend," he told me.

"I want to be your friend too."

He studied me. "But you're not sure," he said.

I swallowed. "Are you sure?"

"I don't know."

"Neither do I," I admitted.

"Fine, we'll take it slow."

"Day by day?" I asked.

"Minute by minute," he replied.

"What should we do this exact minute then?" I asked.

"Find you my Adidas slip-ons."

"Shoes?"

"Yes, so the next minute you can dress and the next we can take the elevator."

"Where are we going?" I asked.

"Farmers Market. How about some breakfast, Hazel?"

CHAPTER TWENTY-SEVEN

Atticus leaned forward and pressed the button for the elevator. We piled in and stood on opposite ends of the car. He pressed the first-floor button and the doors closed. A heavy bass song with piano and horn floated through the speakers, and I started to bob my head without realizing it.

"This elevator music is actually decent," I said absently.

Atticus began to laugh but coughed to stop himself.

I looked at him as he fought a smile. "What?" I asked.

"This is one of my songs. The Muzak version of it, I guess."

I couldn't help it. I burst out laughing. "You have to be kidding."

"I wish I was," he said, allowing the smile.

"So essentially you're getting paid right now?"

"I guess I am."

"Well, then." I looked down at myself. "I can't believe how well your jeans fit." I held out the bottom hem of his T-shirt. "This is a bit big, though."

He laughed. "The slip-ons look a little big as well," he

teased.

"Just a little," I added. The truth was my feet could barely hold on as I walked. I felt like I was wearing snorkel fins. I had to lift my foot up a few inches with each step to keep them from falling off. "Where are we going to breakfast again?" I asked, forgetting his earlier suggestion. I was hoping I wouldn't have to walk too far.

"I thought we could go to the Farmers Market."

So far. "Um, yeah, okay."

He laughed. "Hazel, I'm going to buy a pair of sandals for you at one of the shops downstairs. I just gave you those so you wouldn't have to walk barefoot."

"Oh, thank God," I said, relieved.

We walked out of the elevators and hooked a right into a small shopping center built in his building, including an upscale version of a quik-mart, a dry cleaner, and a small-scale gift-shop type of store. In a crowded corner of the shop were rows of simple flip-flops, and I spotted a pair of black ones. I started to sort through them, the smallest sized shoe at the bottom, and worked my way up looking for the size eight I needed. It was hanging on a hook a little out of reach, so I hopped up trying to dislodge them.

"Here," I heard just behind me.

Atticus reached over me, crowding me in. I could smell his cologne. The scent brought memories forward, making me happy and sad at the same time. As the emotions warred within me, he handed me the shoes. We sat there for a moment, looking at one another.

"Can I borrow some money?" I whispered, remembering I hadn't grabbed my purse from James's office when we'd left the exhibition.

He smiled at me. "No, Hazel, you can't *borrow* some

money."

"Why?" I asked.

He laughed. It was small but it was there. "You are a ridiculous girl, you know that? I'm going to buy them for you, that's why."

"You don't have to do that, though," I said. "I can pay you back."

He flipped the tag over. "Three dollars and ninety-nine cents then," he said. "With tax and interest."

"Shut up," I said, smiling. It dropped quickly, though. I realized just how much I'd been smiling with him and felt guilty for it.

He read the moment. "Hazel," he said.

"Hmm?"

"Let me get these for you. Please."

I nodded. We took the flip-flops to the counter, where he paid for them and had the clerk cut off the ties and the tag. I slipped them on after Atticus handed them to me. He used a plastic bag from the store to tuck his old sandals in. We thanked the clerk and returned to his building lobby. He handed the bag over to a doorman and asked him to have them delivered to his apartment.

We escaped the lobby, pushing open the doors and exiting out into the new morning sun. The sky was blue, the clouds cottony white. People milled about on the sidewalks. An outdoor cafe nearby bustled with clanking dishes and conversation.

"Let's catch the train," he said, glancing down at his watch. "If we hurry, we might make it."

We sprinted toward the station just as the train was pulling in. The crowds were annoying, but we were able to squeeze into a standing spot. We grabbed the railing handles above us as the train whirled out of the station. We stayed quiet, listening to the private conversations around us.

"Girl, he is lying through his damn teeth," one woman told another.

"You don't know that, making assumptions and shit."

The woman looked at her friend like she was nuts. "Damn it, Mya, how many times does his trifling ass have to get caught by you for you to get it through that thick damn head that he is no good and will never change?"

Her friend clicked her tongue and rolled her eyes. "He has urges, Mel. He can't help it."

"You are a damn fool," Mel, the first woman, the smart woman, said. Atticus and I looked at one another and smiled. "Look at these two, " she said softly. We turned as she pointed to us. "Did you see the way that boy was looking at her? You should want that too, Mya. That boy would stop the world from spinning if she asked for it. You can see it in his face."

We turned toward one another. He searched my face for something.

"The one thing you want, I could never give you, though," he whispered, making a single tear slip down my cheek.

I looked toward the window, at the blur of trees and city buildings as we left them behind. The palm of his hand found my cheek as he turned my face toward his.

"This is so bittersweet; I can barely stomach it," I told him.

His hand fell but slid around my shoulders and brought me closer to him. My face found his neck and stayed there, breathing him in, trying to appease the hurt in my chest. It helped. I hated that it helped because that pain for me was proof Juniper had existed, but I also knew I didn't think I could take it any longer without his help. I was weary of standing alone.

"I'm tired of the pain," I admitted.

"Me too, Haze."

"I want to remember her, *you*, without it. I don't expect it to ever go away, but I do want a shift in how I remember her."

"So do I."

"Now arriving St. Paul Station," an automated voice announced. "Doors will open to the right."

He'd kept me held against him the entire ride. I expected him to let me go when they indicated our stop, but he didn't. Instead, he swung me beside him but kept his arm clutched around my body.

We stepped from the light rail and headed toward Harwood. It would be a good fifteen-minute walk but I didn't care.

"What have you been doing with your time?" he asked me.

"Mostly laid in bed. James was kind enough to keep my position for me."

"Sounds like a nice guy."

"He is."

"Those featured paintings took me almost six months," I told him.

"I believe you," he said. "They're stunning, Hazel. Seriously heart stopping."

I nodded, afraid to say anything, to use words without bursting into tears.

"The gallery opened," I said when I'd gathered myself.

"That's amazing, Haze."

"Yeah, we're going to walk right past it," I mentioned.

"Is it open?" he asked.

"Not on the weekends, no."

He nodded.

We were quiet until we met the gallery.

"Saul," Atticus announced, reading its name on the sign above its doors.

"It's on St. Paul Street," I said, laughing a little.

"Ah, so 'of Tarsus'?"

"Exactly. The point of the gallery is to appeal to the masses, which follows Paul's theme as well, I think."

"It does," he agreed with a small smile.

I walked past the door and kept my eyes trained on Atticus's back. He was looking through the glass, chasing the lines of artwork on the walls just through the main gallery walk-through that ran the length of the whole space. He stopped abruptly, almost causing me to run into his back. I followed his line of sight.

"That's yours," he stated, his eyes pinned to a small realism piece I'd just finished.

"It's mine," I confirmed, though it didn't seem as if he needed the proof.

His hands found the glass and pressed, his fingers curling like he could scrape himself through. He glanced at me. It was something hard, confusing. He looked hurt.

"You torture me," he whispered.

I closed my eyes, afraid to look at him. "I know the feeling," I told him.

"Why of us? Why *us*?" he asked me.

"'Cause you're all I think about. I paint what I know. I paint what makes me bleed, Atticus."

"I-I'm all you think about it?" he asked quietly.

"The three of us. We're all I think about anymore."

He stepped back and pointed at the piece hanging solidly, heavily before us. His eyes found the sidewalk below us. "I can't look at it anymore."

He started walking down the sidewalk again but I didn't follow him, didn't know if he wanted me to, until he stopped and looked over his shoulder, holding out his hand for mine. I walked forward and slid my palm in his. It felt good there, safe, secure. We journeyed the seven blocks to the Farmers Market, not saying a word to one another. I wondered what he thought but didn't have the guts to ask him. He looked raw enough that a single word from me would disassemble him, so I kept my words to myself.

When we landed at the Market, I knew *exactly* where he was going. It was one of my favorite places in Dallas. Palmieri Cafe. Ran by an ex-investment banker turned shop owner named Corrado Palmieri. Corrado grew up in southern Italy with a southern Italian grandmother who taught him his way around an Italian kitchen. Everything about the place was authentic, from his espresso machine down to the cups he served it in. It is the best pastry you will ever put in your mouth, savory or sweet, and I couldn't believe Atticus remembered how much I loved the place.

We sat with our drinks at a table after ordering.

"I love this place," I told him.

"I know," he stated.

"I can't believe you remembered."

He took a sip from his coffee. "I remember everything about you, Hazel."

I swallowed. "Do you?"

He nodded once. Palmieri himself brought our food over and set it down with a sweet smile.

"Thank you," we both said.

Neither of us reached toward our plate.

"You want to say something," I commented.

"No, I don't."

"Something sits on the tip of that tongue, I can tell."

He leaned forward. "I have to go to a party tonight." I felt a little shocked and it must have showed. "Come with me."

I studied Palmieri's shop tile. "I don't know, Atticus."

"I don't want to stop being around you."

"What kind of party?" I asked, avoiding his vulnerable words.

"It's for my label. I'm sort of DJ'ing," his words hung.

I nodded. "I don't think so, Atticus."

"Hazel," he whispered. "Come with me. Spend time with me."

"I'll probably just sit around while you did your thing. It'd be pointless."

"I'd like you to come, but I won't make you. Know I'd keep you at my side always, though."

I sipped my coffee. He reached for his pastry and took a bite, chewed, and swallowed before wiping his mouth with a napkin.

"What time is it?" I asked.

He smiled. "Ten."

"I could leave whenever I wanted?"

"Only if you let me make sure you got home all right." I paused. "Any more excuses?" he asked. I shook my head. "Good."

* * *

When Atticus dropped me off after dinner that night, I opened my door to find Etta asleep on my sofa. She had clinical rotation hours at strange hours and slept when she could. Opening the door woke her up.

She sat up. "What's up, buttercup?" she asked, her voice scratchy.

I dropped my stuff on my counter and slunk against the sofa near her reclined feet.

"Atticus was at the showing."

"I know, babe, I was there." I nodded. "Where did y'all go?" she asked.

"He took me back to his new place."

Etta sat up and rubbed the sleep from her eyes. "Whoa, that's heavy." I started to cry and buried my face in my hands. "Oh, oh! Hazel," she whispered, wrapping her arms around me. "Don't cry, Hazel."

I took a deep breath. "We talked about Juniper."

Hazel sat still for a moment. "It was time," she said.

I nodded. "I know b-but I'm not ready."

She gently pulled my head up to see my face. "Yes, Hazel, you are."

"I'm in love with him," I confessed.

Her face softened. "I know, Hazel."

"But he equates pain for me."

"I know, Hazel."

"What am I going to do, Etta?"

"You're going to start living again, Hazel, and I want you let him help you do it."

"I don't need anyone's help."

"Everyone needs help sometimes, Hazel. You're strong, yes, but sometimes you need support. Everyone needs support, and I think he's the only person who can do it for you."

CHAPTER TWENTY-EIGHT

At nine p.m. a knock on my door sounded, causing my heart to leap into my throat. I ran to the door and swung it open. Atticus stood on the other side, looking like every dream I've ever had. I glanced down at the floor, experiencing guilt for feeling attracted to him. I didn't think I deserved to know that feeling again.

"Hey," I said, leaving the door open. "Come in," I said as I turned to grab my clutch, but he caught my hand and pulled me his direction, forcing me to look into his eyes.

"You look incredible, Hazel," he told me.

"Etta dressed me," I admitted.

He looked me up and down, his face turning a soft red, making me blush. "She did good," he replied.

I cleared my throat and grabbed my bag. He offered his arm to me, so I threaded my hand through, then rested my palm on the inside of his forearm. He led me outside, stopping so I could lock my door, and took me to his car. He opened the car door for me and I got in, careful I didn't flash him in my skirt. He rounded the front of his car and I found myself following his profile, his neck, jaw, face, and over his head, back down to study the line of his shoulders. I took a deep, shaky breath when he got in.

"Where is it?" I asked.

"Normandy's," he explained.

I nodded, surprised I hadn't already assumed as much. It made sense. Normandy's had grown even more in popularity since Atticus had struck it big. He was the city's golden boy, and lines wrapped around the block to get in to his brother's bar on weekend nights.

When we turned at the end of the street, it looked like Aidan had hired a valet for the night. Atticus swung in beside the valet and a man opened my door for me. I stepped out and stood to my full height just as Atticus did the same. Loud screams erupted from the sidewalk. Girls left their places in line and began running toward his car. I started to panic before a few bouncers came bounding up, holding the girls back. Atticus threw his keys at the valet and rounded the car, grabbing my hand, and culling me close to him as we crossed through the doorway, held open by another bouncer.

I looked up at him and he smiled, rolling his eyes a little.

"Does that happen often?" I asked him over the music. He shrugged his shoulders as if to indicate he didn't hear me then brought his ear to my lips. "Does that happen often?" I asked again.

He shook his head then brought his own lips to my ear. "It's only here. They know I come here."

"I see," I said. I tried to ignore the seething resentment toward perfect strangers pooling in my belly but my face betrayed me.

Atticus smiled at me, looking a little dazed. "Hazel, are

you *jealous*?"

I bit my lip, tried to fight a smile. "Maybe," I barely said, but he heard me. I know he heard me because immediately he backed me into a dark corner, both his hands on the bits of wall on either side of my face.

"You still like me?" he demanded. I avoided his eyes and stared at his forearm instead. "Hazel, look at me." I obeyed him. "Hazel, do you still like me?"

"Don't make me say it," I begged.

He narrowed his eyes. "I need to hear you say it," he said.

I shook my head. "I can't."

"Yes, you can."

"I can't, though, don't you see?" I asked, my view clouded by burning eyes.

I blinked and two tears streamed down.

"Yes, you can," he urged kindly.

I met his stare and sucked in a breath. "Yes, okay? Very much so, actually."

He dropped his arms; they hung heavy by his sides, and he leaned over me. I had to crane my neck to look into his eyes. "Is that right?" he asked, but I could tell he didn't expect me to answer him. His hands found my face and slid down the sides of my neck, resting there. He searched my face, my eyes. "But you feel guilty for that." I nodded slowly. "We'll have to fix that then," he told me

All the air left the room, it seemed. Suddenly I was very warm all over, which I didn't like. No, actually, I loved it, and I hated that I loved it. The tips of the fingers on his right hand found my hairline and dragged over my temple. He tapped once with his forefinger. "There's a war brewing inside here." His fingers pressed softly. "Stop,

Hazel. Slow down, babe. Just slow down in there."

"I can't," I told him.

He brought his mouth to the skin there. "Yes, you can. Let go of it and let me carry it for you."

I shook my head, fighting tears. "It's mine to carry."

"No, it's not. It's too heavy. You're not meant to shoulder that alone. It's also my job. She was mine as well," he said, breaking the dam. "And so are you. Pile it on me, Haze." My hands found his shirt and squeezed as the tears streamed. I felt myself slipping. I couldn't even hold myself upright the burden was so heavy on my back. He brought me closer to him, wrapped his arms around my shoulders, and held me tightly against him. "Give in to it. Let it spill all over me and I'll weather it for you."

I cried into his neck for God knows how long, but he let me do it. To the untrained eye, it probably looked like we were kissing. Eventually I felt myself relax, and the music and the atmosphere all around us became clear, like a fog had lifted. I raised my head and he looked down at me. Slowly, his arms unwrapped from around me. His thumbs found the skin under my eyes and wiped my dried mascara that had stained there. He kissed beneath each eye and my cheeks, all over the skin of my face.

"I want to take care of you, Haze."

I nodded at him, still a little afraid to talk.

"Atticus!" I heard someone yell out behind us.

He glanced over his shoulder and raised his head in greeting to whoever it was then turned back to me. "It's George, from the label. Do you want to meet him?"

I shook my head. "Let me go to the bathroom first, fix my eyes."

"Go to Aidan's office. Use his private bathroom."

"Okay," I said.

He kissed my neck briefly before turning around. I skirted around him and made a beeline for Aidan's office. When I reached the hall, there were girls lined up near the bar and the overflow spilled near Aidan's office door.

"Excuse me," I said as I reached for the handle, pushed it open, then closed it behind me.

I made my way around his desk, staring at his chairs. I turned around and took in the door. It was the room I'd told Atticus about Juniper. My stomach plummeted to my feet. I went to the corner and opened the door to the little bathroom he had attached to his office. I bent down and grabbed a few squares of toilet paper. I wiped beneath my eyes but they hadn't run as badly as I thought they would. I stood and looked into the mirror, the reflection of the room behind me, and stared at it with new eyes. I remembered how scared I'd been, how I'd wished I'd not been pregnant. That thought sent a spear of guilt through me.

"Juniper," I whispered to my reflection.

Knock, knock, knock. I jumped.

"Hazel?" Atticus's voice rang through the door.

"Coming!" I said, swiping beneath my eyes once more.

I opened the door. "I'm about to go on. You want to sit in the booth with me?"

His eyes looked hopeful. "Sure," I answered.

He took my hand and started to lead me back to the main part of the bar. I quickly glanced back at Aidan's office one last time. The noise of the bar was what got my attention first, then the number of screaming people. I couldn't believe how many people were packed in. What got me, though, was the fact that most were women and they were all chanting Atticus's name. My skin grew warm with anxiety.

"Miguel!" Atticus shouted toward a bouncer. "Protect her first!"

Miguel nodded and stood solemnly behind me. Two more bouncers flanked us as we pushed through the crowd near the wall, attempting to get to the staged booth.

Girls were screaming, pulling at his clothing. He glanced at me and rolled his eyes. My mouth gaped open in disbelief as I shook my head. The crowd around us surged, pushing us toward the wall, making me feel claustrophobic. Miguel the bouncer shoved a few kids back to give us more room. Finally, we reached the setup and Atticus bounded up, turned around, and lifted me next to him. Someone lowered the lights; the neon that lit up the booth became the only light I could see. The music lowered and faded out.

Atticus checked his deck, something I'd seen him do a thousand times, but never for an actual performance. He looked so casual, so comfortable, and I realized he was in his element. He was doing what he was meant to do.

He leaned over the microphone near his lit-up laptop. "Hey, guys, thanks for coming out tonight," he said before pausing for a few seconds then dropping an insane beat, filling the room and shaking the walls. Everyone screamed in excitement and began to bounce in unison while he messed with his decks. I sat on a stool in the corner behind him.

Atticus played song after song, the crowd didn't bother to take a break, it seemed, too engrossed in the music. Atticus turned around and smiled at me. It gave me insane butterflies. He turned back around, spotted Miguel, and made some sort of signal. Miguel worked his way through the crowd then returned to the booth. He smiled at me and handed me a bottle of water. I smiled as I mouthed my thank you and cracked the lid open, taking a swig. Atticus turned back around and winked. I held my water out for him and he took it, placing his lips where I'd just had mine and drinking deep. He handed me the bottle and I rested it on my knee.

The room had grown hot and his T-shirt stuck to his back. His hair laid against his neck, and he kept throwing it out of his face as he worked. One song faded to another, static filled the room, followed by a repetitive digital harp riff, then heavy bass. It was beautiful but made you want to dance at the same time. He had a talent for that.

I nodded my head along with the beat. He looked at me, then bit his lip before holding out his hand for mine. I took it and stood beside him. He bent his mouth to my ear.

"Hold on," he said, before playing with something on his laptop.

He then took my hand, held it out for a second, brought both our hands to the small of my back, and pressed his body against mine. He smiled down at me and I smiled back as we began to sway side to side, the tips of my hair brushing back and forth over the skin of our folded arms.

"This song," I told him.

"You like it?" he asked me, releasing my hand. I brought it up to his shoulder.

"I love it. I think it's one of the best things you've ever written; one of the best I've ever heard."

"I'm testing it out here. I've got an artist ready to sing over the track, but I wanted to see how it did tonight."

"Well, it's going to obliterate the charts, Atticus. Seriously." He smiled but there was something in it, something secret. "What?" I urged.

"It's called 'Hazel.'"

My breaths came quickly. "Oh my God, really?"

"Really." He bent closer to my ear. "Took me six hours to write it. When I get the lyrics recorded, I'll play it for you."

I swallowed. "I look forward to it." He looked at me. I started to open my mouth but closed it. "I'm speechless."

"Don't worry about it," he said, turning and hitting a button on one of his decks. I grabbed his chin and turned his face toward mine. "It's an incredible gift, Atticus. I can't believe you wrote this for me. I'm in awe."

His face bloomed a little and it made my heart skip a beat. "It was the easiest song I've ever written."

We didn't say anything else. Instead, he kept his forefinger slightly bent in the waistband of my skirt near my hipbone to keep me near him as he readied the next song. This simple, innocuous gesture did something to my insides and the palm of my left hand went to my head. The war inside was raging in a vicious battle between *touch him* and *run from him. I want him. You don't deserve him. I want him. You don't deserve him. I want him. You don't deserve him.*

"What are you doing, baby girl?" he asked me, stirring me from the conflict within.

I looked at him. Him with his clean, straight white teeth, defined features, and brilliant eyes. He'd tucked his hair behind his ears, and I found him incredibly irresistible. I didn't want to want him but I did, *so bad.*

"Hazel," he urged.

"You're my friend?" I asked him.

His smirk fell and he nodded. "Yes, Hazel."

I nodded my relief at this. "I'm ready to shed the guilt, Atticus," I pleaded, the bass around us pulsing, reverberating against our skin. "Help me remember her without the pain."

He nodded at me. "I've thought about this," he said. "I think I know what to do."

"Whatever you say, I'll do it."

"We'll go tomorrow then."

I lifted the back of his shirt, grazing the warm skin there barely, then hooked my thumb through his belt loop. He watched me as I did this, a small smile growing wide against his teeth.

I glanced to my left. The girls who'd sat in the hall when I was trying to get into Aidan's door were standing next to Atticus's booth. They signaled to me, so I bent toward them. Before I knew it, a blonde girl had me by the hair and was trying to drag me out of the setup. "Bitch! He's mine!" I heard her yell. I yanked up but a few more girls grabbed hold of me before I had a chance to slip the first's hold. They were actually making progress when I felt Atticus lean over me, his fist connecting with a few of their hands. Their grips were starting to wane and I was able to lift myself up slightly.

"Let her the fuck go!" Atticus yelled.

I saw Miguel and two other bouncers fight through the crowd then scoop up the three girls who had hold of my hair, but they refused to let go. One by one the bouncers peeled the girls' fingers away and dragged them out the front door kicking and screaming. The blonde pointed at me and yelled something, but it was too loud for me to hear. Atticus lifted me up, his face stricken.

"Jesus, Hazel, are you okay?" He ran his hands over my head and face, looking for obvious injuries.

"I'm fine," I answered him, out of breath. "Head's just a little sore."

"Let's go," he said, heading for the edge of the booth.

"No! Finish your set. I'll be fine."

"Fuck it, Haze! I don't care!"

"What about your label?" I asked.

"I've played over an hour. They'll be fine."

"I don't want you to get in trouble, Atticus."

"I won't, Haze. Besides, I don't fucking care right now. Let me get you the hell out of here, please."

He wouldn't let me say any more and edged me to the wall near the end of the booth. He made a movement with his arm and people stepped back to make room for us. He jumped down and held his arms out for me, placing his hands on my waist. My fingers went to his shoulders as I let my body fall forward. He caught me and I slid down his chest. When my boots hit ground, he wrapped his arms around me and elbowed his way toward the back of the bar.

We heard the guy who was supposed to follow Atticus come over the speaker, thanking everyone for him and announcing Atticus was done for the night. The crowd erupted in cheers, and it was a relief they weren't pissed we'd left the way we did. We meandered through the packed floor, people slapping Atticus on the back and shoulder, and girls screaming his name. We rounded the back of the bar, but instead of going through the hall to Aidan's office, he led me through the bar itself and through the pair of swinging doors to the small kitchen.

All Atticus's brothers were in there; we barreled our

way past them toward the back employee entrance.

Aidan smiled at me.

Cillian winked. "Nice to see you again," he said.

"Hi," I said, as Atticus whisked me past them.

Brendan, Liam, and Malachi waved at me.

"You look good, Hazel," Cillian said.

"Thanks!" I yelled as we exited the building.

When we hit night air, we stopped. Atticus searched the parking lot. He pointed at the valet section and started walking.

His brothers followed us out.

"Atticus, wait!" Aidan said. Atticus and I turned toward them. "We have something to say to Hazel," he said. Atticus, who'd kept my hand in his, squeezed it.

We stood there, all of us quiet.

"We're sorry about that day," Liam said, "for everything. We didn't realize what we were saying. We saw our brother hurting and we took it out on you and we're sorry."

"It's okay," I said.

"No, it's not," Cillian chimed in, "but we'd like your forgiveness all the same."

"Of course," I said.

"You okay, Miss Stone?" Miguel asked, after coming through the doors.

"Fine," I said with a smile. He returned inside with a nod.

"What happened?" Aidan asked.

I looked at Atticus. "One of his adoring fans wanted to slit my throat," I joked. Apparently it was the wrong thing to say because Atticus's face looked panicked. "Hey, hey," I told him, placing both hands on the sides of his neck.

"Don't worry. I'm fine. I *promise.*"

His hands lifted and found my wrists then held there. "I don't know what happened," he said. "It wasn't supposed to happen. I'm not big enough for that to happen."

I sighed. "Atticus, I think you are."

"No way, I'm just a producer. We live in the shadows. It's part of why I took the gig. I don't like the spotlight."

I smiled up at him. "You're too pretty for them not to notice, Atticus."

"I'm supposed to keep you safe, though. This hit too close. It's too much."

One of the valet guys must have spotted us congregating outside and brought Atticus's car around, pulling up beside us.

"Thanks, Jason," Aidan told the driver, who'd noticed Atticus's distracted expression and threw the keys at Aidan.

Atticus came to when he heard his keys and held out his hand. "You all right?" Aidan asked.

"Fine. I've just got to get the hell out of here." Aidan threw them at Atticus, who caught them with one hand. "Come on, Haze."

He opened my door for me and I piled in. We started to take off but he stopped abruptly. "Shit," he said.

"What?" He looked at me, he was torn. "What, Atticus?"

"I need to let the label know I'm out for the night. I don't want the waters any more muddied than they are."

"Of course," I said. "Go."

"Cillian!" Atticus yelled toward his brothers. "Come here." He put the car in park and started to climb out. "Make sure those psycho girls don't go anywhere near

Hazel. I've gotta go in and get the label guys sorted out."

Cillian jogged our direction and sat in the driver's seat while Atticus ran in.

"You look good, Hazel," Cillian offered.

I snorted. "You already said that, Cillian."

"Yeah, well, I mean it."

I laughed. "Are you *flirting* with me, Cillian?"

He smiled that smile all the Kelly boys seemed to possess, the one that could make any girl weak at the knees, then shrugged. "So what if I am?"

I barked a short laugh. "Cillian! What is wrong with you?"

He shook his head then sighed. "Jamie broke up with me."

I gasped. "What! No!"

He ran his palms over the steering wheel. "Yeah."

"What happened?"

He took a deep breath and looked over at me. "Fell in love with someone else. Cheated on me."

My hand went to my mouth then fell to my chest. "Oh, Cillian, I'm so sorry."

"It's okay. We were young when we had Nick. If it hadn't been for him, we would have never lasted." He looked at me. "I would have stayed forever, though, for Nick." He shook his head. "Poor Nick. He's such a great kid. He doesn't get why she's never around anymore, and I don't know how to explain it to him. I just tell him I love him and take him bike riding or to the movies or whatever."

"It sounds like you're doing exactly what you should do, Cillian."

"Am I, though? Eventually I'm going to run out of

distractions, and what then?"

"I don't know, but my mom ran out on me when I was a little younger than Nick and I wondered for a while what happened to her, but eventually I stopped wondering why she didn't love me and focused on the ones who did."

He nodded, wrapping his arms around his shoulders. "That's so fucked up, though, Hazel. If I could, I would take away all his unhappiness and carry it on my own shoulders. I'd do anything for him not to suffer."

I smiled at him. "That seems to be a Kelly trait."

He smiled back. "Damn, I thought I had that one on lock or something."

I laughed. "No, all of you boys are like that."

"So, uh, you and Atticus, huh? Is that a for sure thing or —?"

I laughed again. "You haven't been single in a *long* time, have you?"

"No, and it's a bitch out there."

"A little tip? Don't hit on your brothers' girls."

His brows shot up. "So does that mean you're Atticus's girl?"

I cleared my throat, not sure how to respond. "Uh, well, I don't know, but you get what I mean."

He winked at me. "Yeah, Hazel, I think I do."

CHAPTER TWENTY-NINE

Atticus dropped me off at my studio, and I slept harder than I had in more than a year. I didn't know if it was because he was starting to make me feel better or I was just so exhausted, but I didn't wake up one time in a panic. Not once.

I woke at eight, showered, drank a cup of joe, and picked up my pencils. I swiped a hand across a clean canvas. It was my favorite moment when I painted, the promise of something new, of something wonderful, the rush it gives you, the love you feel. I bent over the canvas and traced my outlines. It was another realism piece, but this time it would be different. I didn't know why, but I knew it would be different.

At noon, someone knocked on my door, so I draped a bit of cheesecloth to hide what I was drawing. I lifted the peephole slider and got a fish-eye view of Atticus. My heart started to beat into my throat. I unchained the door, slid the lock, and twisted the deadbolt before throwing open the door.

"Atticus," I said, slightly out of breath.

"I tried to call, I swear," he said.

I pulled the door open farther. "No, it's fine, come in."

He walked in with a bag of something and set it on my counter. He stood still while I bolted the door again, sliding the chain home.

"How's your head?" he asked.

My hand went to the knot that had formed after the girl had yanked my hair. "It's fine," I lied.

He walked in front of me and tenderly ran his hands through my hair, wincing when he landed on the swollen lump.

"It's okay," I told him, dragging his hands down. I nodded my head at the bag. "Is that for me?" I asked, hoping to change subjects.

He glanced backward. "Yeah."

I bit my bottom lip. "Well, can I have it?"

"Of course," he answered.

He took three steps and yanked the bag from behind the bar and brought it over to me, opening it and offering it for me to look at. I peeked inside.

"Oh my God, breakfast tacos from La Ventana's."

"Yes, ma'am!"

I grabbed the bag and skipped to the bar. Atticus instinctively grabbed two plates from my cabinets while I grabbed a spoon and, because I wasn't an animal, my homemade salsa from the fridge. I slid into a seat and he sat beside me, setting a plate in front of me. Eagerly I grabbed a taco from the bag and giddily untucked the wrapper. I reached forward and grabbed the salsa, prying open the lid and setting it between us. I glanced over at Atticus and he was watching me, making me feel self-conscious.

"What?" I asked, aware of myself.

He smiled at me. "You're happy today."

I took a deep breath, the easiest breath I'd taken in a long time. "I guess I am," I told him.

He didn't say anything more while we ate. When we were done, I took our plates to the sink. I began to rinse them when he snapped his fingers.

"I left my guitar in my car. Be right back."

"Okay," I told him, placing our plates in the dishwasher to run later.

I went to my canvas, unwrapped the cheesecloth, and picked up my pencil again. Atticus came back inside and bolted the door again. I watched him walk, his strong, lean legs in a comfortable stride, the swish of his jeans like a song in my head, arriving at my green velvet wingback. He shed his jacket on the floor, fell into his seat, and propped his feet, crossing his legs at the ankles, on the sushi-roll footrest I paired with the wingback. He brought the guitar to his lap, plucking at the strings and turning the tuning pegs with his long, slender fingers until the guitar was on pitch. Everything he did put butterflies in my stomach. I was overly aware of him and it did things to me.

I turned back to my canvas and began to draw, but his proximity made my hands shake and I kept having to erase and reapply the lines. He began to strum the strings, and eventually a beautiful melody came pouring out.

I stopped what I was doing and set my pencil down. "That's 'Hazel,'" I told him.

He smiled but continued playing, only shifting to a minor version of the original. "That it is, madam."

"Is that how you wrote it?" I asked.

"Yes," he answered succinctly.

The song danced across my skin, swam through my head, made me feel drunk. I walked toward him and stood at his feet. He shifted, sitting up a little, letting his feet fall to the floor, and I sat on the footstool in front of him. He leaned forward, his guitar on his thighs, and kept playing.

"Are you ready for an adventure today?" he asked me over the song.

"It depends on what it is," I told him.

"It involves you and those skilled hands."

"Oh, really?" I asked.

"Got a pencil and some paper handy?"

"Yeah," I answered, leaning back and grabbing my pencils. I stood up, grabbed my sketchpad, and sat back down.

Atticus laid his guitar against the outside of the chair, the neck resting in the dip of the wingback's armrest. "Draw me something, Haze."

"Like what, Atticus?"

"Something that honors Juniper."

I took a deep, shaky breath. "Anything?" I asked.

"Anything."

Briefly, the tip of my pencil sat on the surface of the paper before I sketched out Juniper's name hidden in a juniper branch. I filled in the empty spaces with melting juniper berries and dripping paint, gossamer threads, and geometric color blocks. It had an abstract quality to it. It took approximately an hour to finish but Atticus sat still, not saying a word while I worked, and watched my every move.

I shaded in the last bit and held it up. "There," I said, feeling cleansed.

Atticus shook his head at me. "It's like you're not even human," he whispered, making my cheeks feel flushed. "How is it possible that human hands created this?" he asked no one, grasping the sketchpad. "This is ridiculously incredible, Haze." He swallowed. "I think about her, us, all the time," he confessed, looking into my eyes.

"So do I," I revealed as well.

"Feel like taking a little trip with me?"

I laughed. "Why are you being so cryptic?"

"I'm surprised you haven't figured it out yet."

"I'm wracking my brain, dude, but I can't figure it out."

"That's okay," he said, standing up and offering his hand. I took it and he pulled me up. "Do you need to get anything? We'll be gone for a couple of hours."

"Okay," I sang, reaching for a light jacket and my purse. He helped me put it on and opened the door for me then I locked it.

We rounded the corner near my building and came upon his car. I started making my way toward it but he tugged me toward him. "No, we're walking," he said.

I followed him a few blocks down Hall and we hooked a left on Elm and landed at this little hole in the wall.

"What is this place?" I asked. "It's not even marked."

"It's a tattoo parlor, Haze." My eyes blew wide. "I'm getting your drawing done."

"Oh my God," I whispered, my throat gone dry.

Atticus smiled at me. "Come on, Haze," he said, grabbing my hand.

We walked through the narrow door. The entire parlor was about fifteen feet long but probably only six feet wide. The walls were painted brilliantly, lots of Mexican art, just gorgeous. There was one vintage barber chair and a table just behind it lining the right wall. It was small and intimate and beautiful. A man came through from a small curtained section in the back, lots of insane tattoos over his skin, but none of the typical art you see. Just like Atticus's, his were unconventional, a true testament to the art. He had quarter-inch wood gauges in his ears and his brow was pierced. He wore a pair of dark jeans, a short-sleeved print shirt with the sleeves rolled a few times, and a fedora.

He smiled when he saw Atticus. "Hey, Atticus," he said, extending his hand.

Atticus slapped his hand and they did some secret handshake thing, laughed, and patted each other on the back. *Men.*

"Keitel, this is Hazel. Hazel, Keitel."

He held out his hand for me and I took it. He bent at the waist and kissed across my knuckles. "Miss Hazel, nice to meet you."

I smiled. "Same," I said.

He turned and took two steps, rolling a stool with his foot his direction, and sat smoothly. "What are we doing today?" he asked Atticus.

Atticus handed him my drawing and Keitel's eyes bugged as he studied it. "Who in the hell drew this?" Atticus smiled and threw his head my direction. Keitel looked at me. "You drew this?" I nodded. "Whoa, man, this is some shit right here." He looked at me again. "You really drew this?"

I laughed. "Yeah."

"Damn," he said, playfully bowing my direction, "you're a master, dude. Seriously," he shook his head, "this is some grade-A stuff right here."

"Thanks, Keitel."

"*Thanks, Keitel. Thanks, Keitel*, she says. No, man, *thank you*! I don't even know what to say." He looked at me as if something dawned on him. "Yes, I do, actually. You want a job?"

Atticus and I both laughed. "Thank you, but I've got a gig," I said.

"If you ever change your mind," he said. "I'm for real."

"Well, thank you, if I ever feel like changing my profession, I'm all yours."

His mouth opened and a dangerous smile graced his mouth. "*You would*, huh? Listen, what are you doing later?"

Atticus laughed. "Hey now!"

Keitel turned Atticus's direction. "Atticus, I forgot you were here."

"Yeah, yeah," he replied, sitting in Keitel's chair.

Keitel winked my direction and I giggled.

"You're trouble," I told him.

"With a side of mischief."

"I believe you," I said.

Keitel turned toward Atticus. "So where are we putting this? Not much room left from what I remember."

Atticus stood and yanked his T-shirt over his head. My eyes briefly roamed down his chest and stomach then back up. He caught me looking and smiled, his black lip ring dark against his white teeth. He sat back down and cocked his head to the side.

"I've some room on the side of my neck. What about there?"

Keitel examined it and nodded. "Yeah, I think I can do that." He stood. "Let me trace this out. Give me half an hour or so?"

Atticus nodded and Keitel winked at me before disappearing behind the velvet curtain in the back.

I sat on Keitel's stool. "How are you doing?" Atticus asked.

"Today is the first day since Juniper's passing that I feel open."

He grabbed my hand and kissed the heel of my palm. "I'd say that's doing well," he spoke against the skin there.

I nodded, feeling a little teary. He noticed. "Don't cry, Haze."

"They're not hopeless tears, not anymore. They're tears in her memory alone."

His eyes turned glassy and he nodded. "She was really something, wasn't she?"

"She was the most beautiful person I've ever met in my life, Atticus."

He looked as if he'd gone somewhere far away when he answered.

"I love her," he told me.

I smiled as a tear slipped. "So do I, Atticus." I took a deep breath as he brought my hand down and tucked it between both of his on his knee. "Thank you."

"For what?" he asked.

"For her. Thank you for her. No matter how we got her, no matter how short her life was, no matter that I can't have any more other than her, she was worth it. Every single second of all of it was worth it just to hold her those few short, beautiful days."

Atticus's eyes clenched and he brought a white-knuckled fist to his mouth. He didn't say anything, couldn't say anything, it seemed. A full minute passed before he let out a shaky breath and his eyes met mine.

"She was worth it all," he agreed.

Keitel came from behind the curtain and I gave him back his stool after he brought me another chair. He sat down with a pat on Atticus's back.

"Let's do this thing," he said, working methodically, cleaning Atticus's skin, and figuring out how he wanted to place his trace.

He got Atticus's approval on the placement and got to work. Atticus let his head hang as he stared at me. The initial needle to skin made his eyes close briefly. I laid my free hand on top of our already stacked hands and soothed the skin there. He squeezed my hand and opened his eyes, staring directly at me.

"How did you guys meet?" Keitel asked as he worked.

I smiled at Atticus and he smiled back.

"We met at Normandy's," Atticus answered. "I saw her across the room and I knew if I let her leave there that night without trying to talk to her that I'd regret it for the rest of my life." My heart beat wildly against my ribs. "She was with her best friend. She looked unbothered, like she could be there or not, she didn't care, almost as if she belonged nowhere and to no one, and I remembered thinking she was so unlike anyone I'd ever seen, not just in the way she looked, although she is so obviously beautiful it's almost an unbelievable thing, but it was in the way she sat, the way she held herself. It was a confidence I'd never really seen before. She wasn't conscious of herself, and I thought that so attractive, so rare.

"I wanted her," he admitted quietly, making the moment much more intimate than it should have been. I stared at the tips of his lashes as his head hung and wished I could really see him. "So I stood up and talked to her."

"And the rest is history?" Keitel asked, not realizing the gap Atticus had closed between us with the admission.

I cleared my throat. "Our history is, well, it's difficult," I said.

Keitel's needle stilled and both boys looked at me.

"You don't strike me as the drama type," Keitel said. "Either of you."

"It wasn't the kind of drama you create, per se, it was the kind that finds and slams you to the ground unapologetically."

Keitel shrugged his shoulders and shook his head, returning to work. "That sucks," he said.

"It did for a while," Atticus admitted, squeezing my hand again, "but I was meant to find her."

"Yes, you were," I told him.

When Keitel was done, he took Atticus and me over to the mirror and let us see his work. We both stood seemingly dumbstruck. It was our daughter's name. Right there for the world to see. It was our daughter's name.

"It's exactly what I needed," Atticus said.

"It's beautiful," I told him.

Keitel shuffled back and forth behind us, cleaning up his station. "I meant what I said about a job, Hazel," he said. He walked toward us and smiled through the reflection. "I hope you enjoy it, Atticus."

Atticus grabbed my hand. "I will," he replied.

Monday

We parked it outside at Lee Harvey's and had a few beers together. Atticus only got recognized once.

Tuesday

We played miniature golf. I beat him fair and square, though he swears I cheated.

Wednesday

He made me dinner. It was terrible. I didn't have the heart to tell him.

Thursday

Laser bowling. He wiped the floor with me but he didn't gloat. His winner's dance was totally worth it.

Friday

We saw the stage play *An American in Paris*. My girlfriend from school was in it. She got us the tickets. Atticus brought me a bouquet of flowers and a single rose for my friend. He cleaned up real nice.

Saturday

He took me to the state fair. We ate a funnel cake together. Powdered sugar everywhere.

Sunday

We went to the zoo with Etta and Simon. A gorilla charged and beat his fists on the glass we were standing near. I almost peed my pants. Atticus laughed so hard he fell down.

Monday

We went to the midnight showing of *Rocky Horror Picture Show*. Atticus went as Riff Raff. I went as Magenta. We agreed no pictures.

***

Tuesday

I got off early because Atticus didn't have any studio work to do. We bummed around Bishop Arts and ate a piece of pie from Emporium. It was called Smooth Operator—French silk chocolate with a pretzel crust. #heaven

Wednesday

Went to the drive-in at Coyote. I accidentally dropped my corn dog so Atticus shared his with me. We laid a quilt on his hood. We talked about books and art.

Thursday

We went to the aquarium then had a picnic at Dragon Park.

Friday

Shakespeare in the Park. We saw *Othello*. I cried. So did Atticus. He claimed it was dust, though.

CHAPTER THIRTY

Atticus and I spent every moment we weren't working or asleep with one another. It was strange. It felt like we were just starting out again, really, yet a great weight hung between us, a gorgeous daughter who lived within us. Despite all that, or maybe because of it, I'd never felt closer to him in my life. All the bad had flushed its way from our minds and hearts and skin down, down, down into oblivion and we were left with nothing but the good, the sweet, the lovely.

"I'm thinking about having a dinner with everyone next week at Capital. Do you think your grandma could drive up?" he asked me.

"Oh, she would come up for sure," I said, smiling up at him.

"Call her," he said.

I laughed. "Right now?" I asked.

"Yeah," he said, reaching down and yanking on a piece of grass.

"Okay, what day?"

"Saturday night okay?"

"Yeah."

We'd gone a couple hours south for a last-minute trip to the caverns. Etta came with her boyfriend, Simon. We were sitting on a bench outside waiting for them to return from the bathrooms.

I pulled my phone out and rang my grandma but she didn't answer. I opted to text her instead.

Grams, Atticus wanted to know if you could come up next Saturday for a fancy schmancy dinner at Capital. You down? You can sleep at my casa. I hit send then put my phone back in my satchel.

"I wrote her."

"Cool," he said, leaning back.

Etta and Simon came walking down the path toward the little round administration building near the mouth of the cave, so we stood and met up with them inside.

"Two, please," Atticus said to the attendant, handing over his card.

"Thank you," I said.

"My pleasure." He smiled, offering his arm after the girl gave him back his card.

We stood to the side while Simon paid for his and Etta's tickets.

"This, uh, this—" Atticus started, then shook his head.

"What?" I asked.

"Nothing," he said, looking away from me.

"Atticus, cough it up, man. What were you going to say?"

He looked back at me, his cheeks slightly pink. "I was just going to say that this sort of feels like a date, Hazel."

My face warmed and I bit my lip to keep from smiling. "Does it?" I asked, suddenly finding the tops of my boots fascinating.

Etta and Simon walked around us toward the stone staircase leading to the mouth of the cavern and we scurried down after them. Neither of us would look at one another, but I could feel his eyes on me and it did something to my insides, something I hadn't felt since that first night, *the* night.

"Oh my God, it's so beautiful! I'm glad y'all invited us," Etta said.

I looked over at my equally beautiful friend. She was holding Simon's hand, and I felt so happy for her. I looked down at Atticus's hands as they swung at his sides. I found myself wanting one of his to take one of mine. My eyes followed up his arms, his shoulders, the side of his neck, over his tattoo of Juniper's name, and settled on his face. *I wonder*, I thought, *if we could ever be as we were, if it we could ever be simple, if he could ever love me.* I wondered many more things as we followed the sinking path toward the open iron gates below, toward the stalactites and the stalagmites, reaching toward each other, desperate to connect, just like Atticus and me. They had much time to wait, though. I could only hope that wasn't the case for Atticus and me. I didn't know if I wanted to wait anymore. I was tired. Tired of suffering without him, tired of the weight of how I felt for him, tired of dragging it around with me, heavy, and begging to be lifted.

The sun had disappeared as we nestled deeper and deeper into the recesses of God's earth and we found each other in the dull light of the scattered lanterns in a part of the caverns where the ceilings were barely eight feet high. Etta and Simon had gone ahead about a hundred yards where the cavern lifted a hundred feet into the air, studying the nature surrounding them more quickly than Atticus and I could absorb it.

We came upon a stalactite and a stalagmite separated by mere inches. They too looked tired to me. We circled them twice, each of us on opposite sides. Atticus bent his head to peer at me through the gap. I leaned forward and smiled at him but the smile quickly fell.

"So close yet so far," I told him quietly, my whisper betraying me and echoing against the cavern walls. It bounced off our ears over and over.

"At least another thousand years," his answer repeated.

"Such a long time to wait," I said.

"They'll get there," he said.

"Will they, though?" I asked him.

Atticus's eyes softened and he stood upright. He followed the base of the stalagmite around until he was standing about a yard away from me. He stuck his hands in the pockets of his jeans, his T-shirt straining against his shoulders and biceps.

"You know something, Hazel?" he asked me.

"What's that, Atticus?"

"When they meet, those two points, when they finally come together after the wars, the battles, the wrong that has surrounded them in the ripples of their existence, after the longing, the misery, the torture of seeing each other as their future complete, that moment, that second, that instant will be their most vindicating time. It will be quiet; it will be unassuming. No one who sees it will be aware of their perfect collision, but it will be an explosion amongst themselves, for only them to know, for only them to feel. It will be proof they can weather anything, absolutely anything that comes their way. Even if it meant the end of the earth, Hazel Stone, it would not mean the end of the world. They are perpetual. They are forever."

My heart pounded. He took a step closer to me. Another. Another. Until the chasm between *us* matched *theirs*.

"I have missed you more than you could possibly comprehend, Atticus."

His eyes filled with something, an emotion. "I think I could," he revealed.

Tears spilled over my cheeks. "But I don't deserve you."

He shook his head back and forth slowly; the backs of his fingers found my cheeks and dragged across. I turned my head into his skin, desperate to feel him for as long as possible. "No, *I* don't deserve *you*."

I shook my head in disagreement, tears coming stronger. "But I pushed you away."

"You were trying to protect yourself, protect Juniper. I don't blame you for any of it, Haze. It was what it was and it made us who we are."

I nodded, knowing *exactly* what he meant. "Can you forgive me, still?"

"Only if you forgive me?"

"Of course. Of course I do. You know I do."

He placed my face in the palms of his hands. "All is forgiven. All of it. All, Hazel." He took a deep breath.

"Do you still hate my face?" I asked him.

His head lolled softly side to side. His thumbs started at my forehead and dragged down the sides of my face. "No, Hazel, I no longer see my pain there. I only see my future happiness, our future hope."

I let out a groan of emotion, unable to hear that without a physical reaction. "I feel guilty admitting this—"

"Don't. Juniper wouldn't want that for us, Haze."

I nodded. "I don't feel the despair anymore. I feel calm now. I feel the memory without the searing pain. I think—no, I *know* it's because of you."

"We remember her as she is supposed to be remembered."

Atticus brought me into him, wrapping his arms around my shoulders, and I wrapped mine around his neck.

"You're my best friend, Hazel," he whispered to me.

"You're mine, Atticus, my favorite friend, my forever friend… just don't tell Etta."

He laughed against my neck.

CHAPTER THIRTY-ONE

Atticus held my seat out for me and I sat down at the table. It was full with all of Atticus's family, Etta, her aunt, Grams, James, everyone was there.

"I just wanted to say a quick word," Atticus said, standing next to me, his hand on my shoulder. He cleared his throat of emotion. "Hazel and I have been through a lot together," he said, looking down at me. I smiled up at him to encourage him. He looked around the table again. "Our daughter—" he said, breaking down a little then coughing. "She was unexpected, she confused us, she frightened us, but then she became something else. She was early, beautiful, so utterly beautiful, the best thing that had ever happened to either of us, and then she was gone." Atticus smiled at me. "I know she's with us now. I can feel her. Hazel can feel her. She is a part of us and we love her. So, in her honor, I'd decided to have everyone here today because we all need to start over with each other. I want us all to wipe the slate clean and start over." He picked up his pint glass and held it up, so we all followed suit. "For Juniper," he said.

"For Juniper," we all repeated.

"To Haze and me, to all of us," he finished as we lifted our glasses and drank.

Atticus sat down next to me and we watched our joined family and friends talk amongst one another with ease, our histories settled between us all.

"That was pretty, Atticus."

"You know me," he teased.

"Stop," I laughed, "I really mean it. It was an incredible thing to say. It's all incredible. We're making peace."

He sat back in his chair and ran a hand through his hair. "If there is one thing we deserve, it's peace, Hazel."

"Agreed," I told him.

Atticus had reserved a private room at Capital complete with sliding privacy doors. They kept opening and shutting as the waiters came in and out, refilling drinks, setting down bread, taking orders. Atticus took my hand and we sat, content just to be in one another's presence. Dinner came. Conversation flowed. Life was celebrated. Love was felt.

Atticus picked up the tab and the obligatory thank yous from my side and the incessant teasing from his ensued.

All in all, it was incredibly successful. It was everything I didn't know I needed.

When we were done, Atticus held my chair out for me, and as a group, we made our way to the city street, meandering in a group as we waited for the valet.

"Damn, Etta, you're looking good," newly single Cillian complimented my best friend.

Etta crossed her arms under her breasts and snorted. "Cillian, I am very taken."

"What!" he asked. "When did this happen?"

"Almost a year ago."

"Oh yeah? Then where is he?" he asked.

"He's a resident at Children's and couldn't get off for the dinner."

Cillian tripped over his next words, obviously not able to think of anything smart to say, and everyone in our group started snickering.

"Etta, one. Cillian, zip," Atticus teased.

Cillian blushed a little but smiled. "Hey, man, I'm new at this."

"I know, dude. I'm sorry," Atticus told him.

"Grams," I called out for my grandma when I noticed her looking shell shocked, "you okay?

Her mouth dropped open a little and we all turned the direction she was staring. Half a block away was a thin, dirty, barefoot woman with my face and hair.

"Oh my God," I whispered.

Atticus turned toward me. "Who's that?" he asked.

I started to back up, looking for a way to run. Atticus grabbed my hand and held me there. "It's my mom," I said. I looked at my grandma. "Grams, how?"

She shook her head as my mom approached us. "I don't know, baby. I really don't."

"Mom, what are you doing here?" I asked when she came upon us.

Everyone was staring at her. I could see the wheels in her head turning. She loved an audience.

"Mom, get out of here."

She looked at me, eyed me up and down, then stared down Atticus before smiling at everyone else. She turned back to me. "I heard you whored yourself out and got knocked up."

Etta and Sarah gasped. My grandma stepped forward a little. "Tawna, stop this instant!"

My mom swayed on her feet, obviously drunk or high or both. Atticus sidled closer to me but kept my hand in his. "I suppose this is the boy who did it." She studied his tattoos. "Covered in them, just like your dad." She laughed. "Apple doesn't fall far from the tree, does it?" She looked at me. "I heard your baby died."

"Yes," I whispered, and Atticus squeezed my hand.

"I wish I'd been that lucky," she said, stumbling a few steps before righting herself.

Everyone gasped this time. My free hand went to my mouth.

"Enough!" Atticus shouted at her.

She only laughed. "It's just as well your kid died. You would have been a terrible mom."

"Tawna," Grams breathed.

Everyone around us was silent.

"Leave," Atticus demanded quietly, but under his cool exterior, he was fuming. I could see it.

My own feelings didn't match his. I understood why he felt how he did, but her insults hadn't meant anything to me. I'd learned a long time before not to take anything she said seriously. In fact, I'd learned a long time before not to engage her at all, but for some reason I felt compelled to respond that day.

"No," I told her.

She looked surprised. "What?" she asked, in disbelief.

"You're wrong. I wouldn't have been a terrible mom. In fact, I would have been a wonderful mom and for those two days I had my daughter, I was just that. Because I'm not you. I could never do to my kid what you have done to me. You think we're alike, Mom, but you couldn't be more wrong. We are *nothing* alike, because I loved my daughter and I will continue loving her for the rest of my life. *That's* the difference between you and me."

She didn't respond. It was as if she hadn't heard anything I said.

"Do you have any money?" she asked me.

I dug into my purse and gathered whatever cash I had. I held it out for her and she took it.

"Leave. Leave me alone, leave Grams alone. Take my cash and leave. *Leave.*"

She did what she was superlative at and turned away from me, walking in the direction from which she'd come. For an instant I felt like I was on the Leaving Porch all over again, but then just as suddenly I was free of the place. This time I had my daughter with me and I had *Atticus* with me and I wasn't alone anymore.

I looked up into Atticus's eyes. "Take me to the letter painting," I told him.

CHAPTER THIRTY-TWO

We stood in the parking lot, side by side.

"Start there," I told him, pointing to the first word in my letter. "Then move clockwise corner to corner, around and around, and move in as you go. It will make sense once you start reading."

Atticus nodded and cleared his throat.

"*Hello, it's Hazel,*" he began. He turned and smiled at me before looking back at the painting. "*I don't know you yet. I feel like I carry you around with me, though. You're a promise, a hope, and I want you so badly. I've already memorized your skin, your voice, your eyes, your mouth. I know you so well yet I've never met you. I must sound crazy to you but it's the truth because I've felt you. I've opened myself up to the universe and invited you in. I can feel you exist. And I can't wait to meet you, hold your hand in mine, press my lips against yours. I'm eager to love you. No one I know would believe me if I said that out loud but it's the truth. I want to love you. You. I want to love you. I've never really felt I deserved it but I want it all the same. When I do find you, I'll take you here. I'll let you read these words and you'll know. You'll know. I love you.*"

Atticus turned toward me. "I love you, Hazel."

"You do?" I asked him.

"How could you doubt it?"

"I don't count on much, Atticus."

"You can count on that. My God, you can count on that, Haze."

"I love you," I told him, tasting the words on my tongue.

He smiled at me. "It took us some time to get here."

I smiled back at him. "Was it worth it?"

"I'd do it a thousand times more if it meant us falling into place together."

"So would I, Atticus."

"There's only one Juniper, though," he said, though it wasn't necessary. I knew it as well as he did.

I nodded anyway. "Only our little Juniper."

It started raining, but not a small mist, no. No, it was hard, relentless drops and we laughed, holding our palms out.

"There she is!" Atticus shouted to the sky, the tendons in his neck straining against the skin there. "I love you, Juniper!" He looked at me. "I love you, Hazel Stone! I'm sorry, but I can't believe I get to say that to you now!"

"I love you too, Atticus Kelly!"

He took his phone out and The The's "This is the Day" played on full volume. He stuck his phone in the front pocket of his jacket. I smiled at him as he grabbed my hands, and we started dancing in the rain and screaming the lyrics to one another, laughing, and finally feeling free.

Water puddles began to form around us in the uneven parking lot. Atticus grabbed my hand and we stomped in each one, water flying up and drenching our shoes, our clothes, but we didn't care. We got every single puddle in that parking lot, laughing like we'd never laughed before, happier than we'd ever been, loved more than we'd ever felt loved.

Atticus swung me to him, my chest near his, and wrapped his arms around me, bending me backward.

"I love you, Hazel Stone."

"I love *you*, Atticus Kelly."

He studied me a brief moment, his eyes searching mine, then he smiled. That's when his lips touched mine and it was love, it was happiness, it was friendship, it was respect, it was passion, it was allegiance, it was worship. It was everything.

When we finally met, our two points, when we finally came together after the wars, the battles, the wrong that had surrounded us in the ripples of our existence, after the longing, the misery, the torture of seeing each other as our future complete, that moment, that second, that instant was our most vindicating time. It was quiet; it was unassuming. No one who saw us was aware of our perfect collision, but it was an explosion between ourselves, for only us to know, for only us to feel. It was proof we could weather anything, absolutely anything that came our way. Even if it meant the end of the earth, it wouldn't have meant the end of the world.

We are perpetual. We are forever.

The Beginning.

Like Juniper, we are evergreen

ACKNOWLEDGEMENTS

I am so sad to leave these characters because I relate to them so much.

This was a therapy book for me. Write what you know, they say, so that's what I did, which is why getting these characters down on paper felt like releasing a thousand doves into the sky, like a contribution to the world, God willing. Many of you have been through things similar to Atticus's and Hazel's story and I just wanted you to know with this novel, you aren't alone. If your situation is new to you, I can promise you it gets easier as well. It may not be what you want to hear, but it's the truth and eventually you'll turn that pain into memories worth remembering, memories that won't stick you to the earth with emotional daggers.

Everyone has a Cross to bear and these were some of mine. I was glad to carry them, though. They told me everything I needed to know about life, love, compassion because when I get knocked down, instead of getting right back up, I root around for a moment to see if there's anyone else out there with me who needs a hand to hold and then we stand up together.

We're all in this together.

***

I want to thank my incredible editor Hollie Westring. You've been with me for all but two of my books and I can't imagine anyone else touching them. It would be a travesty. Thank you for treating my words with such incredible care.

Matt, I hope I did you justice in this story.

Baby Gabriel, I can't wait to see you again. I love you.

For my earthly littles, take your lives and live them for others. That's the best advice I can give you. When you love others, you love God. There lies happiness.

Courtney Cole, Michelle Leighton, Nichole Chase, and Tiffany King, you are my soul mates but you already knew this. To the moon and back five times.

I love you, Atticus

Listen to Atticus's Mix Tape for Hazel...

Pregnant?
It's going t
be okay.
I promise.
1 (800) 848-LOV

www.ingramcontent.com/pod-product-compliance
Lightning Source LLC
Chambersburg PA
CBHW031119210626
46816CB00016B/1716
9780997876925